TOP SECRET
FOR YOUR EYES ONLY

SUBJECT: Cordelia Gallowglass, second child of SCENT agent Rod Gallowglass, the High Warlock of Gramarye.

BACKGROUND: Father landed on feudal planet Gramarye, his mission to help establish a democratic government. With the aid of Fess, an artificial intelligence in the form of a horse, became recognized as a warlock (see *The Warlock in Spite of Himself*). Despite going native, agent has been successful in laying the foundations of democratic institutions (see files *King Kobold Revived*, *The Warlock Unlocked*, *The Warlock Enraged*, etc.).

CURRENT SITUATION: A second generation of Gallowglass family now coming of age. Children all possess psychic talents, inherited from Gallowglass and his wife, the "witch" Gwendylon (see *Warlock and Son* and *A Wizard in Absentia* for recent mission files on eldest son, Magnus).

PROJECTION: Cordelia, now of marrying age, has exceptional psi powers. Prince Alain, heir apparent to Gramarye, is expected to choose her as his mate. Expect antidemocratic forces to make supreme effort to prevent such a powerful union from coming to fruition (see current file, *M'Lady Witch*) . . .

M'LADY WITCH

CHRISTOPHER STASHEFF

ACE BOOKS, NEW YORK

This book is an Ace original edition,
and has never been previously published.

M'LADY WITCH

An Ace Book / published by arrangement with
the author

PRINTING HISTORY
Ace edition / November 1994

ISBN: 0-441-00113-0

ACE®
Ace Books are published by The Berkley Publishing Group,
200 Madison Avenue, New York, NY 10016.
ACE and the "A" design are trademarks
belonging to Charter Communications, Inc.

PRINTED IN THE UNITED STATES OF AMERICA

10 9 8 7 6 5 4 3 2 1

To my romance consultant,
Genevieve Stasheff,
with the author's thanks

CHAPTER
~1~

"My son," said the King, "thy mother and I have decided that 'tis time thou wert wed."

"As thou dost wish, my father and sovereign." Alain bowed. "I shall inform the lady straightaway."

And he turned and strode out of the solar, leaving his parents gaping after him.

Wooden-faced, the sentry closed the door behind the Prince. The sound jarred King Tuan and Queen Catharine out of their shock.

"Who can he mean?" he asked, round-eyed.

"Who but Gwendylon's daughter?" It was characteristic of Catharine that she didn't mention Rod Gallowglass, Cordelia's father.

"The High Warlock's daughter!" Tuan had the opposite problem. "He must be stopped!" He rose from his chair.

But Catharine restrained him with a hand on his arm. "Let him be, husband. If he doth as I think he will do, he may learn a most signal lesson."

Much as she loved her son, Catharine knew him to be something of a conceited prig. Admittedly, the realization had only dawned on her this last year, when the boy had turned twenty-one and she had finally begun to think of him as a swain going a-wooing. Looking at him in that light, she had begun to realize that her son had some serious romantic defects. They all began with attitude, of course—but if she knew Cordelia, her son might soon have that attitude corrected.

Alain rode the high way toward the High Warlock's castle with a high heart, enjoying the lovely spring day, the cascades of birdsong, and the ribald chanting of his entourage—a dozen young knights in doublet and hose, their swords at their hips. He felt his whole being relaxing, surging upward in delight. It was grand to be young and courting on a day such as this—it even made him feel moderately good-looking.

Actually, he was a handsome young man, though he had been raised with so much emphasis on modesty that he denied it to himself, relying instead on his wardrobe. But he was well muscled, blond, with large blue eyes, a strong chin, and a straight nose; his face was open and ingenuous, though usually too serious.

On a day like this, though, he was perilously close to admitting that he was attractive. He certainly felt so, for all the world must love a lover. And it was such a relief to be away from Runnymede and his parents' court, from intrigue and the need to be formal and wary!

Alain didn't know it, of course, but the girl to whom he planned to propose was even more of a hot potato than a hot tomato. That wouldn't have stopped him—he was a trouble-magnet himself; crown princes always are. Assassins and conspirators lie in wait for them, ready to seduce them into plotting against their parents, or to kill them if they aren't seducible. That was why Alain travelled with a bodyguard of knights, and why his father had made sure he was well trained with sword and battle-axe.

Cordelia, on the other hand, wasn't apt to have any bodyguards around; her parents cultivated the simple and humble image, as much as you can when the King and Queen have insisted that you live in a castle. But she was easily more lethal than Alain could ever be, if she wanted to be—she was, in the eyes of the superstitious peasants, a witch, and a very powerful one.

Actually, she was an esper, a person born with powers of extrasensory perception and, in her case, extrasensory activity. She was a telepath, a projective, a telekinetic . . . and the list went on. About all she couldn't do was teleport.

Of course, it was possible that she might run into something that even she couldn't handle—say, an army or two. If that happened, all she had to do was call for help from the Wee Folk, and a brigade or two of elves, pixies, and brownies would pop out of the woodwork to aid her. If anything stopped them—such as too much Cold Iron, which tends to accumulate around knights—she could always send out a mental call for the rest of her family, and her father would teleport to her, with her brothers right behind. Her mother would arrive a little later, by broomstick. The family had not yet encountered any enemy that could stand against them—provided, of course, that nothing kept them apart.

Rod Gallowglass wasn't quite as adept at using his ESP powers as his wife and children were, because he had spent half his life under the blithe impression that he was an ordinary mortal. Shortly after the birth of his fourth child, he had found out the hard way that he could work "magic," as the local superstitious peasants called the results of his ESP work. He had decided that magic was catching.

Rod Gallowglass's late development was understandable, considering that he hadn't even known there was a planet where there were so many espers, until he came there; he had been born and raised on a high-tech planetoid where the family business was the manufacturing of robots, and had run away from home to spend his twenties bumming around the civilized, modern planets, looking for wrongs to right. Sometimes he wondered how he had ever gotten into this situation. Then he would look at his wife, even now in her fifties, and decide it had just been good luck.

Being a little more honest with himself, he would admit that it had been a matter of needing a purpose in life. He had found one by becoming an agent for the Society for the Conversion of Extraterrestrial Nascent Totalitarianisms, an organization dedicated to spreading democracy by sniffing out dictatorships and other forms of oppressive government, and steering their societies toward one of the many forms of democracy. Exploring the galaxy for new totalitarian governments to topple, he had stumbled across Gramarye. Now he was assigned here for the rest of his life—because SCENT knew how important Gramarye was going to be. Rod, on the other hand, had known how important the beautiful, voluptuous "witch" Gwendylon was going to be, and had married her, cleaving unto her forever—and therefore, of course, to her planet and people, too.

The planet of Gramarye was the only place in the Terran sphere of colonized planets where so many espers existed. All the rest of the Terran planets together had produced only a few rather weak telepaths—so Rod Gallowglass had a very important duty guarding the planet of Gramarye from invasion and subversion by the agents of dictatorship and anarchy.

SCENT believed that one of the prime factors in keeping a democracy alive was speed of communications. If it takes too long to get a message from the parliament to the frontier planets, the frontier planets will eventually set up their own governments and break away. The only way to prevent this is to do away with democracy and resort to some form of government that keeps such a tight hold over its colonies that they *can't* break away—and that tight hold always turns into oppression, in one form or another. So to keep democracy viable, the telepaths of Gramarye were going to be absolutely essential.

Unfortunately, the future totalitarians knew that, too—and so did the future anarchists. Each of them had its own time-travel organization, dedicated to fostering totalitarian governments (VETO) or to destroying governments altogether (SPITE)—and both were directly concerned with keeping Gramarye from becoming a democracy.

Which meant they were out to kill Rod Gallowglass, if they could—and his family. Especially his children.

They had found out, over the last couple of decades, that they couldn't kill Rod—no matter how hard they tried, he always fought them off, and where he might have failed, his wife and her elf-friends and children had beaten off his enemies for him. Together, they were unstoppable—but the Futurians could, at least, make sure his influence didn't go on into future generations. They were bound and determined to kill his children if they could or, if they couldn't, to at least keep them from having children of their own.

So far, the new SPITE chief, Finister, had succeeded in giving the eldest son, Magnus, a very unhealthy distaste for sex in any form, and especially for women as sexual beings. As a result, he had left home to go traipsing around the galaxy, looking for wrongs to right and oppressive governments to overthrow.

Now Finister had set her sights on Cordelia. How she would prevent Cordelia from ever being married, or even seduced, she didn't know—but she would improvise. Half the fun of her job, she had decided, was in finding how things came out.

So Alain rode through a golden morning, blithely unaware of the Futurian witch who was setting her sights on himself and his beloved. Not knowing, he was able to delight in the day.

"How shall you greet the lady, Your Highness?" asked young Sir Devon.

"With cordiality and respect, Hal!" It was such a pleasure to speak so freely, without all that ridiculous and unnecessary formality that the older folk used. "Thee" this and "thou" that, when a simple "you" would suffice! "As I would greet any fine lady!"

Sir Devon didn't seem so sure. "Mayhap, Highness, you should treat her in some degree warmer than that."

"What? And have her forget that I am her sovereign-to-be? Pooh, Hal! It would be beneath my station!"

Hal started to say something more, then bit his tongue.

Alain saw. "Come, come! You must speak your mind with me, Hal—for if my own friends do not, who will? What had you in mind to say?"

"Only that it is a perfect day for so joyous an occasion, Highness," Sir Devon said slowly.

"It is that." Alain looked around him with a broad grin.

Yes, it was a perfect day to become engaged, to kiss a lucky maiden for the first time. The thought was somewhat heady—he had always more or less planned to marry Cordelia, and the notion of actually doing so made his heart sing, though it also roused a nervous fluttering in his stomach. However, he could ignore that—as he could overlook the fact that she wasn't a princess.

He also overlooked the possibility of sending a page ahead, to announce his coming.

Gregory looked up; pale light was beginning to lend color to the leafy roof overhead. He folded up his notes with a satisfied sigh; it had been a good evening's watching, and he had learned quite a bit about the habits of the great horned owl. He rose to his feet with a wince as cramped muscles protested, and noted that he must not be doing enough yoga exercises. If only eight hours of immobility for a night's watch made him stiff, how would he endure the round-the-clock spell of meditation that he knew was coming? His mind was working itself up to that—when it brimmed over with new knowledge, he would have to go into a trance to sort it all out. He didn't dare do that when Mother and Father were home, of course—but they travelled a good deal these days, so he was free to keep night-long vigils in the forest if he chose, or twenty-four-hour sessions of meditation. He knew it would worry his sister Cordelia, but she would only hover over him, not interrupt.

And, of course, there was the problem of trying to contact his eldest brother Magnus, halfway across the galaxy.

He felt the need of that, too, from time to time, and it was very demanding of both body and mind. Heaven knew the lad wrote seldom enough!

His body was making its needs felt in other ways, too. Gregory felt a pang of hunger, and decided, with regret, that he would just have to devote half an hour to taking on some food. He made his way out of the forest and off toward the nearby village, where there was an inn that would be serving breakfast.

As he came into the inn, the serving maid looked up, then gave him a very, very warm smile; her lips seemed to glisten, her eyes to grow larger. Gregory gave her an automatic smile in return, instantly concerned—was the girl beset with a fever? But no, on closer look, he could see no other symptoms—the swellings in her bodice looked natural enough.

He sat at a table, asked her for ale and porridge, then instantly forgot her as he noticed the motion of dust motes in a sun-ray that hinted at a pattern . . .

Something tugged at his attention; irritated, he glanced at the wench's retreating back. He noticed the exaggerated swaying of her hips, and remembered his older brother Geoffrey telling him that when a woman walked that way, she was seeking a dalliance. Then Gregory finally remembered that the look on her face had been one that Geoffrey had told him of, too—but he also remembered his brother's caution that the lass might have a shallow dalliance in mind, or a very deep one, or anything in between, and that a man had to move slowly, trying to read her intentions, for frequently she wouldn't know them herself.

It all sounded very tedious to Gregory, and singularly unproductive. He supposed that he would have to try it some day—but just now, he had far more interesting matters to deal with. He was only sixteen, after all. And, to be quite frank, he couldn't imagine how the physical pleasures Geoffrey described could ever approach the ecstasy of intellectual insight, the long hours of study and meditation that led to the rapture of new understanding of natural phenomena.

Of course, women were natural phenomena, too—but somehow, he doubted that they wanted to be analyzed. And he was quite sure they didn't want to be understood.

The drawbridge was down, the porter sitting at his ease on a stool in the shade of the gatehouse, cutting bits of apple and nibbling at them. He stiffened abruptly at the cry of the sentry in the tower above; then the troop of horsemen came into view, and the guards snapped their halberds down. "Who comes?"

"Alain, Prince of Gramarye!" cried the foremost knight, and behind him, the golden Prince himself sat, cocksure and smiling, head tilted back, resplendent in cloth of gold and velvet, with a plume in his hat.

"Your Highness!" The porter bowed, his expressionless face hiding his surprise, almost shock, at the suddeness of the Prince's arrival. "I regret that Lord and Lady Gallowglass are not within!"

"No matter, no matter," Alain said with careless generosity, "so long as the Lady Cordelia is. Say, are there any others of the family present?"

"His Lordship and Her Ladyship are away for the day, sir. I regret there are none here but the servants, the steward, and myself, saving Lady Cordelia."

"A most excellent notion," Alain said with joviality. "Save her ladyship, indeed—and summon her!"

The porter blanched at the thought of "summoning" Lady Cordelia. He decided to summon the steward instead, and let him deal with the lady. After all, porters were not paid *that* much.

Cordelia was in the stillery, brewing medicines to replace the stock depleted by the winter chills and agues and fevers of all the peasants on the Gallowglass estates. She enjoyed the work, but it was tiring, not to say messy—her apron was spotted with the extracts of various herbs and the mauve and purple from the juices of various berries. Her hair was tied back in a severe bun, to keep loose strands from being caught in the glassware. Her face, too, was smudged with touches of extract, bits of charcoal, and smudges of soot from tending the burners. The solution in the alembic had just begun to boil up into the cooling tube when . . .

. . . the steward stepped through the door and announced, very nervously, "Milady, Prince Alain has come to call on you. He awaits you in the solar."

"Blast!" Cordelia cried, instantly furious. "How dare he come unannounced! How durst he enter just as my brew has come to the boil!"

The steward stood mute, stretching out his hands in bewilderment.

"Well, there's no help for it!" Cordelia snapped, gaze going back to the cooling tube. Drops of distillate had begun to drip into a beaker. "Tell him I will come directly."

The steward bowed and left, relieved.

She would come as soon as the retort was empty and the beaker full, Cordelia decided—two hours' preparation would not be thrown away on a man's oafish whim! As to appearances, well, he would just have to take her as she was.

Still, she patted her hair, wishing she had time to arrange it properly—not to mention donning a pretty gown and washing her hands and face.

Actually, she had very little cause for concern. Cordelia had grown into a very beautiful woman, though she gave it very little thought. There was so much to do—peasants with illnesses, children who must be taught, women who must be aided in their daily burdens. Now and then, she might snatch a few minutes to think about a new dress, or even steal an hour to work at making one. There were even odd moments when she would experiment with a new hairstyle, though those tended to be very, very early in the morning, and only on Sundays.

Makeup? She never thought of it—and never thought it would do her much good, either.

She was half right. Her complexion was flawless, her cheeks rosy, her lips so red that no paint could improve upon them. Her features were those of the classic beauty, and the curves of her body were generous and perfectly proportioned. Her legs were long, her posture straight, almost regal.

Of course, these last were almost always hidden under a work-dress of strong, serviceable fabric. There was, after all, so *very* much to do.

Even the rough cloth could not hide her loveliness, though—from anyone but herself. Cordelia, of course, did not know she was a beauty.

"How dare he?" she fumed to herself, watching the last of the solution boil out of the retort. "What the devil could send him here at such a bad time?"

Alain paced the solar, fretting and chafing. What could be keeping Cordelia so long? His sunny mood was beginning to cloud over, exposing the nervousness underneath. He was remembering that he was proposing a liaison that would last twice as long as he had already lived, and was beginning to wonder if he really wanted that. Still, his lieges, sovereigns, and parents had told him he should wed, so he would.

He consoled himself with the thought that Cordelia had no doubt rushed to dress in her finest and arrange her hair. It wasn't at all necessary, he assured himself—but it was flattering.

So he was jolted to his boot-soles when she bustled into the room, unannounced and without ceremony, in a stained white work-apron and blue broadcloth dress, her hair disordered and her face smudged. He stared in shock as she curtsied, then managed to force a smile. He didn't know which was worse—the annoyance that rippled over her face as she looked up at him, or her distracted air, as though she had something more important on her mind. More important than him!

"Your Highness," she said. "How good of you to come."

Alain stared. "Highness?" What way was that to greet an old friend, a companion of childhood? But the shock gave way to a cold wave of calculation that was new to him, though quite welcome under the circumstances—the emphasis on his exalted station would make her even more aware of the honor he was doing her. "Milady Cordelia." He forced a smile.

Cordelia saw, and withheld another momentary surge of anger. Not bad enough that he had let himself show his dismay at her appearance—now he had the gall to go chilly on her! But she could play that game, too. She gave him a smile of her own, making it very obvious that she was forcing it, and gestured to an hourglass-shaped chair. "Will you sit, my Prince?"

"I thank you, milady." Alain sat and, since they were being formal, gestured to another chair. "I pray you, sit by me."

"You are too kind," Cordelia said with withering sarcasm, but took the chair that he offered her in her own solar—or her own mother's, at least. "To what do I owe the pleasure of this sudden visit, Prince Alain?"

Alain was surprised to feel relief at her use of his name. He decided to unbend a bit himself. "To the beauty of your face and the lightness of your form, Lady Cordelia." He had rehearsed that line several times on his way from his parents' castle, but the effect was somewhat marred by his choking on the words as he gazed at her smudges and stains.

Inwardly, Cordelia was fuming. How dare he praise her appearance when she knew she looked like last week's wet wash? "My thanks, Alain—but you had little need to journey so far to so little purpose."

"The purpose was scarcely small," he returned gallantly, "for you are fair as a summer's day." He said it without choking, this time. "Indeed, 'tis your beauty and sweetness that have minded me to honor you."

"Oh, have you indeed?" she said softly, outrage kindling within her.

"In truth, I have—for my mother and father have deemed 'tis time for me to wed. 'Tis you who are my choice, sweet Cordelia, and 'tis you who shall be future Queen of Gramarye!"

Cordelia sat quite still, staring at him as a maelstrom of emotions churned within her. True, she had always more or less planned to marry Alain, and the thought of being Queen one day was an interesting added fillip—but to be treated with such cavalier disregard, to be the pawn of his whim rather than the queen of his heart . . . ! She felt the anger mounting and mounting, and knew she would not be able to contain it very long.

Alain frowned. "Have you nothing to say?"

"What should I say?" she asked in a very small voice, eyes downcast.

"Why, that you rejoice at your good fortune, that you are sensible of the honor I do you, that you acclaim me as your lord and master!"

I shall acclaim you as a pompous ass, Cordelia thought, but she didn't say so—yet. "Am I to have no voice in this matter, my lord?"

The return to formality was like a stiletto through him. "Assuredly, you are! 'Tis for you to say yea or nay, surely!"

"How good of you to deign to allow me this," she said, syrupy sweet.

Alain relaxed, complacency restored. She was sensible of the honor after all. " 'Tis nothing."

"Oh, aye, 'tis nothing!" The anger boiled up, and Cordelia knew she could contain it no longer. " 'Tis nothing to you, a woman's feelings! 'Tis nothing to you if you humiliate where you should elevate!"

"How now?" Alain stared, thunderstruck.

"I am nothing to you, am I? Only a brood mare, to be bought at your whim when you have a moment to spare from your great concerns? Nothing to you, nothing but a minor matter that you attend to when the mood is on you?" She rose from her chair. "Nothing to you? Only a marriage, only a lifetime's union, and 'tis nothing to you?"

"Nay, certainly not!" He leaped to his feet, stung to the quick. "You twist my meaning!"

"Nay, I attend to the meaning of your tone and your actions, not to your words alone! Why, you great gilded popinjay, you puffed-up princeling!"

"I am your future sovereign!"

"Of my nation, but most assuredly—not of my heart! How could you be, when you have no thought of love or yearning?"

"Do you take me for a heartless wretch?" Alain cried. "Surely I must love you!"

"Oh, aye, surely you must, if your parents command it! Yet had you thought of it before I said the word? Had you never thought to say it, never thought to woo, to court? A fine prince are you, if you can but command!"

The absurdity of the charge struck him. " 'Tis the place of the prince to command, and of the subject to obey!"

"Oh, my apologies, sire!" Cordelia dropped an elaborate, exaggerated curtsy. "Assuredly, if you order me to marry, I must obey, must I not? If you command, my heart must obediently adore you!"

"Why, you heartless witch, you storming shrew! I am your Prince, and I do command you!" Alain shouted, then drew himself up and glared down at her coldly. "I command you to answer me straight! Will you be my wife, or no?"

Cordelia dropped her prettiest curtsy, bowed her head, smiled up at him, and said, quite clearly, "No."

Then she turned on her heel and stalked off back to her stillery.

She slammed the door behind her, leaned against it, and burst into tears.

Alain stared at the doorway through which she had gone, thunderstruck, distraught, and dismayed. Then he remembered that a steward was apt to step through that doorway at any minute, and masked his hurt in a scowl. The scowl raised up a torrent of anger in its wake. He stalked through the archway, and the steward stepped up. "May I fetch you anything, Your Highness?"

"A modicum of sense in a woman's heart," Alain

snarled. "Aside, fellow! I shall seek my horse—'tis a fairer creature than the Lady Cordelia!"

"Surely, Highness!" The steward moved aside with alacrity, then signalled to a footman, who stepped to the stairs and signalled down to the porter.

Alain didn't see; he was aware of nothing but a red haze, his feet following the steps down to the Great Hall automatically. The porter yanked the door open as the prince came to it, and he stormed out, his face thunderous.

In the courtyard, his escort raised a cheer that cut off as though it had been sheared. Sir Devon stepped up, his face dark. "Have they offered you insult, Highness?"

" 'They'?" Alain cried. "No, not 'they'—only she! An arrogant chit of a girl who holds her liege and lord in little esteem!"

"Assuredly she has not spurned you!"

"Spurned me? Aye, as a tyrant would spurn a dog! I shall be revenged upon her, upon their whole house!"

The leader looked shocked for a second, then masked his sudden fear with narrowed eyes and a hard face. He turned back to his fellows. "They have offered our Prince grave insult, sir knights."

He was satisfied to see the same momentary dismay on every face—all of them knew of the magical powers of the Lord Warlock and his family. Moreover, all of them knew Cordelia's brother Geoffrey to be the best swordsman in the kingdom. But even as their leader had done, they all grew stone-faced, and reached to touch the hilts of their swords.

"Say the word, Highness, and your revenge shall be executed," the leader said.

"Oh, not so quickly and easily!" Alain roared. "I shall see humiliation and shame ere I see blood! 'Tis insult I've been given, and dire insult must answer! Away, good friends! For I must think long and hard on the manner of this vengeance! Away!"

Out they thundered through the gatehouse. The sentry on the wall looked up, ready to give the porter the signal that would begin their revenge for the insults given their young mistress. His heart sank at the thought, for he knew that if they raised their hands against the Heir Apparent, the Royal Army would have them sooner or later, and they would all be drawn and quartered. But loyalty was loyalty, and Cordelia was his young mistress, and the daughter of the Lord Warlock, to whom he had sworn his allegiance.

Besides, he was more than a little in love with the lady, as most of the younger men of the castle were.

The steward, however, was older, and a bit more practical. More to the point, he had seen enough of life to recognize rash words that would probably be atoned for in time, and to know that young people frequently say things they do not mean. He only shook his head—so the drawbridge stayed down, and Alain and his young knights rode out unharmed, across the drawbridge, and down the road to the plain.

"What revenge is this he speaks of?" the sentry demanded. "For if I must choose between the Lord Warlock and the King, I know where my loyalties lie!"

"Your loyalty, and my lance," the steward agreed. "Still, he does not speak of action yet, and the time has not come to draw blades."

"But to speak of it to the lady?" the sentry asked, his face uncertain.

"Not to the lady," the steward rejoined. "If I know her at all, she is probably in tears over so disastrous an encounter. Nay, we will speak of it to Lord and Lady Gallowglass, or to either of their sons, should they come home sooner."

Geoffrey came home sooner.

CHAPTER
~2~

"He spoke of *what*?" Geoffrey stared, incredulous. "Surely not even Prince Alain would be so great a fool as to seek revenge on our house!"

"I speak only of what His Highness said, sir," the steward replied.

"And proper and loyal you are to do so." Geoffrey spun away. "I must speak to my sister!"

He boomed through the stillery door. "Cordelia! What has Alain done to you!"

Cordelia looked up at him, tears streaking her face. "Oh, nothing! Only spoke a deal of nonsense, only been as lofty and pompous as ever he was! Do go away, Geoffrey! Leave me to cry in peace! You shame me with your gaze! Go away!"

"Shame you!" Geoffrey spun on his heel and stalked out of the stillery, his face dark, fists clenched.

"Geoffrey, no!" Cordelia cried, leaping to her feet—but she was talking to the stout oaken planks of the door. "I had not meant—oh, blast! Men are such fools!" And she collapsed onto her stool again, weeping afresh.

• • •

In the Great Hall, Geoffrey stood rigid, closing his eyes, visualizing Alain's face, trying to concentrate on it—but his emotions were in too great a turmoil to allow him to teleport. His own sister! That the empty-headed, preening fool of a Prince should have had the gall to insult Cordelia! He could scarcely throttle his rage enough to detect the Prince's thoughts, there was such a roaring in his head. "I shall have to seek him on horseback! Blast and be hanged! 'Tis too slow!"

But there was no help for it, so he strode off to the stables and saddled his roan as a groom leaped to the bridle. Minutes later, the young warlock was pounding out across the drawbridge, hard on the trail of the Prince who had insulted his sister.

An hour later, Cordelia emerged from the stillery, face washed but haggard. As she came into the solar, the steward stepped up, all solicitation. "Are you well, milady?"

"As well as one might expect," Cordelia sighed, and sat down beneath the clerestory window. "I am minded to take some tea, Squire Bruntly."

"Aye, milady." The steward nodded to the footman, who departed for the kitchen.

"And, Squire Bruntly . . ."

The steward turned back to her. "Aye, milady?"

"Where is my brother?"

"I cannot say, milady." Squire Bruntly did his best to look apologetic. "I know only that he rode off posthaste, an hour ago."

"An hour ago!" Cordelia stiffened. "Is it all of an hour since he came to see me in the stillery?"

"It is, milady."

"Where has he gone?"

"I do not know." Squire Bruntly spread his hands, beginning to have a very bad feeling about all this.

"Then I fear I do!" Cordelia leaped to her feet and began pacing the floor. "Blast! Knows he no better than to meddle in my affairs?"

"I am sure that your brother is quite concerned for your honor, milady," Squire Bruntly said, vaguely shocked without knowing why.

"My honor, forsooth! When my honor needs such defending as a brother might do, I shall tell him! Oh, Squire Bruntly! In which direction did he ride?"

"Why, I cannot say, milady—but I shall send for the sentries."

"You need not. Which way did Prince Alain ride?"

"West, milady, back toward Runnymede."

"Then you need not ask which way Geoffrey rode," Cordelia said grimly. "Blast! If only I could teleport, as he can! Well, there's no help for it! I shall return when I may, Squire Bruntly!"

"We shall keep the kettle hot, milady." Squire Bruntly stared after her as she caught up her broomstick and hurried away toward the nearest tower. Now he knew why that feeling of dread had been building within him.

As they had ridden west, the day had darkened, and Alain had calmed a bit, from anger into moroseness. A strange, hollow feeling had been growing inside him; where butterflies had been struggling out of their cocoons, there was now only echoing darkness.

Very dark indeed. There was a lethargy, a hopelessness, that had never been there before. Could Cordelia really have meant so much to him?

Yes, he realized. For year after year, she had been his playmate, when the two families had met for feast-day or parents' conference. She had played with the boys as vigorously as any, and Alain had fallen in love with her before he was seven. Of course, he had told himself, that had been only a child's infatuation—but when she had undergone the teen-age metamorphosis from child into young woman, he had been taken all over again; his head had seemed lighter whenever he had looked at her, watching her move and hearing her talk had become entrancing again. Of course, he had been tongue-tied, unable to talk with her then, except in the old, familiar ways of friendship, never as boy to girl, so he had never told her of his feelings. Instead, he had consoled himself with the thought that, since he was a Prince and Heir Apparent, he could have his pick of any of the girls in all his parents' kingdom, and of course he would choose Cordelia. It had never occurred to him that she might say no.

However, with a new and brutal self-honesty, he realized that he had never seriously thought that she could be in love with him. Oh, yes, he was Prince and Heir, and would some day be King—but he was lumpen compared to her. She was a fairy, light and dancing; he was an ox, plodding through life with nothing but a dogged determination to do what was right—right for his subjects, right for the kingdom, and right for her. Not for himself, of course—that was one of the most important principles in being a knight and a nobleman, let alone a King: to sacrifice one's own comfort and pleasure for others' good. So his father had taught him, and it had never occurred to him to question it, in spite of his mother's jaundiced looks and jibing. She had never truly denied it, only joked with Father that he was too intent on duty, to the point of being dull and boring. Her sallies always resulted in his giving a ball, and spending half the evening dancing with her, jesting and chatting and listening to her, in a strenuous attempt to prove he could be exciting and romantic still.

He had never done very well at it, Alain thought. He had heard that his father had been handsome and gallant in his youth, and the son could certainly believe it when he looked at the sire—but he noticed that no one had ever said his father was dashing or romantic, and he could easily believe that Tuan had never been so. Always solidly dependable, always serious and devoted, but never much fun.

Nor was his son, Alain reflected—and never would be, in all probability. Worse, he didn't even have the advantage of being handsome.

But he could be gallant. Iron resolve hardened within him; he would treat Cordelia in the future as though she were a goddess; he would bow to her, he would speak her fair, he would shower compliments upon her. He would even send word ahead.

A shout broke the air behind him, inarticulate, angered.

"Highness!" Sir Devon snapped.

Alain looked up, startled, and turned around, to see Geoffrey Gallowglass pounding after them down the road, cloak flying behind him in the wind. Alain turned his horse, a glad cry of welcome on his lips, but Geoffrey was roaring, "Caitiff! Hound and swine!"

"How dare you speak thus to our Prince!" Sir Devon bellowed back at him, and the other five young knights took place behind him, forming a living wall between Alain and Geoffrey.

Suddenly, Alain remembered that Geoffrey was the brother of the lady who had so lately scorned him, and that in his hurt, he might have spoken more harshly to her than he had intended.

Geoffrey crashed in between Sir Devon and Sir Langley, throwing his weight against Sir Devon in a body-block. Horse and rider shuddered; the others were knocked aside, and the horse stumbled.

With an inarticulate roar, Geoffrey whirled to chop down with his sword at Sir Langley, who was just recovering his balance from the unexpected shock. He looked up, appalled, then brought up his sword barely in time to parry. Then Geoffrey whirled his sword down to slam against the knight's shield. The strength of his blow knocked the blade back against its owner, slashing Sir Langley's forehead. He fell, senseless.

Then Geoffrey was beyond the group of knights again, turning and halting his horse, glaring at them, eyes narrowing. They shouted and spurred their horses—but two of the stallions collided with each other, and the third knight's sword suddenly wrenched itself from his grasp, then rapped him sharply on the head with its hilt. He slumped in the saddle, and his horse slowed, feeling the loosening of the reins. He fell, limp as a sack of meal. The horse, well trained, stepped over him to shield him with its body.

The other two young knights had steadied their horses and regained control—but one's shield suddenly yanked his arm up high, then knocked him on the head. He fell.

The last knight paled as he galloped toward Geoffrey, but he didn't rein in; he even managed a battle cry of bravado—a cry that turned into a yawn as Geoffrey glared at him. His eyes fluttered closed, and he fell forward in his saddle, sound asleep.

Sir Devon struggled back up to his feet, weaving and woozy, but game.

Geoffrey turned to him with narrowed eyes.

"Hold!" Alain was jolted back to his senses. " 'Tis me with whom he fights! Stand aside!"

Geoffrey turned toward the Prince.

"But, Highness . . ." Sir Devon cried.

"Aside!" Alain stormed, and the thrill of battle sang through his veins. He turned to his erstwhile friend Geoffrey with an almost savage delight; this would be the perfect outlet for the rage and frustration of Cordelia's rejection. "He is mine!"

"Then have at thee, boorish Princeling!" Geoffrey bellowed, and slammed his horse into Alain's.

But Alain had already seen the maneuver used against Sir Devon, and was braced for it. He rocked in the saddle but held his seat, and parried Geoffrey's overhand slash, then parried another, and another . . . the blades rang, strokes fast and furious, the horses dancing around one another, the knights of the bodyguard crying out in anger and alarm.

Geoffrey was staring in surprise, and Alain felt a thrill of satisfaction; the Gallowglass had not expected him to be so able an opponent! The satisfaction was strong enough to urge him to use Geoffrey's own trick against him—he spurred his horse and slammed it into Geoffrey's mount with a suddenness that took the young warlock by surprise.

So did Alain's shoulder in his short ribs.

Geoffrey reeled in the saddle. Alain reached over to

shove with his left hand, and with a very ungraceful scrabbling and grasping, the young warlock fell off his horse.

He landed and rolled up to his feet, sword still in his grasp, face red with embarrassment and fury—to see Alain dismounting and turning to him.

"Oh, very chivalrous!" Geoffrey snarled, and was on him.

Now the blows flew thick and fast, thrust and parry and slash and counter. There was no use of horses as weapons now, but only naked steel, sword and dagger against sword and dagger. But Alain was quickly on the defensive; he gave ground, and gave ground again, astounded to realize that he was fighting for his life, that his sword was beaten back again and again, that Geoffrey's blows came so thick and fast that it was all he could do to parry, not even having time to riposte.

Sir Devon cried out and spurred in.

"Hold off, Sir Devon!" Alain cried, but not soon enough; Geoffrey leaped aside, whirled, and caught Sir Devon's foot as the knight galloped by. He heaved, and Sir Devon came crashing down from the saddle. Geoffrey spun back, ready to ward off Alain's blow, but the Prince was standing on guard. "I would not dishonor myself by striking at a foeman's back!"

"Would you not?" Geoffrey snapped. "Then your sense of honor shall cause you to be slain some day, Highness!" And he leaped in to the attack again.

Alain saw his one chance to regain the offensive, and took it, leaping aside from the blow and thrusting at full extension—but Geoffrey twisted to parry in a gyration that Alain would have thought impossible, and slashed backhanded at the young Prince's chest. Alain parried in the nick of time, then parried again and again, giving ground with each stroke. His companions howled their alarm and pressed in, but Alain bawled at them to hold their places.

Then, suddenly, Geoffrey's blade swirled around his own, his hilt twisted in his hand and wrenched against the fingers, and his sword went flying away through the air.

Aghast, he stared at the point of Geoffrey's blade, six inches from his face.

The young knights cried out in alarm and spurred their horses.

"Back!" Geoffrey roared. "Or my hand might slip!"

The knights reined in, hard.

"Now," grated Geoffrey, "you shall apologize to me on my sister's behalf, Your Highness, and swear to take your apologies to her in person, or I shall witness the color of your entrails with my own eyes."

Alain tried to glare back at him, but he remembered the rash words he had snapped at Cordelia, and dropped his gaze in chagrin. "I do most humbly apologize, for those were rude words indeed that I spoke, and the lady deserved them not in the slightest." He lifted his head, looking back into Geoffrey's puzzled gaze. "As to fear of yourself or your blade, why, if you think me a coward to have apologized at sword's point, then stab with that point, and be done! You have sneered at the notion of honor, so I shall not be surprised you have so little of it yourself, that you would slay an unarmed man!"

Sir Devon gasped, gathering himself for a desperate spring—but Geoffrey's eyes only narrowed to slits.

Before he could speak, Alain went on. "Yet be advised, young warlock, that your sister's words had a sting of their own, and did stab me most unexpectedly."

"Did that warrant your insults and threats of revenge?" Geoffrey countered, grim-faced.

"I spoke in anger, hurt, and shame," Alain replied. "I spoke rashly and foolishly. Surely, Geoffrey, you know that I would never dream of hurting Cordelia—and to realize that I have done so is cause for great shame! I shall apologize as honor dictates I must, apologize to the lady most abjectly!"

"Why, how now?" Geoffrey eyed him warily. "Will you do what honor dictates, when your station contradicts it?"

"Honor is of more import than rank," Alain returned. "In truth, I cannot honestly claim royal station if I have lost honor. Nay, I shall apologize to your sister as soon as I may come to her."

Geoffrey tried to maintain the glare, but had to let it drop, and his sword's point with it. He eyed his old friend with disgust. "Why, how can I stay angry with you, if you behave so admirably? You are a most aggravating opponent, Prince Alain!"

"And you a most astounding one," Alain returned, suppressing a tremor of relief. "I have never been beaten before, save in childhood duels with yourself. You humiliated me, for you were two years my junior—and you have done so again now."

"You have deserved it," Geoffrey said grimly.

"I know that I have." Alain frowned. "Yet we have not duelled since we were twelve, for my father forbade it."

"Aye." Geoffrey smiled. "He forbade it as soon as we were old enough to be truly a danger to one another. One must not imperil the heir to the throne."

"You would not have slain me!"

"Not with purpose, no. Accidents have happened with swords ere now, though, and will happen again. 'Tis a dangerous game."

"But how could you win so easily?" Alain protested.

"Partly by my own skill." Geoffrey's anger had largely abated. "The other part was your overconfidence."

"None have won against me save you!"

"Of course they have not." With friendly exasperation, Geoffrey explained, "Who among your courtiers would dare to defeat the Heir Apparent, Alain?"

Alain stared. "You do not mean they have let me win!"

"Certainly they did! Would any man in the Court dare to antagonize the future King, whose favor will determine each man's fortune?"

Alain looked away, numb and confounded. "I had thought myself the epitome of courtesy and chivalry!"

"Well, mayhap in your daily conduct." Geoffrey relented. "Yet surely not when you are angered. Your speech with my sister was somewhat less than charming, Alain."

The Prince looked up again, alarmed. "Less! How rude

was I, Geoffrey? I came so filled with enthusiasm and excitement that I may, ah, have overlooked the niceties."

"Niceties?" Geoffrey grinned. "Forsooth, Alain! You did not send word of your coming, you did not ask to be admitted, you virtually commanded the lady to appear and, worse, informed her that she was your choice! A lover should plead and sue, not command!"

"Should he indeed?" Alain stared. "I know naught of this."

"That," Geoffrey said drily, "is somewhat apparent."

Alain's gaze wandered again. "I had never thought to court a lady! Princes' marriages are arranged for them; I did not think to have choice, nor to have to woo, and therefore never learned the way of it."

"No, you surely have not." Geoffrey felt a stab of sympathy for his friend. "A lad does not dictate nor condescend to the lady whom he loves, Alain, and well she knows it. She must be sure that he yearns for her so greatly that he will cherish her always."

Alain frowned, puzzled. "How do you know so much of it?"

Geoffrey answered with a knowing grin. "Ah, well, my friend, I am not a Prince, nor do I have so exalted a sense of forbearance as you seem to have."

"You do not mean that you have courted ladies!"

"Well, not ladies," Geoffrey allowed. "With them, I have only flirted, stealing no more than a kiss or two. With ladies of one's own station, one is apt to be constrained to become a husband, if one seeks to dally. With commoners, though, there is less expectation, and greater willingness."

"You have flirted with chambermaids and milkmaids, then?"

"I will own to that," Geoffrey admitted, "and to having won their favors."

Alain ached to ask just how extensive those favors had been, but it would have been rude. The sudden, overwhelming realization struck him: any favors he had won from women had been almost by accident—and intoxication. "Alas! If I am not the chivalrous knight I had thought myself, however am I to win your sister's love?"

"Chivalry does not always have a great deal to do with it," Geoffrey allowed. "Do you truly wish to win Cordelia, though? Or is it only that you have been ordered to?"

"I have not been so ordered!" Alain cried vehemently. "She is my choice, my heart's desire! I have known that I loved her since I was fourteen!"

Geoffrey sat still a moment, absorbing the fact of his friend's passion. Then he said quietly, "Well, well. You have kept your own counsel well, have you not?"

"So have I been bred." Alain looked away. "My father has taught me that a king must indeed do so, for his bosom will need to hold many secrets."

"You have kept this one too well. I doubt that my sister knows anything of it."

"But how am I to tell her?" Alain cried. "I cannot merely step up to her and declare it!"

Now it was Geoffrey's gaze that wandered. "No-o-o-o," he agreed. "That would be unwise. You must create the right mood for such an announcement, if you wish her to believe you."

"Why, how is this?" Alain stared, astounded. "Is there no love arising by itself, from a woman? Might not she fall in love with me ere I have even spoke a word?"

"She will, if she is your one true love," Geoffrey said. "If she is not in love with you, no persuading of yours will ever create that love, though your conduct and bearing may inspire it. When all's said and done, it is what you are that will win the lady—and if you wish to win her, 'tis a matter of what you can become."

"I cannot be anything but myself!"

"That is true," Geoffrey agreed, "and you were best to wait for the lady who loves what you are, rather than try to become what she loves. But you may have sterling qualities that would inspire her love, if only you could show them. When all's said and done, winning a lass is a matter of how you present yourself. That, and learning to be romantic."

"What is this 'romance'?" Alain asked, frowning.

Geoffrey spread his hands, at a loss. " 'Tis as much a fantasy as a reality, my friend. The troubadours know it— 'tis not a matter of lying, exactly, but of making the plain facts more appealing, of surrounding the bare bones of life with a pleasing form. 'Tis this that awakens desire in a lady—candlelight, and viols playing, and a dance that whirls her away."

"You speak of deliberate planning, of cozening," Alain protested. "Must I persuade her that what I say is true?"

Geoffrey shrugged. "Her future, her entire life, depends upon it, Alain. She must be sure."

"Then however am I to win her?" Alain cried in despair. "For I have no gift in persuasion, no silvered tongue, no ability to charm! I am only a blunt, plain-spoken soldier who knows how to guard his words!"

"Guarding one's words is not altogether what the ladies want," Geoffrey advised him, "though you must choose those words well. They wish you to be borne away by a flood of passion so strong that tender, caring words burst out of you."

"And all my training has been to keep words in!" Alain turned away in misery. "I shall never win her love, then! I shall never win *any* woman's love!"

Now Geoffrey felt the first faint twinges of alarm—of concern for his friend but, moreover, for his sister. He knew Cordelia had always thought of Alain as her personal future property, and frankly, the young Prince was the only man whom he thought worthy of his sister—not because he was the future King, but because he was as dependable as a rock and, beneath all his pomposity, good-hearted and warm. Geoffrey didn't doubt that, if they were married, Alain would treat Cordelia like the precious thing she was. He felt a sudden need to boost his friend's ego. "It is nothing inborn," he said, "no quality within you. It is only that all your life, all your experience, has been spent in the safe confines of your parents' castle, the controlled and artificial world of their court."

"Artificial!" Alain looked up, amazed and affronted.

" 'Tis quite a work of artifice, a thing made by people, not by God," Geoffrey explained. "Hunger and ugliness are banished and kept out; oppression and cruelty are veiled and harnessed by custom and manners. You have never faced real danger without others to ward you, nor dealt with the world on its own terms."

"What terms do you speak of?" Alain demanded sharply.

Geoffrey realized that there were suddenly more concerns than Cordelia on his mind. "Terms of danger, my Prince—the danger of cruel men who murder and steal, the dangers of famine and disease. You have never seen how your future subjects live, nor to what authority they must answer. You have never gone through your kingdom solely as Alain, not as the Prince."

"Why, thou dost paint me as a stock of a man, a painted stick, a hollow effigy!"

"Even so; you have said it."

"How dare you!" Alain cried, the anger of his defeat finally bubbling over. "How dare you speak so to your Prince!"

Geoffrey nodded with grim satisfaction. "Even now you do it—even now you seek refuge behind your title. As to how I dare, why—I have only answered the questions you asked. Do you truly ask me how I dare to answer them honestly?"

Alain stared at him, then spoke, seeming numb. "No. I cannot fault you for that, can I? Indeed, I should praise you for the truthfulness all others near me do lack."

Suddenly he turned away, once again in despair. "But how can I ever face her again? If I am truly so shallow, so puffed-up and pompous, how can I ever hope to win Cordelia's heart? How, if I am so superficial and vain?"

"Become a true man," Geoffrey answered, "one of flesh and bone, with hot blood in your veins."

"Why, how can I do that?"

"Go off on a quest of your own, friend, to discover what you truly are—with none to ward you, and no sign of your true rank."

"I would not know how to bear myself, nor where to go," Alain protested.

Geoffrey threw up his hands in exasperation. "Why, then, I shall show you! Come, and we shall go adventuring, you and I—but come straightaway. Do not go to your home to shift your clothes, nor to pack your gear, but come away now!"

" 'Tis even as you say; my parents would never hear of it." With sudden resolution, Alain said, "Why, then, I shall learn the way of it—of courting, of living, of being true! Come, old friend, let us go!"

Sir Devon watched, amazed, as the two young men rode off into the forest side by side. Clearly, the Prince had forgotten Sir Devon. The knight felt a moment's rage before he remembered how preoccupied Alain had been, how sunk in gloom; then Sir Devon's resentment melted like ice in tea, for he had been raised on romances like any other young gentleman of Gramarye, and knew that all can be forgiven the lover who is driven to distraction. He allowed himself a moment for a sad smile, then sighed and called his horse. Alain might have been forgiven, but Sir Devon still had his duty—to report what had happened to Their Majesties.

He rode away down the road. Scarcely had he passed beyond the first bend when Cordelia came shooting into view on her broomstick. From her higher vantage point, she could see a break in the trees, where Alain and Geoffrey were riding away together. For a moment, she stared; then a hot surge of indignation reddened her cheeks, and she banked into a sharp turn, heading back toward Castle Gallowglass, growing angrier and angrier with every mile she flew.

CHAPTER
~3~

"How could he! How could he go gallivanting off with one who has but lately given his sister insult!"

Cordelia was pacing the floor of the solarium, fuming, tiny slippers tapping. Rod and Gwen sat by, watching their daughter and biting their tongues. At least, Rod was biting his.

"Perchance," Gwen suggested, "thy brother had already rebuked Alain, and punished him."

Cordelia looked up, instantly dismayed. "Oh, say not so! I know the manner of Geoffrey's rebuke." She frowned. "Nay, he could not have, or there would not be enough of Alain left to sit a horse!"

"Unless Alain apologized," Rod pointed out.

Cordelia stared. "Alain, apologize? That stuffed, self-important popinjay, lower himself to apology?"

"I think thou dost wrong him in that, daughter," Gwen said gently. "He is chivalrous enough to apologize, if he could be brought to see that he had wronged you."

"Even if he had, 'twas to *me* he should have apologized—not Geoffrey!"

"Why, that is so," Gwen said, puzzled. "Wherefore would he not seek thee out?"

"Scared," Rod opined. "I would be, too, if a pretty girl had just rejected me flat out."

Cordelia turned to him, puzzled. "Why should this be?"

"Just a quirk of the male mind. We're sensitive about being told we don't matter."

Cordelia frowned. "But I did not."

"Sure—you just told him 'no.' Right? No explanations, no excuses—nothing but a flat 'no.' "

"There was more than that." For the first time, a trace of guilt crept into Cordelia's expression.

Rod was silent, waiting—but Cordelia was silent, too, lost in recent memory, and mortified.

Finally, Gwen broke the silence. "Thou hast ever been quick and sharp of tongue, daughter."

"Oh, but I so rarely mean what I say in the heat of the moment!"

"Aye—'tis naught but the telling remark, the barbed retort, that matters, is't not? Yet hast thou thought of the hurt thy hasty words may do?"

"Surely he knows that rash words are not meant!"

"Alain? No," Rod said. "I don't think he knows anything of the kind. Very serious young man, that. In fact, I wouldn't be surprised if he thinks angry words show how a person really feels."

"Oh, but he cannot!" Cordelia wrung her hands. "He cannot truly think that I meant what I said!"

"Are you sure you don't?"

Cordelia stilled, considering. Then she said, "He is somewhat pompous . . ."

"And insensitive," Rod agreed. "Are you sure he's right for you? Shouldn't you be going after a man with a bit more of a sense of fun?"

Gwen flashed him a glare.

"But he could be changed!" Cordelia cried. "I could make him see his true nature, lessen his conceit, teach him to think of others' feelings!"

Rod shook his head. "Never think you can change a

man, daughter. Oh, he will change, in time—but not necessarily into what you want him to be."

"Marriage itself will change him!"

"Aye, marriage will," Gwen agreed, "but not on the instant, and not always in the way thou wouldst wish."

Rod cast her a rather guilty glance. Fortunately, she wasn't looking.

"But I have always known I would wed Alain!"

"Thou art not pledged to him," Gwen said sternly. "Look at the man he has become, daughter, and say if thou truly dost wish him."

"I do! Oh, I know I do! Have I not lain awake thinking of him? Have I not watched him year by year, and considered him?"

"Hast thou ever asked thyself if thou dost love him?"

"We will love one another in time!"

Rod shook his head. "Don't ever bet on that."

"Are not all royal marriages so made?"

"Catharine's wasn't," Rod pointed out.

"Aye," Gwen agreed. "She married for love, and I doubt not she doth hope that her sons will also."

"I know that I want him!" Cordelia cried. "Is that not enough?"

And, "No," both her parents said together.

"Oh, be still!" Cordelia stormed. "You understand nothing, you are too old! You have forgot what 'tis like to be young!"

Her parents ground their teeth, and tried to remember what Cordelia had just said about not meaning what she said in anger.

"The worst of it is that I must now follow them." Cordelia started pacing again.

"Follow them?" Rod stared. "In the name of Heaven, why?"

"It might not be the course of wisdom, daughter," Gwen hinted.

"Wisdom is for crones, old men, and Gregory! I must follow to see that no harm befalls my Prince!"

"Surely he is safe with thy brother," Gwen objected. "Naught could touch him there."

"Naught but Geoffrey's soldierly nonsense! He will fill Alain with swagger and bluster, I doubt not—tell him that no man's a man unless he can drink a gallon of wine and still bed a wench!"

"Cordelia!" Gwen gasped.

"He will, Mother—you know he will!"

"Maybe not quite in those terms," Rod hedged.

"Terms! What matter the terms?" Cordelia stamped her foot. "Nay, 'tis what he may do that worries me! By your leave, my parents, I must fly!" She turned and strode out of the solar without waiting for an answer.

It was very still behind her, for a few minutes.

Then Rod released a long breath and said, "Well! What do you think she's really planning to protect him from, dear?"

"Wenches who are pretty and willing," Gwen retorted. "What else?"

"I think she'll find that her usual array of witch powers doesn't do her much good there. Think she can learn new techniques?"

"How to enchant a lad? I have no doubt that she can, if she wishes to."

"Yes, but knowing our daughter, she's too honest to want to, if she isn't in love herself."

"Dost thou truly fault that?"

"Not in the slightest," Rod sighed. "But I can't help wondering if she's going to be enchanting for Alain. What do you think of the chances?"

"I think that she may make the greatest mistake of her life," Gwen answered, "or the wisest choice."

"Let's hope for wisdom, in spite of what she thinks of it." Rod shook his head. "I'm only glad that in my case, wisdom and love happened together." He squeezed her hand and smiled into her eyes.

Gwen smiled back, reflecting that it had taken her a great deal of effort to make him understand that.

• • •

"He is gone! What! Off into the forest? Alone?"

Tuan forced down a surge of irritation. He understood that to his wife, "alone" meant with fewer than twenty bodyguards. "Be of good cheer, my sweet. He could not be more thoroughly warded if he had an army with him."

"Oh, thou dost place far too much faith in this boisterous boy of Gwendylon's! How could they stand against a whole troop of bandits, they two alone? And they are quite like to meet such, there in the greenwood!"

She had been carrying on like this since Sir Devon had reported what had happened.

"To dare to strike at the Heir!" Catharine ranted. " 'Tis treason, 'tis a crime most foul, 'tis . . ."

" 'Twas a disagreement between two youths," Tuan interrupted, "and our own lad was not blameless, if thou wilt consider."

"Well . . . aye, he may have spoken rashly and in haste! But the Crown Prince may not be assaulted!"

Privately, Tuan thought it had probably done his son a world of good, and was rather proud that he had stood up for so long against Geoffrey Gallowglass—for King Tuan was a knight born, bred, and trained, and knew well the warrior-worth of the middle Gallowglass boy. "Blows or not, they are friends again . . ."

"Through our son apologizing! A Prince, to apologize! 'Tis unheard of, 'tis humiliation, 'tis . . ."

"Most chivalrous," Tuan finished for her. "Howsoe'er it may or may not have become him as a prince, it is most fitting for him as a knight, and I am proud of him for it."

"Oh, thou wouldst be, thou! Men! Hast thou no care but thy game of honor?"

Tuan stiffened. "That honor is the protection of many a lady, and giveth her the respect that is due her. If our son hath transgressed in this, at least he hath had the grace to make amends . . ."

"Or shall, if he doth live! Husband, art thou a fool? Canst thou not see his danger?"

"Danger, when he is a swordsman most excellent himself, and is accompanied by the best in the land?" Tuan smiled. "Be of good cheer, my sweet. He shall come forth from this wood hale and sound, and more sure of himself than ever he hath been."

"Oh, to be sure! That is what our son Alain most truly doth need—an even greater opinion of himself!"

"In truth, he doth," said Tuan quietly, "for though he may believe himself to be good, he cannot *know*. He is untried, and therefore unsure of his own worth."

"Men!" Catharine threw up her hands in disgust. "As though naught but thy ability with the sword proves thy worth!"

Tuan reflected that she had been glad enough of his ability with weapons, when she had stood at war with her noblemen. "There is also the matter of his being an object of desire in the eyes of the lady he loves—and he hath but now found that in that regard, he is naught."

Catharine stopped abruptly, frowning down at her knotted hands. She was silent a moment, then said, "Doth he love her, then?"

"Be sure that he doth," Tuan said softly. "Hast thou seen his eyes when he hath watched her at a banquet or a ball, and thought she did not see?"

"I have," Catharine said, her voice low, "and have watched Cordelia's face, too, as she watched him when he was engaged in talk—or in dance, with another damsel."

"Is she too in love?"

"I cannot tell," Catharine said slowly. "She is jealous, aye, though whether it is for love, or for others' interest in something that she doth regard as belonging to her, I cannot tell."

"If 'twere only a matter of property, would she have cast him off but now?"

Catharine shrugged. "If he came upon her unannounced, when she was in such disarray? Aye, any woman would have turned him away."

"I know so little of women," Tuan sighed, "but to me, that hath more of the sound of love than of covetousness."

Catharine shrugged, irritated. "I fear, husband, that our son is lacking in gallantry."

Christopher Stasheff

"He is," Tuan admitted, "as he is lacking in knowledge of his people."

That stung Catharine in one of her most tender spots—for she was, in spite of her willfulness and temper, a diligent ruler who tried her best to rule for her people's good. "Thou dost speak truth. He hath never been among the folk." Then hysteria surged again. "But how can I risk him?"

"You must," Tuan said, gently but inexorably. "He cannot be a good man if he hath not tested his true mettle—and he cannot become a good King if he knoweth naught of those whom he would rule."

"But the price!" Catharine cried, anguished.

"The price must be paid." Tuan still strove to be gentle. "He must come to know at least a little about his people, and what their lives are truly like. He must rule more folk than the noblemen he hath grown to know, after all, nor must he govern only for their benefit."

"I know that thou hadst some months among the poor," Catharine said, low—she still felt guilty for having banished her lover, even though he had forgiven her instantly. He had smuggled himself back in from exile, and lived in hiding among the commoners of the capital town. Then he had proved himself in war, for her sake.

Tuan nodded. " 'Tis for this that I have ever had as much sympathy for the poor as thy tender woman's heart hath given thee. But our son will not, if he goeth not among them whilst he can."

"It is true," Catharine admitted, "and I have been glad of the caution and respect for the common folk that thou hast brought to accompany mine ardent wish to better their lot." She looked up at Tuan. "Dost thou truly believe he must undertake this quest, to become a good monarch?"

"And a good lover," Tuan amended. "Aye, it is most necessary indeed."

"Why then, let it be!" Catharine threw up her hands in surrender. "But if he must go, husband, thou must needs assure he will not go unguarded—or, at the least, no more so than is necessary."

"I shall have a squadron of knights ever at hand, in case of need," Tuan promised.

"But how shalt thou know if there is such need!"

"That," said Tuan, "I shall leave to Brom O'Berin."

Brom O'Berin was the Lord Privy Councillor, but in secret, he was also the King of the Elves. To his human friends, he was a dwarf—but to his elfin subjects, he was a giant. He managed to straddle both worlds without being torn apart—but his love for a diminutive mortal woman had nearly rent his soul, when she died. What had kept him going was the child she had left behind, whom he had seen raised in secret, not knowing he was her father, for he feared she would be ashamed of him. He swelled with pride when he saw her with her husband and her children, for she was Gwendylon, now Gallowglass, and her half-elven blood made her the most powerful witch of her generation.

A few years later, his caring for his natural daughter was supplemented by his love for his foster daughter—for he was the King's jester, and took the little princess under his wing. She had grown up to become Catharine the Queen.

So Brom had a double interest in the current quest—his grandson, and the son of the woman that he loved almost as much as his daughter.

He made sure they would be very safe.

"Still, my lord," said Puck, "the Prince should concern thee as much as the warlock."

"Should he truly, Robin?" Brom turned a dark gaze upon his right-hand elf. "Geoffrey is my grandson, after all—and more to the point, Cordelia is my granddaughter."

Puck's brow puckered in puzzlement. "Aye, my lord, she is—yet wherefore is that more to the point? She is not at risk on this quest."

"Nay, but her happiness is. I find myself wary in regard to Alain—moreover, in his fitness as a suitor."

"He has ever been summat of a spoiled brat," Puck admitted.

Brom nodded. "He spoke with far greater anger to the lady than a gentleman ought."

"Well, true—but she had refused his suit, and quite abruptly, with no graciousness to cushion the blow. Still, I will own that even a squire should have shown more self-restraint, let alone a prince."

"Is it so easy, then, to believe that Alain is unworthy of her?" Brom demanded.

Well, now, Puck wasn't related—and more importantly, he had been baby-sitter for the Gallowglass brood when they were children. He knew their inner selves quite well. "I love the lass dearly, as do any who know her—yet I must own that she, too, has her faults."

"Oh, aye, a temper ever too ready! Yet should she not thereby wed a man with great inborn patience?" Brom shook his head. "I had thought Alain to be such."

"Why, so he is, like his father before him," Puck answered, "under most circumstances. Yet we speak now, my lord, of a wound to the heart—and, though 'tis not easily seen through the maze of Alain's vanity, he is in love with her."

That brought Brom to a halt. "Aye, he is, and hath been since that he was a child. It is well thou dost bring it to mind, Puck, for I am like to forget it, he hath learned to hide it so well."

"What else might he do?" Puck sighed. "The lady hath ever been bright and cheery with him, but hath never shown a single sign of being a-love with him. Thinking him to be her property, aye, but in love?"

"Mayhap I should not be unhappy to see them parted," Brom mused. "Indeed, even a prince of mortals may not be worthy of a lass who is herself a princess of Faerie, though she knoweth it not."

And of course, as they both knew, the folk of Faerie were worth far more than mere mortals.

"Worthy or not, were he to die, her heart would break," Puck pointed out.

"Aye—but would it not also break if she kept a pet dog

that were slain? For she hath a most generous heart."
Brom's visage was dark.

Puck knew the kind of storms that darkness could presage, and quailed within—but he spoke up bravely. "There is no question, then, my lord—they must be warded, protected."

"Even so," Brom said heavily. " 'Tis my duty to the Queen . . ."

"If a King of Faerie could be said to have duty to any other monarch," Puck muttered.

"I have sworn allegiance to her, Puck, and I love her, though not so intensely as mine own daughter. Nay, we must protect her son—and my grandson. Go thou to watch over them, and summon a legion of elves if need be."

"I go." Puck bounced up—then paused. "Yet how if need *not* be?"

"Then I will rejoice to hear it. Send word of their journey daily, Robin—most particularly as regards the bearing and conduct of the Prince."

Puck eyed his sovereign with foreboding. "And if his comportment doth not meet thine expectation?"

"Then," said Brom grimly, "I shall find some way to bring his suit to disaster."

A devilish grin lit Puck's face.

"Aye, thou hast had a dozen manners of mischiefbringing spring into thy mind on the instant, hast thou not?" Brom said, with dry amusement.

"No, my lord," Puck said truthfully. He had only had six schemes for sabotaging Alain's courtship burst fullblown into his mind.

"Hold them in abeyance until I bid thee," Brom commanded, "and ponder on ways to aid his suit, should I decide he is fitting."

Puck made a face; helping lovers was far less to his taste than sabotaging them.

"Away, now, to ward!" Brom commanded.

Puck darted away down the tunnel, and was gone.

Brom turned back to the long stone staircase that would take him up to the secret door into the royal castle. He still had to command the seneschal to send out a troop of knights to follow an hour's ride behind the prince. As he climbed, he considered Puck's reliability, especially considering the elf's inability to refuse a chance to play a practical joke, should the occasion offer. No, everything considered, Brom decided that he should occasionally go himself, to check up on Alain's welfare and progress.

Tuan had similar concerns, though he wasn't about to voice them to Brom, and certainly not to Catharine—she would have denied his comments hotly, taking them as an attack upon her son and, more pertinently, on her ideas about rearing him. But Tuan was the offspring of a country lord, and had been hardened by combat in the field. He had been worried for some time that his son was becoming a court fop, removed from the realities of life, concerned more with the cut of his hose than the sufferings of the poor or the political machinations of the aristocrats. Everything considered, the chances of any real harm befalling Alain seemed quite small compared to the benefits he might gain from the excursion—not the least of which was the companionship of Geoffrey Gallowglass, who had grown up to be everything Tuan had hoped his sons would be. Admittedly, Geoffrey was several things Tuan would *not* want Alain to be, too—he had heard tales of the boy's roistering and wenching—but he trusted to Alain's good breeding and inborn sense of rectitude to help him resist those traits.

Above all else was the invaluable knowledge that Alain was travelling with a swordsman who could beat him handily, and who had no more respect for his station than if he had been the lowest beggar on the road. Indeed, if that beggar had been able to put up a good fight with his quarterstaff, it was quite possible that Geoffrey would have had more respect for him than for the Prince. Geoffrey respected the man and his inner qualities, not the station. Tuan wasn't entirely sure that was a good attitude, but in the present circumstances it was ideal.

No, all in all, the King had high hopes for the trip—it

might be the making of Alain, both as a man and as a human being.

Still, there was danger.

He couldn't come right out and say any of this to Rod Gallowglass, of course, but he could propose a friendly hunting trip.

"Let us leave the ladies to their own devices for a while," he said as the two of them walked in the courtyard of Rod's castle. "It is too long since we rode the greenwood together, to remember the true troubles of the world."

Rod couldn't remember their ever having gone hunting together, but he knew a cue when he heard one. "After all, what could be more natural than that the King and his Lord High Warlock should go hunting together?"

"My thought exactly!" Tuan grinned. "And on the way, Rod Gallowglass, we might discuss our mutual concerns—perhaps even our hopes."

"And just happen to be going in the same general direction as our sons." Rod nodded. "Of course, it would be beneath our dignity to travel with fewer than a dozen knights as an honor guard."

"Quite so," Tuan agreed. "Certes, 'tis true that each of us hath oft gone abroad among the common folk alone, and disguised—but this would be more in the nature of a meeting of state."

"Of course. Any time we get together officially, it's always a meeting of state—and the fate of our children just happens to fall under that heading, too."

"It does. Thou art not opposed to the match, then?"

"Cordelia and Alain? Not at all—though I would have appreciated it if Alain had followed the social formula of asking my permission before he proposed. Might have staved off the current disaster."

"Aye." Tuan nodded heavily. "I have told him aforetime that being royal doth not allow him to trample on custom . . ."

"But his mother has told him that princes are above tradition, eh? Well, I think he'll begin to see that customs grow up for reasons." Rod frowned. "But there's another side to it, too, my liege."

"Aye." Tuan's face darkened. "Are they in love?"

"Such a short little word," Rod sighed, "but it can create such difficulties, can't it? Especially if it's not there."

Tuan shook his head, perplexed. "How can he have gone to ask her to be his wife, if he did not know her to be in love with him?"

"Oh, they have more or less grown up with the idea that *of course* they'll get married some day," Rod sighed. "After all, how many young folk of their age are there among the nobility of Gramarye?"

"A hundred, perhaps," Tuan said slowly.

"Yes, and a properly inbred bunch they are! Besides, half of them regard Alain as a hereditary enemy, simply because their fathers rebelled against you and Catharine at one time or another."

"Aye," said Tuan, "and the other half live so far from Runnymede that 'tis a wonder we have seen them once in a year. Still, my boy hath seen other lasses his age. I wonder that his devotion to thy Cordelia hath never swerved."

"It would be normal," Rod admitted, "but Alain is an unusually conscientious lad, and very loyal." He did not add "humorless and dull," though he might have. "He may feel that once he has pledged himself to Cordelia in his heart, he can't even look at another lady."

Tuan shook his head. "If it is not love, then the Archer will smite him soon or late."

"Better to have it sooner," Rod agreed. "I'll tell you frankly that I'm not all that sure that the match would be best for either of them; they may not be right for each other."

"Cordelia is certainly of acceptable rank to be a queen," Tuan said quickly, "and more than acceptable in her own person. Indeed, I would be honored to call her my daughter-in-law."

"And I couldn't ask for a more worthy or more responsible mate for her." Rod tactfully didn't mention that he really didn't want his daughter to marry a selfish prig like

Alain. Of course, if she had really been in love, he wouldn't have argued. "However, though they may be of the right quality for each other, they may not be right in personality. After all, so far as I know, neither of them has ever fallen in love with the other."

"Oh, I have seen the odd glance between them," Tuan said, "and the lilt to her voice when she speaks, and the toss of her head."

"Flirting, sure," Rod said, "but even that might have been due more to a shortage of other young folk their own age than to any real interest."

"So we must watch them in more ways than one, eh? Well, I shall tell Catharine of my departure. I doubt not she will be relieved to have some small time to herself."

Catharine might have been pleased if she hadn't seen through the ruse in an instant. Fortunately, the Lady Gwendylon had come to discuss the situation with her. They were sitting in Catharine's solar when Tuan breezed in and dropped his little bombshell.

"Surely thou wilt not be too aggrieved, my love? Thou shalt not? Why, there's a wench for you! Come on and kiss me!"

Catharine's protests were smothered, and by the time she caught her breath, Tuan was out the door and gone.

"Oh! The idiocy of men!" she fumed. "Thinks he that I cannot see through his ruse? Hunting, forsooth!"

"In a manner, they do," Gwen sighed, "though 'tis our sons they hunt, not the deer."

"And the dear knows when we shall see them again! Pray they do not let the boys know they are followed!"

"I shall—and I shall pray the same for Cordelia."

Catharine turned to her, stunned. "Surely she doth not follow them, too!"

"She doth," Gwen returned. "She hath little trust in her brother."

"Well, therein may I agree with her," Catharine said judiciously, "for Geoffrey is more filled with masculine nonsense than most—if thou wilt forgive the observation, Gwendylon."

"When did truth need forgiveness?" Gwen returned, though she could have added, "Frequently."

"They are so ridiculous!" Catharine fumed. "They will likely follow a day's pace behind—too distant to protect 'gainst assassins, too close for the boys to know they must trust to themselves!"

"Aye, 'tis most ridiculous," Gwen agreed, "but then, so are Geoffrey and Alain. Still, I doubt not that Brom's forces will be near. The young men will be protected, never fear." She knew, far better than Catharine, exactly how ubiquitous and effective Brom's troops were—his personal forces, at least. She had been raised by the elves, and they had no secrets from her, except the name of her father.

"Well—I warrant the men can do the boys no harm," Catharine grudged.

"We must let this issue pass, as we do so many that are really of no consequence," Gwen agreed.

"Still . . ." Catharine turned to her with a glint in her eye.

Gwen braced herself. "Aye, Majesty?"

"Why should not the followers be followed?" Catharine said, with a wicked smile.

Slowly, Gwen's own smile matched the Queen's. "Aye, Majesty. Be assured, I shall look in now and then on mine husband—and on thine, too."

So Alain and Geoffrey went a-wandering wild and free, two knights errant in search of adventure, on what must surely have been the best-supervised quest of all time. In fact, it was a virtual parade, with Puck shadowing his lord's grandson (not to mention his granddaughter's suitor), a dozen royal knights following a few hours behind the Heir Apparent, the two fathers trailing their sons with a score of knights, and the Lady Gwendylon keeping an eye on the two husbands.

But in front of them all, of course, went Cordelia.

CHAPTER
~4~

They rode in under the trees, Alain saying, "But where shall we . . ."

"Hist!" Geoffrey turned to him with a finger across his lips, then beckoned. He turned his horse off the trail and pushed through the underbrush.

Alain stared, taken by surprise. Then he pushed on after Geoffrey, aching to ask what they were doing, but keeping his lips pressed tight.

The underbrush thinned out, leaving room for the horses to walk, though Alain had to duck under boughs. Fortunately, he could watch Geoffrey in front of him, and be ready for the next low-hanging limb. They had to skirt a few trees that had branches down to the ground and step carefully over fallen logs, but they kept on going.

Finally, Geoffrey's horse half-slid, half-walked down to a stream. He stepped in. Alain followed, dying to ask what they were doing—or rather, why; the "what" seemed obvious.

They walked upstream for a quarter of an hour or more; then Geoffrey turned his horse to climb back out onto the same bank from which they had come, though a good way farther into the forest. He reined in and waited for Alain to come up with him.

"Wherefore have we perambulated so?" Alain asked.

"To lose pursuit," Geoffrey told him. "I doubt not that knight of your bodyguard may waken to find us gone, but will follow our trail into the wood. We do not wish him to be able to trace us far."

Alain turned thoughtful. "Aye, even so. Sir Devon would take it as his charge to find me, whether I wished it or no."

"And he will be most reluctant to return to your parents with word that he has lost us," Geoffrey agreed. "Nay, he will seek to follow—and when he cannot find our trail, he will take word to the King and Queen."

Alain's mouth tightened. "No doubt he will, and they will send a whole troop of knights to dog our footsteps."

"Therefore shall we leave them no footprints." Geoffrey grinned. "Mayhap we shall muddy our trail even further, then double back to watch them casting about to find us. Would that not be pleasant?"

Alain's first instinct was to protest against taking pleasure in troubling good men who were only trying to do their duty—but Geoffrey's smile was infectious, and he found himself grinning. "It would be amusing to watch."

However, Geoffrey could read his mind—only figuratively, this time, though he could easily have done it literally. "Be easy in your heart—they will not be greatly upset. Still, if we are to be accompanied by a small army, there is scant purpose in wandering."

"True enough," Alain admitted. "Nay, let us lose ourselves thoroughly."

They did.

An hour later, Geoffrey reined in and pronounced them properly hidden. "Now, Alain, we must set to work disguising ourselves."

"Wherefore?" The Prince frowned.

"Why, because you wish to go knight-erranting, do you not? To seek out wicked folk to punish, and good folk to aid, and damsels in distress to rescue?"

"Indeed I do! I must prove myself worthy of your sister!"

"Well, what wicked knight would dare to win against you, if he recognized you as the Crown Prince Alain?"

Alain's brow creased as he thought it over, then nodded. "Aye, there is sense in that. How shall we disguise us, then?"

"Well, to begin, you might take off your coronet and hide it in your saddlebag."

"Oh, aye!" Alain sheepishly tucked away his low crown.

"Now, as to your garments," Geoffrey said. "They must be leather and broadcloth, not silk and velvet. You must be dressed for long journeying, not for court—a good woolen cloak against the chill of night, and stout high boots."

Alain glanced down at his low but very fashionable boots and nodded. "Where shall we find such?"

"In a village, if it be large enough. Let us fare forth to the nearest town."

They rode on through the forest, and as they did, Geoffrey tried to explain the nature of courtship. "You must begin by flirting," he counselled, "and do not yet be serious."

"But," said Alain, "if I compliment a lady and seek to kiss her . . ." He blushed. ". . . what shall I do if she says yes?"

"If the offer's made, you may treat it only as one more flirtation, and respond with some gallantry, such as 'Ah, would that I could! But if such beauty as yours is like to blind me, I shudder to think what more would do!' Then touch her and draw back your hand sharply, as though from a hot griddle, crying 'Ah, fair lady! Only a touch, and my blood boils to burn me!' "

Alain goggled. "Where did you learn that bit of extravagance?"

"Why, it came to me even now, as we spoke."

"Alack-a-day!" Alain sighed. "I have no such gift of silver to my tongue!"

"You will be amazed how quickly it comes, Alain, most thoroughly amazed—if you begin to play the game, and enjoy it."

Alain reddened. "I could not!"

"Of course you could, and shall. But remember—'tis only a game, but fully a game. Enjoy it, as you would enjoy tossing a ball—for the words are like the ball, and you've but to toss such compliments back and forth."

"Tell me a few more, I beg you!" Alain implored. "For I would not go unarmed into my first fray!"

Geoffrey shook his head. "You must not think of it as a fray, mind you, but a game. If a lass eyes you, so . . ." He made a moue and batted his eyelashes.

Alain burst out in laughter that mingled shock and surprise.

"Aye, that is the spirit!" Geoffrey grinned. "If she looks at you like that, then you must look at her like this!" His eyes widened a little, seeming to burn as his mouth curved slightly. "Then she will respond, thus . . ." He made sheep's eyes at Alain. "And you must sigh and reach out to touch her hand, ever so gently." He pantomimed a delicate touch.

Alain laughed heartily. Then, gasping, he said, "I never could! I never could do so in seriousness!"

"Oh, do not! A straight face is like the side of a cold fish, and seriousness might be mistaken for ardor! No, you must let your amusement show, but like this . . ." He gave a low and throaty laugh.

Alain tried to imitate him, but it came out as a rusty chuckle. Nonetheless, Geoffrey nodded encouragement. "Well begun! Now, you must speak of her eyes and her cheeks, saying the former are like stars and the latter like roses . . ."

"Even I have heard those a thousand times!"

"So has she, friend, and will protest such, but in truth, she never grows tired of hearing them. Still, if there is more novelty in your saying, she will like it all the better. Mayhap you should take her hand upon your own, and tickle the palm whilst you nip the fingers with your lips . . ."

"Surely I could not!" But Alain's eyes were glowing now, the color was rising in his cheeks, and his seriousness seemed banished for the moment.

Encouraged, Geoffrey went on. ". . . and you shall tell

her that her skin is smoother than the current of a placid stream and as cool, though it inflames your blood . . ."

And on he went, manufacturing extravagant compliments by the yard. Alain clung to his every word, filing each away for future use. They rode through the forest, Geoffrey explaining the multitude of gallantries available for the courting of a lady, up to and including the way in which the knight Don Quixote had sent his vanquished enemies to his lady Dulcinea as proof of his valor and the purity and intensity of his love.

However, he did not tell Alain that Don Quixote had been mired in delusion. All lovers are, so it did not matter. Of course, Geoffrey was not in love when he flirted—but he hoped ardently that Alain would be. For, although love had touched Geoffrey only once or twice, he knew the signs, and knew also that he saw them in Alain. In fact, he knew that he had seen them for several years.

On the other hand, he also knew that Alain had been busily denying them. He seemed to think that such emotion, being swept away on such a tide, was unworthy of a man destined to be a king. His tutors had done their job too well.

Geoffrey was determined to undo it.

Then a woman screamed, ahead of them on the trail. Men shouted, and there was the clack of quarterstaves.

Alain and Geoffrey stiffened. Then Alain gave a gleeful shout. "So soon!" He drew his sword.

"Be sure which side is in the right before you strike!" Geoffrey was already spurring his horse.

"Do not slay unless we must!" Alain called back from half a length ahead.

They crashed through the brush screen just as some outlaws knocked the quarterstaff spinning from a carter's hands. One of their number leaped in to seize his wrists and force them up behind him, bending him almost double. Two others were pulling a woman down from the seat of the cart with lascivious, gloating laughs. She was still screaming.

There were at least a dozen bandits, and only the one carter with his wife.

"No doubt who has set upon whom!" Alain whooped and rode into battle with Geoffrey a step behind him.

The outlaws turned, startled, but set themselves quickly. Most had swords—badly nicked or honed down thin, but swords nonetheless, with bull-hide shields.

The others had bows.

Arrows flew about the two knights. They ducked and dodged. Then they were in among the bandits, laying about them with their swords.

Alain knocked a blade aside, then stabbed down. The bandit, a young fellow in a jerkin with a mane of black hair and a beard, raised his shield to block, as Alain had expected. The Prince's sword pinned the target, holding it up as he kicked a foot free of the saddle and lashed it lightning-quick into the bandit's jaw. The outlaw's eyes rolled up as he fell, almost wrenching the sword from Alain's grasp.

But quick though the Prince had been, another bandit had been quicker. He landed on Alain's back with a howl, arms hugging the Prince's neck, pulling him backward. Alain fought to keep his seat even through the choking and swung back with his blade—back and around with the flat of it. The outlaw cried out, and abruptly the pressure was gone. Heart singing, Alain turned—to see a sword jabbing up at his belly with a grinning bandit behind it. He rolled aside, but the blade sheared through his doublet, staining it with blood. Pain stung hot along his ribs, and fueled fear—but also anger. Alain shouted and caught the blade in a bind as the outlaw tried to riposte, circling his own sword, twisting and sending his enemy's blade whirling away. Other outlaws cried out, ducking the spinning steel, as Alain turned to the next opponent.

A staff cracked against his skull.

The world spun about him; pain wreathed his head. Alain fought to stay in the saddle, to keep his hold on his sword. Dimly, he heard a yell of triumph, felt hands seize his legs . . .

Fortunately, they seized both legs, and the tug-of-war lasted long enough for the world to steady about him. Then he slapped down with his sword and pounded down with his

left fist. Both blows connected, and the outlaws fell away.
Alain turned to follow up with the point of his blade . . .

And saw all the outlaws rolling about on the ground,
groaning and clutching their heads, or out cold.

Alain sat still and stared for a minute that seemed to
stretch out to ten. Then he looked up across the collection
of moaning men to Geoffrey, sitting smugly across from
him, winking. Alain grinned like an idiot.

Then he remembered his duty and his dignity, and composed his face gravely, turning to the carter and his wife.
"Are you well, goodman, goodwife?"

"Aye, thanks to thee, Sir Knight." The middle-aged couple huddled together, his arm about her. The woman was
weeping, but through her tears cried, "Bless thee, bless
thee, good sirs!" Then she saw the red streak along Alain's
side and gasped, "Thou'rt hurted!"

"Hurted?" Alain looked down—and stared, shocked. He
had never seen his own blood before. But he remembered
himself, and forced a smile. " 'Tis naught, belike."

"Aye, but let us be sure!" The woman hurried over to
him, drying her tears on her apron. She pushed the slashed
cloth aside and probed carefully. "Nay, naught but the skin
is cut. Still it must be dressed, good sir!"

"I shall tend to that," Geoffrey assured her.

She looked up at him doubtfully. "Knowest thou aught
of nursing, Sir Knight?"

"As much as a knight must know," he assured her. "You
may trust him to me, goodwife."

She subsided, stepping back to her husband, but didn't
look convinced.

"Tell us thy name, that we may boast of thy deed and
spread thy fame," the man urged.

Alain opened his mouth to tell him, but felt a nudge in
his short ribs. He glanced back over his shoulder and saw
Geoffrey frowning, with a shudder that could be inter-
preted as shaking his head. That was right, Alain
remembered—they were supposed to be incognito. He
turned back to the carter. "I may not tell you my name,
good folk . . . um . . ."

"Until his quest is done." Geoffrey stepped smoothly into the breach.

"Even so," Alain said with relief. But how then were they to gain glory?

"Say that 'twas the Knight of the Lady Cordelia who gave you rescue." Then Geoffrey remembered that his sister had not given Alain permission to claim her as his sponsor, and that their last meeting had certainly indicated anything but. "Or one who would be hers, at the least."

That made the woman look up to stare in wonder; then she began to smile, softly.

Women and romance, Geoffrey thought with exasperation, but reflected that his more clumsy friend was scarcely any better off. He turned to the outlaws. "What shall we do with these?"

That brought Alain to his senses. He turned, staring down. "What indeed?"

"They must be gaoled," Geoffrey prompted.

"But we are on quest! Must we ride guard upon them, to the nearest sheriff?"

"We cannot leave them to wander the countryside and prey upon travellers again, my friend."

"No, we cannot," Alain sighed. "Ho! Blackbeard!" He leaned down to prod the biggest outlaw with his sword.

The man moaned, but forced himself to sit up, one hand pressed to his head. " 'Twas a right shrewd blow, Sir Knight."

"Be glad he did not use the sword's edge," Geoffrey snapped. "What is your name?"

"Forrest, sir."

"I require your name, not your haunts! Speak truly!"

"Why, so I do, sir. 'Forrest' is the name my mother gave, and my father blessed." The bandit grinned, showing a wide, even expanse of white teeth. "Belike 'twas the name that gave me the thought of the life in the greenwood."

Alain surveyed the man, something about the bandit catching his interest. Forrest was tall, six feet or more, and broad-shouldered. His face was open and regular-featured, with thick black hair and a black jawline beard. His eyes were large, well spaced, and deep blue, his nose straight and well formed. He wore hose and cross-gartered sandals, instead of the usual peasant's leggins and buskins, and in place of a tunic wore only a sleeveless jerkin that showed a broad expanse of chest and the bulging muscles of arms and shoulders. Alain found himself wondering if it was by luck that he had defeated this man.

"You are a gentleman gone wrong," Geoffrey stated. "What is your family's name?"

"None of any consequence, for I doubt not they have disowned me."

"Mayhap they have not. What name?" Geoffrey added iron to the question.

"Elmsford," the bandit sighed.

"How came you to this pass?"

Forrest shrugged. "I am a youngest son of a youngest son, who had need to seek his living however he might."

"You could have found a way more honorable!"

"I did; I pledged my sword to a lord. He took us all to fight his neighbor, and we lost."

Geoffrey frowned. "Here is no shame."

"So I thought—but the neighbor sought to smite down all who had opposed him. I fled to the greenwood for my life, and lived as best I could."

"Wherefore you did not throw yourself upon the King's mercy?"

The bandit grinned, teeth startlingly white in the expanse of beard. "The King is at Runnymede, sir, and though 'tis near to us here, 'tis far from the estates of my former lord. I have been many months seeking this greenwood, but have now so many crimes on my conscience that I dare go no farther."

"Certainly the King's shire-reeve was near enough!"

"Aye, and under the hand of the lord who sought my life."

"You shall go to the King now, and woe betide him who would stop you! Do you speak for all of this band?"

The bandit looked around, but nobody seemed to want to dispute it. "Aye, Sir Knight."

"Then go to the sheriff at . . ."

"Nay." Alain stopped him with a touch. "Go to Castle Gallowglass . . ."

Forrest looked up sharply, and Geoffrey whirled about to stare at Alain. The bandits scrambled to their feet with groans of fear. "The witch-folk!"

Geoffrey turned to scowl at them. "Aye, the Lord Warlock and his family. Mind your manners about them, or you'll have no heads to mind with!" He turned back to Alain with a look that clearly said his friend was mad.

" 'Tis even as your Don Quixote did," Alain reminded him. Then, to Forrest, "Go to the Lady Cordelia, and surrender yourself to her there. If she bids you go to the King's prison, then you must go—for trust me, you do not wish to transgress against her."

"Be sure I do not!" Forrest bobbed his head, not smiling now.

"Be cautious and filled with respect," Alain admonished him. "Say to her that . . . that he who hopes to prove himself worthy has sent you."

The carter's wife clapped her hands, eyes shining. Geoffrey restrained an impulse to look up to Heaven for help.

" 'He who hopes to prove himself worthy.' " Forrest nodded, lips pursed in puzzlement. "Yet why not send your name, good sir?"

"Because . . . because I shall not use it again in public, till she has heard my suit!" Alain smiled, pleased with his first attempt at improvisation. Geoffrey nodded judicious approval.

The bandit bowed, his face wooden, and Geoffrey guessed he was hiding his reaction to the quixotic gesture. "As you bid me, sir."

"Go straightaway, and do not stray from the path," Geoffrey told him. Then he raised his voice. "You, who thread the forest's roots and stitch the green leaves for your garments! Come forth, I pray thee, by the pact of kindred blood!"

The outlaws stared at him as though he had gone mad, but the wife drew back against her husband with a low moan. For a few seconds, the whole forest seemed to be waiting, still and silent.

Then leaves rustled, and a foot-high mannikin walked out along a branch. "Who art thou, who dost seek to summon the Wee Folk?"

Now it was the outlaws who moaned and shrank away, while the wife and husband watched, spellbound.

"I shall not use my name openly again until my companion uses his," Geoffrey told the elf, "yet I ask the favor by the bond 'twixt he who rides the iron horse, and the king who goes about among his peers disguised."

The outlaws glanced at one another and muttered, but none knew what he was talking about.

The elf, though, must have recognized the references to Rod Gallowglass and Brom O'Berin, for he said, "That will suffice. What would you have us do?"

"Accompany these men to Castle Gallowglass," Geoffrey said, "with a whole troop of your kind—and if they stray from the path, I prithee discourage them."

The elf's eyes glittered. "Aye, gladly, for never has a one of them left a bowl for a brownie! How strongly would you have us 'discourage' them?"

"Well, I would not have you slay or maim them," Geoffrey conceded. "In all other respects, whatever mischief allows, why, do."

"Here is no work, but play! Aye, surely, young warlock, that we shall do!"

Forrest's head lifted; he glanced sharply at Geoffrey.

"Yet do not allow any others to detain them," Geoffrey said. "I wish them to arrive at Castle Gallowglass, not to be taken on the way."

"We know the lord whose lands lie between this forest and that castle, and he knows us, to his sorrow," the elf said. "None shall trouble them, save us."

"I thank you." Geoffrey inclined his head.

"It will be our pleasure." The elf bowed, stepped back among the leaves, and was gone.

Geoffrey turned back to the outlaws. "Get you gone, then—and seek to despoil none, nor to flee an inch from the path. I doubt not you have some coins about you; what food you need, see that you pay for. Be off!"

Forrest bowed again, barked a command to his men, and set off down the road. They straggled after him reluctantly.

A whistling sounded from one side of the road, a hooting from the other.

The bandits jumped, and started moving considerably faster.

"Well thought, Geoffrey," Alain said. "I thank you."

Geoffrey shrugged. "The gesture was perhaps extravagant, but will no doubt prove effective."

"I doubt it not." Alain turned back to the carter and his wife. "Go your way, now, without fear of these brigands. They shall not trouble you more."

"Aye!" The carter ducked his head, touching his forelock. "I thank you, Sir Knights!"

"And I you, for the chance of glory." Alain inclined his head, and Geoffrey was tempted to tell him chivalry could be taken too far. "Farewell, now, and travel safely."

"And you, good sirs." The carter turned to help his wife climb up onto the seat, followed her, sat down and picked up the reins, then clucked to his mule, and the cart ambled off down the forest road. The couple turned back to wave before the leaves swallowed them up.

" 'Twas well done, Alain, and a good beginning!" Geoffrey clapped him on the shoulder. "Come, let us ride."

"Aye!" Alain cried with zest. "Adventure waits!"

The road curved, and an elderly knight wearing a hooded robe stepped out to bar the outlaws' way. At his back stood a dozen knights.

The outlaws halted. "We have done as you bade, Sir Maris," said Forrest.

" 'Tis well for thee," the old knight said grimly. "You are free of the King's dungeon now, and thy poaching and thievery are pardoned. See to it you do not fall into such error again."

All the outlaws muttered denials and avowals of future honesty, and Forrest said, "We will not, I assure you."

"Cease this talk of 'you' and 'your'!" Sir Maris snapped. "Canst not say 'thee' and 'thou' like honest men?"

Forrest composed his face gravely. "Pardon my offense, King's Seneschal."

Sir Maris eyed him narrowly, not missing the implication that if Sir Maris weren't the King's Seneschal, Forrest would thumb his nose at the old knight's demands. But Sir Maris *was* the royal seneschal, and had had long experience of arrogant young men, Prince Alain and Lord Geoffrey among them. "What did the young knights bid thee do?" he demanded.

"To surrender ourselves to the Lady Cordelia, at Castle Gallowglass," Forrest responded.

Sir Maris heaved a sigh of exasperation. "The folly of youth! Well-a-day, then, thou must needs go! But think not to take a single step off the road, or my men shall fall upon thee like hawks upon sparrows."

Forrest bowed, poker-faced. "Even as thou dost say, Sir Maris." He straightened up, called to his band, and led them on their way. Why should he tell Sir Maris that they were flanked by a troop of elves? Let his knights find out for themselves—preferably the hard way.

Ever so carefully, he opened his mind, listening to the babble of thought that surrounded him. Yes, the elves were still there, and rather indignant about all the Cold Iron that was going to be keeping them company. He was rather sorry that he had had to throw that fight with the two young knights—he was reasonably sure that the stockier one had been Geoffrey Gallowglass, and he would have welcomed the opportunity to try his own "witch powers" against those of the Lord Warlock's son.

Sir Maris watched the band of ruffians out of sight. He did not trust Forrest or his band an inch beyond his sight. Unfortunately, they would be many inches beyond the sight of himself or his knights; it would not do for little Cordelia to see her suitor's trophy-offering being escorted by Royal retainers. He sighed and turned back at the creaking of a cart. Now for the carter and his wife.

"Here is another florin to match that which I gave thee aforetime," he said. "Didst thou do thy part well?"

"Oh, aye!" said the wife. "The two young men believed all that we did, by the look of them."

"By the saints," said her husband, "I believed it myself!"

Sir Maris's gaze sharpened. "Did those bandits offer thee harm?"

"Nay," said the woman quickly. "Well, no more than was needful. They did not truly hurt us, sir, nor would they have meant to."

"Not with thee and thy knights so close by," the carter grunted.

Sir Maris nodded. "So I promised—so I did. But did they affright thee?"

"Aye, sir, even though I had known them from their cradles." The goodwife shuddered. "They have become rough men indeed! And all for poaching—'twas that which sent them, every one, to the greenwood! Still, I did not truly fear them—naught save that black-visaged scoundrel who was not of our village, and did call himself 'Forrest.' "

"What did he?" Sir Maris snapped.

"Naught," the carter said slowly. "Naught that he *did*."

"Aye," said his wife. " 'Twas in his look, and in his manner of speech. Though he smiled fair, there was something of the devil-may-care about his eyes, that did speak of danger. Still, he did *do* naught."

"Well, if he did naught, then I shall do naught to him," Sir Maris grumbled, "though I would I had some strand of excuse to hang him by."

"Nay, no cause, truly," the carter sighed.

"And the others?" Sir Maris peered at the woman keenly. "Didst thou think they gave thee true cause to fear?"

"Nay." At last, she laughed a little. "I've known them all since they were lads, and they all knew that if any among them had truly offered me harm, I would have told their mothers."

CHAPTER
~5~

"Milady!" The porter bowed a little as Cordelia strode in. The Gallowglass servants generally didn't do more than incline their heads, but with the mood Cordelia was in, it was best to play it safe.

"Here, Ganir!" Cordelia tossed him her cloak. "And thank you. Where are my parents?"

"In the solar, milady."

"Mercy." Cordelia paced up the stairs.

Rod and Gwen looked up as she came in the door. "I do not mean to interrupt . . ." she began.

"Of course you do." Gwen dimpled. "And we could wish no happier afternoon than to have you do so. Could we not, husband?"

"Of course," Rod said. "Back so soon?"

"Oh, aye!" Cordelia threw up her hands. "What else am I to do? That lummox of a brother of mine told Alain about the heroes of legend, who sent their defeated enemies to their lady-loves as proof of their worth!"

"So we are about to be hit by an invasion of defeated enemies?" Rod fought to keep a straight face.

"A troop of bandits! Ruffians! Outlaws! And I must be here to receive them, so I cannot follow as I should! What other dangerous silliness will they fall into unwarded?"

She had a point, Rod decided. For a second, he wondered if Geoffrey might have arranged it this way. Then he dismissed the thought as unworthy—such manipulating would have been far too subtle for his direct, brash son.

Gwen gave a slow nod of approval. " 'Tis an honor not unworthy—to see the lambs defended and the wolves caged, in thy name."

" 'Tis a plaguey nuisance! 'Tis a monstrous inconvenience! 'Tis an imbecilic imposition!" Cordelia paced to the fire, glowering down at it.

Rod thought the lady did protest too much—and indeed, as he looked at her face lit by the fire, he thought he saw some glow of pleasure, of satisfaction, albeit carefully hidden.

Gwen knew she did, and that without reading her daughter's mind—not literally, anyway. " 'Tis romantic," she murmured.

"Aye," Cordelia admitted. Finally, she smiled.

They rode on through the forest, chatting of this and that—but Geoffrey did most of the chatting. Alain listened, round-eyed and constantly feeling that he should not be hearing such things. Geoffrey was telling him all the things he had never said at court, about revels with villagers and tavern brawls and willing wenches at town fairs. Alain's eyes grew larger and larger, as did the feeling that he should tell Geoffrey to stop—but he abided, partly in fascination, partly in the conviction that somehow, mysteriously, all this would make him a better suitor for Cordelia.

An hour or more they passed in this study. Then the trees thinned out, and they saw the thatched roofs of a village ahead.

"Come!" Geoffrey cried. "There will be hot meat and cold ale, I doubt not, and perhaps even that change of clothing you wish!"

Alain agreed enthusiastically—it had been a long time since breakfast—and they rode out of the forest, down the single street of the village. A peasant who saw them looked up in alarm, then gave a glad shout. "Knights!"

"Knights?"

"Knights!"

"War-men to aid us!"

The villagers crowded around, showering the two young men with cries of gratitude and relief.

"Why, what is the matter?" Geoffrey called over their clamor.

" 'Tis a monster, Sir Knight! 'Tis a horrible ogre, only this morning come upon us!"

"Only this morning, you say?" Geoffrey frowned; something there struck him as odd.

But Alain was delighted. "Have we come to our first adventure so quickly, then? Surely, good folk, be easy in your hearts! We shall find the monster and slay him for you! Shall we not, Sir Geoffrey?"

"Oh, certainly," Geoffrey seconded. He realized suddenly that, whatever its source, this most convenient monster would certainly give Alain a good chance to prove his courage and skill. Geoffrey couldn't have planned it better himself. "Yes, surely we will fight the ogre for you—if he is evil."

"Aye, if he is evil!" Alain sobered; he might have been about to strike a harmless being, simply because it looked frightening. That would have been very poor behavior indeed, for a knight-errant. "What has he done?"

Well, actually, it turned out that the ogre hadn't *done* all that much, really—only knocked a haystack apart, and made off with a sheep. Of course, he had also taken the shepherd, a boy of about twelve, who had been hiding in the haystack with the sheep, and that was what the townsfolk were really concerned about.

"He will eat the lad!" one woman cried, while another comforted the mother, who could not stop crying.

"His father has already gone out to slay the monster,"

an old man said grimly. "I doubt not he will be slain, if thou dost not speed quickly, good sirs!"

"Why, then, let us ride!" Alain cried, eyes alight with anticipation.

"Aye! To the fray!" Geoffrey wheeled his horse about and rode off after Alain, amazed—not so much by the Prince's eagerness as by his total lack of fear. Was he only hiding it well? Or didn't he really understand what he was up against? Probably the latter, Geoffrey reflected—ogres were nothing but pictures in books to Alain, as much fantasy as a real fight was. The trouble was that Alain didn't know that the battles in the books, and the monsters, weren't real. How would he react when he came face-to-face with the genuine article?

Pretty well, as it turned out. They followed a peasant to the haystack in question—or what was left of it, at least—then tracked the ogre down. It wasn't hard—he had left footprints in the grass an inch deep and two feet long.

"If his feet are double the length of mine," Alain said, "will he be twice my height?"

"Likely he will," Geoffrey said, trying to sound as grim as possible. Didn't the callow youth understand what he was getting into?

He certainly must have understood it when they came in sight of the ogre. Newly arrived or not, he had found a cave already—a hole in a rocky outcrop toward the top of a hill, and the flinty pathway led up to him in zigs and zags. He sat by a fire where, with one of his four hands, he was turning a spit with some sort of meat on it, while he gnawed a leg-bone with one of the others.

Now Alain paled, reining in his horse. "Pray heaven that is not the boy's leg he is chewing!"

"I shall." Now Geoffrey turned grim in earnest as he drew his sword. "Ah, for a proper lance and armor! But we shall have to manage with what we have."

The ogre heard the sound of steel whisking loose from a scabbard and surged to his feet with a roar, brandishing the leg-bone in one hand and catching up a huge club with another. The other two clenched into fists and shook in the air toward the two young men. To Geoffrey, those extra arms seemed to have life of their own. The ogre wasn't twelve feet tall after all, but only ten—*only* ten! What he lacked in height, though, he made up in bulk. He must have been four feet wide across the shoulders. He needed the extra shoulder room, on the other hand—and the other hand, and the other, and the other.

Then Alain howled a battle cry and spurred his horse. He charged up the mountainside, sword swinging high as he shouted, "For Gramarye and the Lady Cordelia!"

The romantic fool, Geoffrey thought, alarmed, even as he spurred his own horse—but even in his exasperation, he had to admire Alain's bravery.

For the first time, he found himself wondering what he was going to say to Cordelia if he had to bring back the dead body of the man she'd been planning to marry since she was five.

The ogre roared and charged down the slope as fast as Alain was charging up. Geoffrey cried out in alarm—there was no possibility of a misunderstanding here; that ogre was out for blood! The huge club lifted for a blow that would flatten the horse like a housefly, and the leg-bone shot toward Alain's head.

But the Prince chopped the bone out of the air with a sweep of his sword, then shouted to his charger. Undaunted and well trained, the warhorse charged straight at the ogre.

The huge club wound up and slammed down.

Alain swerved at the last second.

The club churned up the ground. With a roar of frustration, the ogre yanked—but the cudgel stuck. Enraged, the monster bellowed, grabbed it with two hands, and set itself to pull.

Alain darted in to stab the monster's bottom.

The ogre howled, snapping straight upright, one of its free hands slapping its buttock. The other swatted at Alain as though he were a fly.

Alain danced his horse back, but not fast enough—the

huge palm slammed into his chest, and he reeled in the saddle. His horse leaped back beyond range. Alain struggled for breath.

Geoffrey saw he was needed. He howled like a banshee and came riding in, waving his sword.

The ogre looked up, startled, then roared and snatched at its club.

The club still refused to move.

This time, the ogre grabbed it with all four hands—then, as Geoffrey galloped in, loosed one fist to swing backhanded at him.

Geoffrey dodged, but not far enough—the blow glanced off his head, and he saw stars. Holding onto consciousness, he backed his horse clear.

The ogre gave a mighty heave and pulled the club out with a shout of triumph.

Alain caught his breath and charged in.

He swerved around to the front, being too chivalrous to attack an opponent from behind without warning, and Geoffrey groaned at his friend's idiocy. He set himself to gallop back to the fight, but Alain charged in so fast that the huge club slammed down right behind him, giving the Prince just time enough to stab up, as high as he could—right into the ogre's midriff. It screamed, a ghastly sound choked off as its stomach muscles gave out. Alain darted back out, but the ogre, disabled or not, slammed a roundhouse blow at him that cracked his shield and made him reel in the saddle.

Strangling and gasping, the monster waddled after him, murder in its eye, club lifting in all four hands.

Geoffrey shouted and charged.

But Alain rallied, lowered his head, extended his sword like a lance, and charged again.

The ogre gave a strangled cry and swung, but it was so weakened that it overbalanced and fell—right on top of Alain. Its whole body slammed down with every ounce of its impossible size and weight. Alain disappeared under a mountain of flesh.

"Alain!" Geoffrey cried in horror, and leaped off his horse, sword swinging high to chop off the ogre's head . . .

Then a gleaming sword-tip poked out of the monster's back, and the ogre went limp.

Geoffrey almost went limp himself, with relief—but not quite. A dead ogre didn't prove a live Prince, after all. He grabbed an arm and threw all his weight against it, rolling the ogre up on its side.

Alain scrambled clear and climbed to his feet. He looked about, crying, "My sword!"

"There!" Geoffrey grunted, nodding toward the ogre's chest. "Pull it out, and quickly! I do not know how long I can hold him up!"

Alain dived for the sword, set a heel against the monster's chest, and heaved. The blade slid free as easily as though it had been in its scabbard, and Alain went staggering back.

Geoffrey let go with a grunt of relief.

"I did it!" Alain stared down at the huge corpse in disbelief. "I have slain a monster!"

"That you have," Geoffrey said sourly, "and with full measure of danger, too. Might I ask you, next time, to wait for your reserves?"

But Alain's face was darkening, elation giving way to remorse. "It looks so shrunken, lying there . . ."

"Shrunken! 'Tis ten feet long and three times the bulk of a man—nay, more! Make no mistake, Alain—that pigface would have slain you in an instant, if he could have!"

That lightened the Prince's mood considerably—but he still brooded, though with puzzlement now, not guilt. "How is it he does not bleed?"

"Well asked," Geoffrey admitted. He had been wondering about that himself.

None of the ogre's wounds showed the slightest trace of blood—nor of ichor, nor any other sort of bodily fluid, for that matter. They were as clean as cuts in bread dough. In fact, the ogre's body looked far more like that substance, than like flesh or meat.

"Still, 'tis no wonder," Geoffrey said, searching for

something reassuring to say—and found it. "The monsters of Gramarye are not made as you and I were, Alain."

"Not made as we were?" The Prince transferred his frown to Geoffrey. "Why, how is that?"

"Not made by mothers and fathers," Geoffrey explained, "or if they were, those parents, or their ancestors, sprang full-blown from witch-moss overnight. God did not make them as He made us, from lumps of protoplasm formed by countless eons of random changes that were shaped by the role He planned for them. No, they were made by the thoughts of a granny who was a protective telepath, but did not know it, shaped as she told a bedtime story of monsters and heroes to her babes—or by one person telling such a tale to many others, and of the many, there were several who were projectives but also did not know it. Their thoughts, together, formed the monster out of witch-moss."

He had told Alain about projective telepaths years ago—and about all the other psionic talents the espers of Gramarye had at their disposal. Of course, his father had warned him not to, and Geoffrey could understand why, in the case of the ignorant, superstitious peasants who would have reacted by saying that a witch was a witch, no matter what you called her. But Alain was neither ignorant nor superstitious—at least, not by local standards—and Geoffrey and his brothers and sisters had reasoned that he needed to know what his subjects really were, if he was to rule them well when he was grown.

So Alain understood Geoffrey's explanation, nodding, though his brows were still knit. "Naetheless, would such witch-moss creatures not have blood in them?" He knew that the substance they called "witch-moss" was really a fungus that responded to the thoughts of projectives, turning itself into whatever they were thinking about.

"Not if the granny who told the tale did not think of blood. Difficult to imagine, for we who loved to hear tales of bloody deeds even in our cradles, but there are many who do not. Nay, there's no doubt the creature was only a construct, naught more, and one brought to life only last night, or the villagers would have seen him ere now."

"Well, there is no glory in slaying a thing that is not real, is there?" Alain asked, disappointed.

"Oh, it was real, Alain! Be sure, it was real—and you would have been sure indeed, if that club had touched you! Do you not see the hole where it plowed into the ground? What do you think it would have done to your head? Nay, made by grannies or by God, this was a lethal brute, and 'twas an act of great daring to slay it!"

Alain seemed reassured, then suddenly stood bolt upright, eyes wide. "The child! The shepherd-boy! We must find him! Pray God it was not . . ."

He could not finish, nor did he need to. Geoffrey nodded grimly; he had also wondered at the source of the legbone the ogre had wielded. "Aye, let us search."

They climbed up toward the ogre's cave, Alain calling, "Boy! Shepherd! You may come out now with safety! We have . . ."

"You waste your breath." Geoffrey caught his arm, pointing.

Alain looked, and saw the shepherd boy pelting away across the field, already little more than a dot of dark clothing against the amber of the wheat.

"Praise Heaven!" the Prince sighed. "He is safe!"

"Aye. I doubt not the lad was penned in the cave, and seized his chance to flee when the ogre charged down upon us. He will surely bear word to the village—if he paused to look back."

"What boy would not?" Alain smiled.

"A boy who flees for his life." Geoffrey was very glad to see the curve of Alain's lips; he had begun to wonder if the Prince was going into shock. "We must go tell them ourselves. Someone must bury this mound of offal, and I have no wish to tarry long enough to undertake the task myself."

Alain nodded; Geoffrey didn't need to explain. The Prince knew as well as he that a royal search party was very probably already after them, and he had no wish to cut short his adventuring.

Geoffrey clapped Alain on the back and turned him toward his horse. "Come, away! For what other feats of glory await you?"

But Alain hung back, glancing at the ogre. "Should I not hew off its head and send it to the Lady Cordelia, as proof of my love?"

Geoffrey tried to imagine Cordelia receiving the ugly, gruesome trophy and shuddered. "There is no need, and I do not think she would find it aesthetic. Be assured, she shall hear of it soon enough!"

She didn't, as it happened. All the elves who had been watching the encounter were too late to tell her of it before she left Castle Gallowglass to follow the boys again. But Puck himself brought word back to Brom O'Berin.

" 'Tis well." Brom nodded, satisfied.

"The mission is accomplished, and none hurt but the ogre." Puck strutted as he said it.

Brom eyed him askance. "Here is turpitude indeed! Have you no remorse, no sorrow for the creature you made?"

"None at all," Puck assured him. "It had no mind, look you, only a set of actions implanted in its excuse for a brain. It would charge when it was charged, strike when it was threatened, and naught more—save to die when its time was done."

"And was very clumsy into the bargain?"

"Tremendously. It could strike no object smaller than a horse, save by luck."

"Bad luck indeed! 'Twas with that I was concerned."

"Be easy in thine heart, O King," Puck said, grinning. "Surely thou dost know that I would take no chance with the Prince's life."

"Aye, unless thy sense of mischief got the better of thee!"

"Well, it did not in this case," Puck said judiciously. "A score of elves hid with me in the bracken and all about the field of combat, to protect the Prince and thy grandson with their magic, should mischance befall. Yet 'twas without need; 'twas not mischance that befell, but the ogre."

"Aye, and nearly crushed Alain in its fall!"

" 'Twas not so massive as that," Puck protested. "Indeed, for its size, 'twas quite tenuous."

"As is thy report." But approval twinkled in Brom's eye.

The villagers cheered as soon as the two young knights came in sight.

"I take it the shepherd boy did watch the battle," Geoffrey said.

Then the people were on them, clustering about their stirrups, reaching up to touch their defenders.

"All praises be upon thee, young knights!"

"Save thee, my masters!"

"A thousand blessings on they who saved the boy!"

"Blessings and praises, and what soe'er they may ask that we can give," said one buxom, dark-haired beauty with a look in her eye that sent a thrill through Alain, one that held his gaze riveted to hers as hot blood coursed through him, awaking sensations that he found both intimidating and fascinating at the same time.

Then she transferred her gaze to Geoffrey, and Alain went limp with relief—but the sensations were still there, with a strength that shook him.

Geoffrey had no such trouble, of course. He met the girl's gaze and grinned slowly.

Alain turned red and cleared his throat. "Aye! You may give the monster burial! A score of your men, with shovels and picks!"

"We shall, we shall straightaway!" cried a man. "But what wouldst thou have for thyselves, good sirs?"

Alain glanced at Geoffrey, saw he was still eyeing the peasant wench, and sighed. If his father's party caught up with them, well, they would, and that was that. "I would have a bath," he told the man, "and food, and strong clothes fit for travelling. Then, though, we must be on our way."

"Must we truly?" Geoffrey said, gaze still on the wench. "Might we not stay the night? There will be few real beds for us in the weeks to come, Alain."

The girl's smile broadened; then she dropped her gaze demurely.

"Why, as you will," Alain sighed—but he found himself eyeing the peasant lass, too, and forced his gaze away. It did no good; the sensations she had raised still shuddered through him. He did his best to ignore the feelings and said, "Still, my companion, let us first bathe."

The village didn't have a bathhouse, of course—such an item would have counted as a major technological breakthrough in the Medieval Europe after which Gramarye's society had been modeled. Such whole-body washing as was done occurred in the local mill pond. The villagers didn't seem to have all that elaborate an idea of privacy, but fortunately, there was a screen of brush around the pond that the miller hadn't gotten around to clearing for several years. On the other hand, from the smothered titters and giggling that rose from the scrawny leaves, Geoffrey guessed that the brush didn't screen them all that thoroughly. He grinned, enjoying the attention of the unseen audience as he languorously caressed his muscles with a cake of soap—but Alain turned magenta with embarrassment, all over, and made sure he didn't let anything more than his torso appear above the waterline. That did inhibit the bath, of course, but it was an improvement over the sweat-and-grime coating with which he had climbed into the pool.

Then, though, there was the problem of climbing out.

It didn't bother Geoffrey in the slightest—he just waded ashore, though he did catch up the makeshift towel so quickly that his nudity was only revealed for a second. However, that was long enough to still the giggling chorus. It began again as a series of hushed murmurs as he turned his back, tucking the towel around his waist as an improvised kilt, then holding another out to Alain.

"I thank you from the bottom of my heart, Geoffrey," the Prince muttered as he stepped out of the pool into the cover of the towel.

"Well, from your bottom, anyway." Geoffrey grinned. "You look quite well in that sacking the miller provided us, Alain."

The Prince gave him a murderous look and caught up another towel, rubbing himself dry with furious haste.

Geoffrey grinned, taking his time about towelling, playing to his hidden watchers. The murmuring voices were properly appreciative.

Alain caught up his clothes and went quickly toward the cover of the mill. Geoffrey caught up with him, and they went through the door together.

"You are quite shameless," Alain grumbled as they dressed in the safety of the millhouse. "How can you enjoy displaying yourself like a joint of beef?"

"Why, I find it quite stimulating." Geoffrey was still grinning. "My blood tickles through me when I know that lasses do watch and admire me—tingling in every limb, at the hint of the pleasures that may follow, if they find enough to admire."

"Shameless, as I said," Alain growled. "Surely you are too chivalrous to seek after such pleasures as you mention!"

"To seek after, no," Geoffrey said, "though if they are offered freely, I am delighted to accept."

"Have you no decency, no regard for others' feelings?"

Geoffrey blinked, surprised at Alain's vehemence. Then he said slowly, "Well, some regard, surely. I would never think to force my attentions on a wench who did not want them, nor on a virgin, no matter if she did wish it, nor how greatly. I seek to give only pleasure, Alain, never hurt—and if there is reason to think the lass wants more than the sheer fun of it, I'll not come near her, for then is there chance indeed of hurting her heart."

"But all women believe, in their hearts, that there will

be more than a night's sport—that the man will then take care of them forever after! They do, Geoffrey, even if they admit it not, not even unto themselves!"

Geoffrey took his time framing the reply, choosing his words carefully. "They want something more than the pleasure of their senses, that is true. But marriage? Nay! No peasant woman truly believes a lord will wed her, Alain—no woman of sound mind, at least. In this instance, what they want is a night with a hero, that his glory may adhere to them afterward."

"Aye, and expect him to adhere to them, too, for all their lives!"

"Hope for it secretly, mayhap—so secretly that they admit it not, even unto themselves. If they see him again, they will hope for at least a nod, a few tender words, a half-hour's intimate talk. But, 'expect'? Nay. Unless she is mad, no peasant wench would truly expect a lord to marry her."

"Still, secret or not, expectant or not, there will be mayhem done to her heart, whether she knows it or not!"

"Or will admit it or not?" Geoffrey shrugged. "There, I cannot say without reading her mind far below her surface thoughts—and even I shudder at so profound an invasion of privacy. If she knows it not, neither do I. I can only judge by her actions, by the deeds and the farewell smiles of those I have seen, by the boasting, covert or overt, among her friends."

"Surely a woman would not boast of being used by a man, even a hero!"

"Well, I have never heard a woman boast of a bedding," Geoffrey admitted, "though I have seen them cluster about a hero, and hint most plainly to be admitted to his bedchamber."

"Mayhap." Alain scowled. "I cannot deny it. But does not each lass hope that he will cleave unto her forevermore, no matter how plain it is that he will not—that to him, she is only one among many?"

"Mayhap," Geoffrey sighed. "I cannot say. There is no accounting for the daydreams women may spin for themselves, nor may men truly comprehend them. I only know that I count it no shame to take what is offered freely, and think that if it is so offered, I give no pain."

But Alain only shook his head as he buttoned his doublet, muttering, "I cannot believe it!"

As he followed the Prince out of the mill and back toward the village common, Geoffrey reflected that Alain's attitude paid credit to his upbringing, but not to his understanding of the world as it really was.

The village common was decked with streamers of cloth and bunches of flowers around trestle tables. The village girls, decked in bright skirts, dark bodices, and white blouses, were just finishing putting up the decorations, chattering and exclaiming to one another. The village youths and men raised a cheer as the two young men came in sight.

"Hail the slayers of the monster!"

"Hail the saviors of the child!"

"Hail the courageous and mighty knights, who have saved our village from peril!"

Alain looked about as they closed in, applauding and cheering him. He was dazzled by all the adulation. He, who was used to the deference and flattery of the court, had never received so much heartfelt praise due only to his deeds, not to his station. He turned from one to another with an incredulous, widening smile . . .

And a village wench planted a kiss on his lips, firm and deep.

He jerked his head back, shocked, but she was turning away herself by that time, and another was taking her place. Alain looked up to Geoffrey for help, saw him with a girl in his arms, mouth to mouth, and mentally shrugged. What harm could a kiss do? And would not the girls be insulted if he refused? Surely, he did not want to hurt their feelings! He turned back to give the peasant lass a courteous peck on the cheek—but she had other ideas, ones that took a bit longer. So did the next girl, and the next.

Alain finally managed to reclaim his lips and, yes, his whole mouth, from the last admirer, dazed and incredulous to hear the men still cheering all about him. Were none of them jealous? Were there no sweethearts among the girls who had just kissed him? He realized, with a sense of amazement, that he was rather enjoying the whole affair.

They ushered him to a table and sat him down. Before him, a whole pig was roasting over a fire. The aroma reached him, and he breathed it in eagerly, suddenly realizing how hungry he had become.

And how thirsty. A girl thrust a flagon into his hand and her mouth against his—only this time, however it may have looked to the outside world, her tongue trickled fire slowly over his lips.

Then she straightened up with a glad laugh, and to cover his confusion, he took a deep draft from the tankard. It was new ale, nutty and strong. He came up for air. Geoffrey slapped him on the shoulder, chuckling. "Drink deeply, my friend, you have earned it."

And Alain did, wondering whether country ale always tasted so good, or if it was only so after a feat of valor. Indeed, all his senses seemed to be heightened—the village lasses seemed to be prettier, their cheeks redder, their eyes brighter and more inviting. The aroma of the roasting meat seemed almost solid enough to bite, and the piper's notes sounded far keener than they ever had, stirring his toes to movement. He took another draft of ale; then a girl was pulling him up from the bench, laughing, and another took his other arm. They led him to a flat, level green, and began to dance. Alain knew the steps—he had seen them often enough, at festivals, and his parents had seen him schooled in the more stately steps of the court dances. He began to imitate the girls' movements, slowly and clumsily. Then he noticed that other girls had stepped out to dance with the young men, and he could copy the boys' movements. He did, with increasing sureness and speed, turning back to his partner. Her eyes glistened, her teeth were very white against the redness of lips and tongue as she laughed, and he found himself caught up more and more in her movements and his own, thought suspending, sensation claiming.

Then, at some unseen signal, the girl whirled away, and another took her place. She leaned forward to give him a quick kiss, clapping his arm about her waist, and moved through the same steps, but much more quickly now. He gazed down into her eyes, feeling his own grin widening, and let himself be swept up in the movements of the dance. Dimly, he noticed that Geoffrey was dancing, too, but it only seemed to be of passing interest.

Then, suddenly, the dancing was done, and the girls were leading him back to the place of honor, thrusting another tankard of ale into his hand. He took a long, thirsty pull at it. As he lifted his head, Geoffrey scoffed. "Pooh! That is no way to drink village ale, Alain! You do not sip it as though it were a rare vintage—you pour it down your throat!" So saying, he lifted his own tankard, tilted his head up, and drank it down—and down, and down. Finally the tankard exploded away from his lips and thumped down onto the table, empty.

"Aye, that is the way of it!" a village youth next to him cried with a laugh, and lifted his own tankard to demonstrate.

"Come, confess it!" Geoffrey cried. "You cannot even keep pace with these stalwarts!"

"Oh, can I not!" Alain retorted, and tipped up his own tankard. The ale was good, very good—but he did begin to wish he could breathe. Nonetheless, he was hanged if he'd admit defeat, so he hung in there, swallowing the rich dark tide, until suddenly he gulped air. He thumped the tankard down, drawing a very deep and welcome breath, and was amazed to hear the villagers all cheer. He looked up, smiling, not quite believing it, then grinning as he saw they were delighted to see him enjoying himself. A fresh tankard appeared next to his hand. Across from him, Geoffrey raised his mug in salute, and Alain felt a sudden surge of determination not to be outdone. He clinked his tankard against Geoffrey's, then copied his motions as he swung the vessel up. He swallowed greedily, though to tell the truth, he was liking it less than he had at first. When the tankard was done, he slammed it down, almost in unison with Geoffrey. The two young men stared each other in the eye, and Geoffrey grinned. After a moment, so did Alain.

Then the tankards were whisked away and full ones set in their place, but Alain was saved, because a trencher of sizzling pork was slapped down in front of him. "Eat, as a hero deserves!" someone cried, and he did.

He ate, he drank, and the notes of the pipes filled his head, along with the scents of the meat and the ale. Things seemed to be blurring together a bit, but the villagers were such warm and friendly folk that it didn't worry him. He chewed the last sliver of pork, and a girl was pulling him from his seat, laughing, out to the dancing. Laughing, too, he feigned reluctance, then fell into the steps with her, mimicking the extra sinuousness with which she moved, and if she took advantage of the dance to thrust herself against him, why, it seemed only polite to return the gesture.

Then Geoffrey's face was there again, laughing, raising his tankard in salute, and Alain was raising one in return, the nut-brown ale cascading down his throat, then the tankard gone, and the girl back, her eyes heavy-lidded, her smile inviting, her body constantly against his as the dance moved them, till they seemed to churn as one. Fire threaded itself through him, tingling in his thighs, his hips, wherever his body touched hers.

Then she was holding up another mug of ale, and he was drinking it down, lowering it to look into her eyes, and they seemed to be huge and seemed to draw him in, and her lips were red and moist, so moist, but she was not holding them up to him now, but drawing him by the arm, out and away from the dancing, away from the fire, to a place where shadows gathered, where their bodies crushed soft bracken beneath them, and the music of the dance was distant, so distant, but her mouth was warm, very warm, encompassing him, and her touch thrilled him, so it seemed only right to return that thrill, if he could.

CHAPTER
~6~

The whole castle was agog, bubbling with excitement, for the elves hadn't made any pretense of keeping a secret. A brownie had popped up at the kitchen door to announce that their unwelcome guests were almost upon them.

Cordelia hurried out into the courtyard and took up her position in a patch of sunlight, doing her best to look stern and regal. She was resplendent in a white damask gown; the sunlight glowed in her auburn hair, carefully set off by a plain bronze circlet.

The bandits trudged in through the gatehouse, stumbling with weariness and coated with dust. Cordelia stared, appalled. Had they walked all night?

Then the foremost bandit looked up, saw her, and stared. Suddenly, the weariness fell away from him.

Cordelia gazed back, amazed. Her first view of the bandits hadn't prepared her at all for this. He was quite the most handsome man she had ever seen—though that may have been as much due to the hint of wildness in his face as to the actual set of his features.

Or it may have been some other attribute; there was a

lot of him to admire, more than six feet, and most of it muscles. His legs were exceedingly well formed, she thought dizzily, and that sleeveless jerkin left one in no doubt as to the bulging muscles in his shoulders and arms, though she did have to guess at the massive chest beneath it. His face was open, his black eyes large and long-lashed, his nose straight though perhaps a little short, his lips full and red through the black jawline beard which blended into the wealth of black curls on his head. His teeth flashed white as he smiled, and the dangerous gleam in his eye as he looked at her struck like a crossbow bolt, arousing sensations inside her that she had never been aware of before, and wasn't at all sure she liked.

Of course, she wasn't at all sure that she didn't like them, either.

She stood a little straighter and tilted her chin up, looking down her nose at him. "What do you here, sirrah?"

"Why," said the bandit, "my men and I have come to surrender ourselves to the Lady Cordelia Gallowglass at the behest of him who defeated us in battle."

"Indeed," Cordelia said, with her best attempt at frostiness. "And what is his name?"

"Ah! My lady, that would he not tell us!" the bandit chieftain lamented. "He said only that he was a knight who sought to be worthy of you, and would not use his name in public until he has proven his worth."

Cordelia stared. Such a poetic flight was quite unlike Alain—and coming from the lips of this rogue with the tilted eyebrows and the knowing smile, it set up strange quiverings inside her. "Indeed! You have walked all night to tell me this, sirrah?"

"Alas! We have—for the Wee Folk would not let us rest. Whene'er we sought to halt, or to sit for more than five minutes, they were upon us with pinches and stings."

Cordelia tried to glare at him while she considered. "I might pity you, if there surely had been no reason for . . ." She withheld Alain's name, not quite knowing why. ". . . for the young knight of whom you speak to beset you so harshly. What misdeed had you done?"

"Oh, no greater than to seek to rob a poor carter of his goods," the bandit said, trying to look apologetic.

"And to reive his wife of her virtue," squeaked a small voice near Cordelia.

Her eyes widened, glaring. "How durst you, sir!"

"Ah!" the bandit said, the very picture of remorse. "I would have stopped my men ere long! We had first to subdue her husband, though, and must needs see that she not seek to aid him."

Cordelia's indignation boiled over. "You have deserved every pinch and every sting that the elves have given you, sir, and far worse, I doubt not. Mayhap I should give you some more of them, myself!"

The bandit chief stepped back, alarmed. He had some notion of what Cordelia might be able to do if the spirit moved her. He braced himself, ready to defend against a telepathic attack.

Her eyes widened; she felt the stir of his mind against her own. "You are a warlock!"

An incredulous muttering sprang up behind him. He glanced back at his men, then shrugged and looked up at her. "I had not sought to make it a matter of general knowledge, my lady—but yes, I am a warlock."

"For shame, sir! A warlock, and one nobly reared, for so I can tell by your speech alone! For you, who were born gifted in both rank and talents, to abuse your powers thus, by preying upon the weak when, by virtue of birth, you had ought to defend them!" Cordelia blazed.

"I know." The bandit chieftain bowed his head. "I had meant to spend my life in defense of they who could not defend themselves, my lady, to use my gifts for the general good—but circumstance has decreed otherwise."

"Circumstance? Nay, tell me!" Cordelia bit off the words sharply. "What circumstances could these be that would turn you from the obligations of your station?" She reddened, suddenly incensed as she realized what the rogue was doing. "You seek to play upon my sympathies! Be sure, sir, I am not so easily gulled as that! But what shall I do with you?"

She narrowed her eyes. "What mischiefs might Puck himself invent? Can I be as ingenious as he?"

"I do not doubt it!" the bandit said quickly. "But I pray you will not! Nay, if there is a gram of woman's pity in you, forbear! Send us to the King's dungeon, if you will—set us to a year's hard labor—but do not seek to emulate the Wee Folk in your treatment of us, I beg of you!"

Cordelia gave him a look of contempt. (She thought she did it rather well.)

The bandit only looked up at her with wide, pleading eyes, and a look of intense remorse.

Cordelia made a sound of disgust. "Well, indeed, we shall see that the punishment does fit the crime! Get you to Sir Maris, the King's Seneschal, and tell him of your deeds. Tell him, too, who has sent you. Then, whatsoever punishment he shall give you, see that you bear in patience."

"Aye, my lady." The bandit chieftain bowed his head to hide his relief. "You are generous."

"Begone," she said, "before I forget my generosity."

"Begone?" He looked up and, for a moment, his face was drawn, exhausted. Then he recovered his poise, forced himself to straighten, and inclined his head. "As you wish it, my lady. Come, my men." He turned away.

"Oh, bother!" Cordelia stamped her foot, hands on her hips. "Nay, do not play the martyr! I will not be so cruel as to send you out with no rest at all. Go, go sit down against the courtyard wall! Guards!"

The Captain of the Guards stepped up beside her. "Aye, my lady?"

"Keep watch over these men, and if they seek to move more than a yard from the places where they sit or lie, have at them! Steward!"

"My lady?" Everybody was on hand, of course, watching and waiting to be called upon.

"See to it these men are given gruel and water. Let them rest till noon, then send them out."

"In the heat of the day, my lady?" The steward looked appropriately horrified.

"Aye, even in the heat of the day!" Cordelia declared,

with some heat herself. "'Tis the least they deserve, who have sought to wreak havoc on the weak." She turned back to the bandits. "Rest then, and begone." And, in a whirl of skirts, she turned and stalked away into the castle.

Forrest watched after her, reflecting that, if this was not the most beautiful woman he had ever seen, she was certainly not far from it. The vivacity, the fire within her, made her quite the most fascinating female he had ever encountered. And she was a witch!

He had heard stories of the delights that lay in store for those who lay in love, warlock and witch, their minds melding as their bodies did. He wondered if such ecstasy awaited those who found themselves in such an embrace, even if they were not in love.

Then, with a start of dismay, he realized that for himself, at least, the question was academic. He fell in love easily and frequently—and he knew the signs well. He had fallen again . . . And from the look in her eyes when they first saw each other, he thought that Cordelia might have, too.

"You make it sound as though it were a trade to which a man might be apprenticed, Geoffrey!" Alain complained—almost, Geoffrey thought, scandalized.

"Well, 'tis not quite so methodical as that," he said, grinning. " 'Tis more a matter of an art for which one must have a talent."

"As you have, to be sure," Alain said wryly. "But even given that talent, there still seems to be a great amount that is simply knowledge."

"Knowledge for some men, instinct for others." Geoffrey shrugged. "If you enjoy the game for its own sake, you learn it quickly enough. If you do not, you shall never play it well, no matter how many years of study you invest."

"It can be learned, then!"

"The forms, at least," Geoffrey agreed, "though they are worth little without the true spirit. If you would court a lady, you must dine by candlelight and, if 'tis possible, with a fiddler or three nearby, but out of sight, playing softly."

"But her duenna . . ."

"Ah, we are assuming that her duenna is not there." Geoffrey raised a forefinger. "We do not speak of ladies only, after all, but also of village wenches. Still, if you would win the heart of a fair lady, you must need find some time to whisk her away by herself for conversation, even if 'tis only for the quarter of an hour. A sheltered nook in her garden will do, or a bower—and have your fiddlers seeming to stroll by, or mayhap a lad who shall play soft songs of love on a flute."

"This by candlelight, or the light of the moon?"

"The moon is better," Geoffrey said judiciously, "if 'tis full, or nearly. But candles will do, and that quite well."

"But what would I say?" Alain asked.

"Why, you must praise her eyes, her hair, her lips, the roses in her cheeks," Geoffrey said. "It would help if you had written a poem to her beauty and committed it to memory."

"I have small gift for versing," Alain said ruefully.

"Oh, there are poets aplenty who will scribble you a whole book of verses for a piece of gold, my friend—and if you do not trust your memory to work in her presence, you may surely bring the paper along to read."

"But will she not know that 'twas not I who wrote it?"

"She may suspect," Geoffrey said carelessly, "but she will not seek to prove it—if you do not give her occasion to. Speak of love, or if you think you have it not, speak of the feelings that rise within you when you look upon her."

"Why, there am I in confusion." Alain frowned, gazing off into space. "If I look at your sister as she stands today, I do feel most strangely within—and some of those feelings, I would not speak of to her brother." He blushed furiously. "Nor to any other being, mayhap, save my father."

"I rejoice to hear it," Geoffrey said softly.

"Yet most swiftly rises, over the image that she is, the face and form of the child she was." Alain turned to him in consternation. "For she was indeed a comely little lass, Geoffrey, as I am sure you remember."

"I would not have called her 'comely,' " Geoffrey muttered.

"Nay, of course not—you are her brother. Still, the sauciness, the scoldings, the brightness of her laughter—all that arises when I look upon the grown Cordelia. It seems . . ." He broke off, shaking his head.

"Come now, you can say it!" Geoffrey coaxed. "Out with it! Speak it, then—nay, speak both, speak all, for I see you are a very welter of feelings now."

"Aye, and they go at cross-purposes." Alain scowled at the back of his horse's head. "On the one hand, there is the feeling that the impish girl is still within the gentle form I see before me, and although that has its attractive side, it is also somewhat repugnant—for she was ever as quick to turn and scold as she was to speak in mirth."

"I would say that child is still there within her, of a certainty," Geoffrey said slowly, "for I have heard my father say that we all are children within, and that 'tis tragedy beyond speaking if that child dies."

"Aye, I have heard our chaplain say that, too." Alain gazed off at the countryside. "That we all must strive to keep alive the child within us—for Christ said that we must become as little children if we would enter the kingdom of Heaven."

"Become," Geoffrey reminded, "not remain."

But Alain wasn't listening. "I am not sure how I felt toward that child, though, Geoffrey."

"Oh, stuff and nonsense!" Geoffrey said, with a flash of irritation. "You did trail behind her like a besotted mooncalf when you were twelve, Alain."

"Well, aye, I mind me of that," the Prince admitted, embarrassed. "I speak now of a younger age, though, when she dared to speak to me as though I were a lad with an empty head."

"Oh, aye, but she did that when you were twelve, too—and fifteen, and seventeen, and is like as not to do it again even now!" Geoffrey scoffed. "Be sure, she will. If that truly does repel you, Alain, seek elsewhere for a wife."

"Well . . . I would not say 'repel,' " the Prince said. "It does nettle me, though—sometimes. At others, it is as much a matter of spice as of bitter. There are thorns on the stem, so to speak—but the man would be a fool who would not brave those thorns for the beauty of the rose."

Geoffrey smiled, amused. Alain did have something of the poet's gift within him, after all. "Yet what is the feeling that does counter such ardent praise?"

"Why, simply that she was near to being a sister!" Alain burst out. "Or the closest that I ever had, at least—for she was the only female child near to my own age that I saw with any frequency. How can one be in love with a *sister*? 'Tis against nature, when one has known a lass too well, too long, and too young. Why, there may be good fellowship, but never love—or, at least, not the sort of love that must be between a man and a wife."

"Yes, I see," Geoffrey said, nodding, "though I am not at all sure that you would think it against nature if we were speaking of peasant folk who lived in a small village, where all know one another from earliest youth. When that feeling comes upon you, try to remember in your heart the mooncalf that you were when you were twelve. Surely, you did not then seem to find her too sisterly."

"Well, there is some truth in that," Alain said. "But if I were truly in love, Geoffrey, would I not lie awake o' nights, dreaming of her face, her form? Would I not find food to be of small appeal? Life itself of no joy? Would I not spend my days in moping about and sighing?"

"Aye, if you were a fool," Geoffrey said. "In truth, whenever I see such a man, I cannot help but think that 'tis not love he feels, but sickness. What *do* you feel, when you lie awake dreaming of her face and form?"

"Why, I am near to crying out in madness, that she seems to entice, yet mock!" Alain burst out, then broke off suddenly, staring. "You have tricked me, Geoffrey!"

"But only for your own benefit," Geoffrey said.

Cordelia couldn't resist coming out to see her guests off. In the end, she relented, and told the guards not to expel them at noon, but to let them rest until two o'clock. She chafed and fretted at the delay in following Alain and Geoffrey—but also found herself thinking constantly about

Forrest and seeing him and his men off. She told herself the strange feelings that churned within her were only nervousness, and anticipation of seeing such a gang of blackguards out her gate.

Nonetheless, as the time approached, she found herself moving across the outer bailey to where Forrest reposed, a little apart from his men, stretched out in the shade of the kitchens. But he opened his eyes as she came near, and for a moment, she found herself trapped by that ebony gaze, mischievously admiring as it traversed her from head to toe, insouciant and arrogant with the knowledge that he was attractive to her.

Cordelia knew that so surely that she also knew it must have been a sort of psychic leakage, an unconscious projection of his that was bound to make a woman want to come closer—and the most maddening thing was that it worked. She flushed and stepped closer, her voice as cold as she could make it. "You are no peasant. What do you among this gang of thieves?"

Forrest sat up, running a hand through his hair and shrugging. "I live as I can, milady."

"Surely you could live better than as a robber!"

"So I thought." Forrest drew his knees up and clasped his arms about them. "I joined a lord's retinue—but he went to war against his neighbor, and lost. Then the neighbor hunted down those of us who refused to turn our coats, to slay us—so I fled to the greenwood."

It was a harrowing tale, and Cordelia found herself fascinated as well as sympathetic. She tried not to let any sign of it show in her face. "But you are a warlock! Surely you could have found a way by the use of your powers!"

"Could I indeed?" Forrest's smile curdled. "We are not all like yourself and your brothers, milady—oh, yes, we have heard of you, all young witchfolk have heard of you, even to the farthest corners of Gramarye, I doubt not! The sons and daughter of the High Warlock and High Witch? Oh, aye, we all have heard of you! But few indeed are they who have so many talents as you, or in such strength! Myself, I can read minds, and craft witch-moss if I concentrate my thoughts with all my might, but little more. The former can be of value in telling me when my enemies are coming, but that does not always guarantee victory. The last is too exhausting to be of much use as more than an amusement."

Cordelia's heart went out to him. "But you are still branded with the sign of difference."

"Only figuratively, praise Heaven!" Forrest grinned again. "And then only if I let it show. I have become expert in dissembling. Indeed, I warrant you would not have guessed, had you not been a witch yourself."

"I had not thought . . ."

"Aye." Forrest shrugged. "How could you, when the only witchfolk you have met have been those of the Royal Coven, or the few who dared to try to seize all that they might, no matter whom they hurt? They had the power, milady, that most of us lack." He shrugged. "Too little to be of use, too much to let us feel safe in our likeness to others—that is your garden variety of witch."

Cordelia longed to tell him that the proper word was "esper," for those born with psionic talents, but knew she must not, to anyone who did not already know of the great civilization on the Terran planets outside of Gramarye. "But you are a gentleman, at the least, and more likely the son of a lord, if I mistake you not!"

"You do not." Forrest inclined his head. "But I am a youngest son, and my father is a lord attainted in the first rebellion against Queen Catharine, before either of us were born."

"The Crown did let the rebel lords keep their lands and titles . . ."

"But they were ever suspect thereafter." Forrest raised a finger. "And their eldest sons were taken as royal hostages, to learn loyalty to the Crown—but not their younger. My father told me with regret that I had my own way to make in the world, though he would help me as he could."

"Surely there were many positions open to a lord's son!"

"Honorable positions?" Forrest shrugged. "I had a choice between the church and the army—anything lesser

was not honorable, and I am not cut out to be a priest."
Again, his gaze raked Cordelia, making her feel as though
he had touched her, lightly, caressingly.

She tried to hide a shiver. "Nay, you are not," she said
tartly. "Still, you could have accepted service with the
Crown!"

Forrest grinned. "I have said it was the eldest who was
taken to Court to learn manners and love of the King and
Queen, milady, not the youngest. No, I found myself re-
senting them highly, they who had shorn my father of respect, and myself of opportunity."

"Did you not think the King and Queen were merciful?
They did not behead the rebel lords for traitors, after all.
By custom and precedent, they could have hanged or be-
headed all the lords, scattered their armies, and attainted
their wives and children, so that none might inherit."

"Aye, I know, and given the estates to those who had sup-
ported them loyally in the war." Forrest nodded, chagrined.
"They were merciful, even as you say—but the shame of the
parents clung to the sons, and it was no great boon to me to
have my eldest brother set even higher above me."

Cordelia remembered how brothers could vie against
one another, and had heard of families in which the rivalry
was much sharper than in her own. "You did not at least
lack for meat, nor a roof over your head! In truth, you did
not lack for comfort!"

" 'Tis true," Forrest admitted, "but only till I was
grown—which is to say, sixteen. Then was I set on mine
own, for my father died, and my eldest brother had no
great love for me. You may say 'twas bad luck that I
pledged troth to the wrong lord and had to run for my life,
making a living by my wits—or you may say 'twas mine
own recklessness that drove me to the greenwood. I could
not argue, in any case." He looked up at Cordelia, and
suddenly, his eyes seemed huge, seemed to devour her,
and with alarm, she felt herself turning weak inside, felt a
warming and a thrilling in the blood, far worse than she
had felt for the very first time so short a while ago—or far
better—and his words made it even sharper. "Were I not

so attainted and so ashamed, were I not cast down to banditry and poverty, I might dream of suing and sighing, of wooing and courting so beautiful a lady as yourself."

The blood roared in her ears, but she knew extravagant flattery for what it was—and loved it, in a part of herself that she tried desperately to deny. She heard herself saying, as though from far away, "A man's lot is never lost. Faith and industry, and honest striving, can resurrect the fortunes of any nobleman, no matter how low he has fallen. You must never give up hope, sir."

His eyes fired with that hope she had spoken of. "Surely, my lady," he breathed, "if you say it, I shall hope—and strive to clear my name, and prove myself worthy of regard."

She stared at him, stiff, her face burning.

He added, softly, "The regard of my King, of course."

But he fooled neither of them—nor did he intend to.

They stared at each other for seconds that seemed to last for an uncountable time, until Cordelia felt she must break from the strain. Clutching her hands at her waist, she said, "Then go, sir, with your men, and prove your proud words."

He stood up slowly and stepped close. His scent seemed to enfold her, the scent of sweat and dust—and something else, some musk she did not know. He towered over her, so close, so close, but not close enough . . . "If you say it, my lady," he breathed, "I shall." And he held her gaze for one more long, long moment until finally she gave ground, stepping back a little, to break the strain.

Forrest smiled sadly, and turned to bawl at his men.

They came to their feet with groans, most shaking themselves from sleep, and a scullery boy passed among them with a bucket and a ladle. Another stepped behind him with a basket of rolls. Each outlaw took a roll, took a drink, and looked up at Cordelia in gratitude, muttering, "Mercy, Lady."

"Gladly given," she answered in her most lofty manner, wondering for the first time, with desperation verging on panic, why her mother and father didn't come out to help her with this.

Then Forrest bawled orders at his men, chivvying them

into some sort of order and shooing them out through the gatehouse. But before the shadows swallowed him up, he looked back for a long, last look at Cordelia, and his eyes seemed to glow.

Then he turned away, and was gone.

The whole of the outer bailey seemed to exhale in one vast sigh of relief.

All except Cordelia, who stood rigid, staring after him.

Above, at the solar window, her mother beamed down, and her father scowled.

"She did that rather well, my husband," Gwendylon said.

"Yes, she did," Rod answered. "And so, unfortunately, did he."

"Ah, yes." Gwen's voice was entirely too cool. "He doth seem to have gained her interest. However, it will do her no harm to find some other suitor after her affections."

"Well . . . if you say so." Rod did not look convinced. "But I don't like the look of him."

"Or the look he gave our daughter? I cannot say I am surprised. Yet be easy in thine heart, mine husband—she is warded against those who would use her, as well as any maiden may be."

"And no better. Why didn't you go down there and help her out?"

"Why did not you?"

"Mostly because of your hand on my arm restraining me, every time I started for the door."

"Well, that is true." Gwen smiled, dimpling. "After all, 'twas to her they were bound to surrender, not to us."

"True," Rod admitted. "Still, I think she could have used a little support."

"She is experienced with those who would do her harm, and is quite ready to deal with them herself, mine husband. We cannot always shield her—but I will admit 'tis best for her to experience such men as he, when we stand near."

"Oh, you bet it is," Rod said softly.

The bandit troop passed out from the gatehouse and down the winding road, descending the mound on which the castle stood. There the road split, the eastern fork straggling off into the wood, toward Runnymede. They trooped off eastward with it—but as soon as they were in under the trees, there were mutterings in the ranks.

"We could go now, and none would ever be the wiser!"

"Now could we fade in among the greenwood leaves, and none should ever find us!"

Pebbles whizzed from the roadside. One clipped the last speaker on the pate as it passed, knocking his hat off. He cried out, pressing a hand to his head, then bent down to pick up his hat—and a stick popped up out of the roadway to spank him very soundly on the rump. He straightened up with a howl, pressing his other hand to the injured anatomy.

"I think the Wee Folk have not forgotten us," said Forrest. "We are not quite yet free to go where we will."

"Then when shall we be?" cried one of the bandits.

"Why, you heard the lady—when we have spoken to Sir Maris!"

Sure enough, a few rods farther on, the roadway opened out into a small clearing, and there stood Sir Maris with his dozen knights at his back.

"The lady bids us bring ourselves to you for punishment, Sir Seneschal." Forrest bowed a little.

"She has done well," the old knight grated. "We are freed of any need to require thee at the King's dungeon."

"But you promised . . ." one outlaw burst out, before another clapped a hand over his mouth.

"Aye, I gave my word," said Sir Maris, "and gave it in Their Majesties' names—so thou art free to go. But see to it thou dost not rob, nor steal, nor poach, ever again!"

"We shall not, sir," said Forrest, and the whole band behind him mumbled hasty denials.

"Thou, sir, most of all!" Sir Maris glared at Forrest. "Thou, the son of a nobleman, lowering thyself to banditry by the roadside! Thou shouldst be red with mortification, to stand before a knight! Thou shouldst be afeard to admit thou wert ever dubbed a knight bachelor!"

"I am ashamed." Forrest lowered his head—coincidentally hiding his expression.

"Well, mayhap there is some saving grace left within thee," the old knight grumbled, leaning on his staff. "Go thou, and mend thy ways, then—and see that thou dost make better use of the life and fortunes God hath given thee! Be mindful, whene'er thou art tempted to despoil those weaker than thyself, or those come for a moment within thy power—what would any one of these men of thine give, to have been born as thou wert? Be grateful for what thou hast, sirrah, and do not berate God for not having given thee more."

A flash of annoyance showed in Forrest's eye—resentment, quickly masked. He bowed again. "I shall take your words to heart, Sir Seneschal."

"See that thou dost! Farewell—and never come before me again with complaints of misdeeds being levied against thee! Go, go one and all—into the greenwood! You are pardoned, you are free to seek honest labor within the King's domain! Go, and never stray again!" He raised staff and hands, dismissing them.

The bandits knew when to take their chance. They faded in among the trees, one and all.

Including Forrest. He picked his way through underbrush, then strode quickly over last year's fallen leaves until he was a hundred feet from the roadway. There he stopped and listened, and heard faint sounds that must have been his men gathering together again. He set off in the opposite direction. At last he was freed from their weight, hanging about his neck—at last he was freed from the need to care for them. If they still wanted him to lead them badly enough, they could come and find him.

He hoped they would not. He wanted the freedom to be himself again, to try to build his own future once more. He had decided to take Sir Maris at his word, and make better use of his time, indeed. He strode off through the woods, circling back toward Castle Gallowglass, the image of a lissome form and a beautiful face under a wreath of auburn hair burning in his mind.

He intended to court Cordelia.

CHAPTER
~7~

"Alain? Ala-a-ain! Alain!"

Alain opened his eyes, and the light seemed to lance through to his brain. He squeezed them shut, then forced them open a crack. The light still pained him, and that infernal voice was booming in his ears, sending pain rolling through his head. "Alain! Praise Heaven! I feared I had lost you!"

"So did I," Alain gasped. "More softly, Geoffrey, I prithee! There is no need to shout!"

"Why, I do not." Geoffrey grinned, recognizing the condition. He knelt and slid a hand under his friend's back, pulling him up. "Drink, now. 'Tis time to break your fast."

"Bury me," Alain groaned, "for I have died." But he took the tankard obediently and drank. Then the taste hit him, and he yanked the tankard down and spat. "Pah! 'Tis the same vile potion with which you slew me!"

" 'Tis good country ale," Geoffrey rejoined, "and 'twill go some way toward making you whole and sound again." He was still grinning. "But wherefore did you hide . . . Oh, I see."

Alain frowned. What was he talking about? He followed the direction of Geoffrey's glance, and saw the bracken flattened in what must surely be more room than he needed by himself—and saw the stockings that lay there, forgotten as the wench had tiptoed home in the false dawn. Alain stared. "But . . . but I did not . . ." Then memory struck, and he buried his face in his hands and groaned. "I did!"

"Why, then, be glad!" Geoffrey slapped him on the shoulder, albeit gently. "You have slain a monster, you have drunk deeply, and you have lain with a wench! You live, Alain, you are alive as you never have been!"

"I am dead, as I never have been," the Prince groaned, "or nearly. You do not understand, Geoffrey."

"Oh, but I do. Quite well."

"Nay, you do not! I am the Prince, it is given to me to take care of my people, to guard their welfare—not to use or abuse them!"

"I doubt that you did," Geoffrey said slowly.

"But you have said it yourself!"

"I have said no such thing," Geoffrey replied with asperity. "I told you to be glad of what you have done, and I say it still. The wench was more than willing—she was eager! I saw myself how she passed beyond flirtation to invitation, to leading and chivvying. What happened after she led you away, I cannot say, for I did not see—but if you could remember, I think you would find that she did urge you on even then, and did never say, 'Hold!' "

"Nay, she did." Alain pressed a hand to his forehead. "The memory comes now—she did say, 'My lord, how naughty! You must not!' "

Geoffrey smiled slowly. "And what did you do?"

"Why, I drew back, and took my hand from her, as any gentleman would."

"And what said she to that?"

"She took my hand and pressed it back where it had been, saying, 'Nay, you must—if you wish it.' I assured her that I did . . ."

"And thereafter she told you where she wished you to put your hands."

Alain blushed furiously. "Aye, though not always with words."

Geoffrey shook his head. "You are wrong to torment yourself with spasms of conscience. She wished it, and you were too drunk to refuse her, or to deny your own desires. There is no cause for you to feel guilt in anything save having drunk to excess—and therein must I share the blame, for I egged you on to it."

"My guilt is my own, for whatever I have done, I could have chosen not to!"

"Yet you would not hesitate to share the glory." Geoffrey grinned, shaking his head. "Well, bear in mind the wench's name, and that of this village, so that if she does prove by child, you can see that she is provided for. That much obligation you may claim, though I would not think it necessary. Still, if she knew who it was had lain with her last night, I have no doubt she would boast of it, and raise the child with pride."

Alain started to pull on his hose. "Then I must tell her!"

"Nay, nay." Geoffrey restrained him with a hand on his shoulder. "*If* she should prove by child, I said. If she does not, she will keep the memory of this night to herself, I doubt not—or if she chooses to share it, 'twill be as a boast, that she shared the bed of the knight who slew the monster."

Alain hesitated, half into his hose.

"Nay, do pull on your clothes," Geoffrey urged, "for we must be away."

"Ought I not . . ."

"Nay, you ought not, for she may try to presume upon your good nature." Geoffrey did not add "and innocence." "Did you say a single word about love, or desiring anything further of her?"

Alain scowled, clutching his head, forcing the memories up from the alcoholic murk. "Nay. As I remember it, I could scarce say a word."

"Then do not seek her out again, for if you do speak of love you do not feel, or of desiring further acquaintance with her, you would hurt her heart when you left. As it is, she will remember a night's sport, and so will you—and since that is all she desired and more than you promised, she will have nothing bitter in her heart. Speak again, and she may. Come, be of good cheer!"

Alain stood, fastening his hose-belt about his waist, but he was still dark of face, brooding.

Geoffrey eyed him narrowly. "What else, then?"

"What a vile excuse for a man am I!" Alain burst out. "To bed one woman while I love another! Indeed, how can I truly say I love Cordelia, if I go slavering after every shapely form like a dog in heat!"

"I would scarcely say that you went slavering," Geoffrey said drily, "or that it was you who went after her. Still, 'tis a sad fact, Alain, and mayhap the bane of our species, that a man can desire many women, even though he loves only one."

"But does this not mean that I am not truly in love with her?"

"Not a whit," Geoffrey assured him. "The troubadours would have it otherwise, I know—they sing to their patron-ladies that a man's desire springs from falling in love, and that the man will *only* desire her with whom he is in love—but the truth is otherwise. It is for me, at least."

Alain looked up. "You have been in love with one, yet desired others?"

Geoffrey shrugged. "Either that, or been in love with many at one time, or never been in love at all—have it as you will. I fear that fidelity is as much a matter of self-control as of love, Alain."

"Well—I am schooled in that, at least." The Prince seemed somewhat reassured.

"Too much so," Geoffrey told him. "Indeed, I rejoiced most amazingly to see you drop your armor of chivalrous discipline for a few hours, Alain. There is more to life than rules and duties."

"I have been told that." Alain looked him straight in the eye. "I have been taught that a wise ruler must recognize that impulse toward excess in his people, so that he may understand and be merciful if they do not cleave to the letter of his laws."

"Have you been told, too, that men may be tempted and fall?"

"Aye." Alain looked away. "But I think that I never truly understood it before."

"That may be, that well may be," Geoffrey agreed, "but you do understand it now."

"Oh, aye! Most thoroughly!" Alain turned away in self-disgust. "Surely I am not worthy of the Lady Cordelia."

Geoffrey sighed. "I thought you had but now said that you could understand that men could fall."

"Well . . . aye, but . . ."

"Then what matter this one lapse, so long as you are faithful after you wed?"

"But how can I be sure that I will be? I had thought love was my assurance, but . . . Geoffrey! How if I am not in love?"

"If you can even ask the question, then you are not," Geoffrey said, with inexorable conviction, "and if you are not, then 'tis far better you learn it now, than after the wedding."

"I am in love with her!" Alain said. "I must be, for I have planned it for years!"

" 'Twas your head did that planning, not your heart. Yet if your love is sure, it will stand the test."

"What test is that?"

"The test of conversing with pretty maids and beauteous ladies, even of kissing them now and again. You must risk your heart, Alain, or you may never truly find it." Geoffrey clapped him on the shoulder. "Come, don your doublet, for the day draws on apace."

"Aye, if you say it." Alain shrugged into his doublet and turned away, fastening the buttons as he went.

Geoffrey followed him, reflecting that a quick exit might be advisable, in case the wench came back looking for her hero. He trusted neither her, nor Alain's conscience and sense of duty. Besides, they had a world to wander, villains to chastise, damsels to rescue . . .

Beautiful damsels, and pretty maids all in a row. A long row, Geoffrey decided. If he was going to trust his sister's happiness to Prince Alain's heart, he was going to make sure that heart had been tried in the crucible first.

In the vastness of the forest, a woman cried.

Alain snapped rigid, like a bird dog hearing the flap of wings. "A damsel in distress!"

"Aye, from the sound of it." Geoffrey turned toward the sound, too. "Let us beware of traps, though."

"Ridiculous!" Alain scoffed. "Who would think to trap two knights with a woman's cry?"

"Who would think to summon drakes to the arrow by simulating the cry of a duck?" Geoffrey returned. "Nonetheless, we must go—but with tactical soundness, shall we not? Let one go posthaste, and the other go carefully."

"Then I shall take the posthaste." Alain grinned and plunged into the thicket at the side of the road. His horse neighed in protest, but fought its way through. Geoffrey followed the path made by Alain's horse, but rather more warily.

He could hear the sobbing through the trees—forlorn, heart-rending, almost as though the woman who wept was trying to choke her sobs down, but not succeeding.

Alain rode through the brush and between the trees until they opened out into a river meadow, a broad expanse of clover dotted with wildflowers and bordered along the stream by weeping willows. Under the largest sat a damsel, head bowed into her hands.

Alain slowed, going softly, wondering if he had the right to interfere—and Geoffrey came up behind him. They were so silent in their approach they were almost upon her before she heard the horses' hooves. She leaped up in fright, then gasped in fear and backed away under the willow branches.

"Fear not, fair maiden." Alain reined in his horse. "I would not hurt a lady in any way."

"We are knights," said Geoffrey, "sworn to protect the weak and punish the wicked."

"If any man has wronged you, tell us," said Alain, "that we may challenge him to mortal combat."

The damsel stopped withdrawing, at least. Alain's eyes were fast upon her, and it was scarcely a wonder. She was slender; long lashes swept across her eyes, so pale they seemed gossamer; her golden hair fairly glowed in the sunlight, sweeping down to the middle of her back. Her little heart-shaped face was the perfect setting for such huge, lustrous blue eyes and her small, pert nose. The width and fullness of her lips were surprising, seeming somewhat out of place—but making a man ache to lean down and kiss them. When she looked up at him, he felt a stirring within him, and had to fight to keep it from emerging as a shudder. She was, after all, a beauty—very much a beauty. She wore a bliaut and a kirtle, high-necked, full-sleeved, that should have been very modest, but was made of some fabric that molded itself to her body with every gentlest breath of wind, revealing the lush contours beneath.

Geoffrey glanced about, trying to discern some hint as to why the damsel wept—and why a lady of gentle breeding should be alone by a riverside. He did see a palfrey, tethered to the willow, grazing beneath its branches. Other than that, there was no sign.

"Lady, we shall protect you," he called out. "How is it you have come here alone?"

"Alas, good sirs!" She stepped forward timorously, coming out from beneath the branches of the willow—but only a little way. "There was a man—my true love, I thought—who bade me meet him here this morning, as the sun rose. But the dawn has gone, the sun nears the noon, and he has not come."

Geoffrey frowned, having something of a nasty suspicion as to what had happened—but when it came to a motive, he could only understand the most obvious, and it didn't make sense. "Wherefore would a gentleman fail in rendezvous with so beautiful a lady as yourself?"

The lady lowered her eyes, blushing, then looked up with a sigh. "Ah, sir! I can only believe that he is a true love turned false, or was never a true love at all! I blush with shame to think that he only toyed with my affections!" And she heaved another sigh.

Alain caught himself staring; the heavy sigh had done

wonders. Her gown clung to her figure, after all, and her figure was very much worth clinging to. He found a desire to do so himself.

Indeed, a very great desire.

"The man who forswore a tryst with you must have been a fool indeed," he breathed.

"A fool," Geoffrey agreed, "or a very shrewd villain. Have you a sister, milady?"

"Aye, sir—a younger sister." Her eyes were wide in wonder. "How could you know?"

"You have no brother? It is the firstborn grandson who will inherit?"

"Nay, sir—it is she who weds first." Then the maiden gasped, covering her mouth with her hand. "You do not believe . . ."

"How did word of this tryst come to you?" Geoffrey asked.

"Why, from my sister! 'Twas she who brought me word from my lord . . . No! You cannot think that my own sister would betray me!"

"And that she even now importunes upon him?" Geoffrey shook his head sadly. "It has happened before this, and will happen again."

"But wherefore should she deal so cruelly with me?"

"Why, to have your lover for her husband, and your father's estates for her own," Alain said gently, his eyes full of sympathy.

The damsel stared in shock, then burst into tears.

Alain leaped down off his horse and ran to take her in his arms, patting her back, soothing, making comforting noises. He looked up and glared at Geoffrey over the damsel's head.

Geoffrey felt a surge of annoyance, and fought to keep his face impassive. Was the man truly so great a fool as that?

Or, perhaps, merely inexperienced.

Geoffrey knew that Alain had had very little acquaintance with girls his own age, and that only under the very rigid rules of court formalities. But perhaps he was not so great a fool after all, for it was he who was holding the beautiful maiden in his arms—and she certainly was a beauty.

Geoffrey tried to smile, but it came out as a grimace of distaste. "Come, maiden," he called. "Where is your home?"

The damsel's sobs had slackened. Alain stroked her hair, murmuring inanities, looking stunned. "There, now—life shall go on, and you shall find a truer love than he. Come, let us dry these tears." He pulled a handkerchief from his own sleeve and dabbed at her cheeks. "Five years since, you shall look back on this day with amusement, and bless the mischance, the betrayal, that held him from you—for you shall find your true love, I doubt not, and discover him to be a far better man than he who turned from you to your sister only because you were not there, and she was."

The disturbing thing, Geoffrey decided, was that Alain really meant every word of it. In this case, it was not that he had acquired the gift of flattery—it was a genuine sympathy, a real caring for a person who was suffering. Though, Geoffrey reflected cynically, Alain's sympathy might not have been quite so strong if the damsel had not been quite so beautiful.

"But has he truly turned to her?" she cried, eyes brimming full again.

Alain stared down at her, feeling his heart turn over in his breast—but it was a heart that was pledged to Cordelia, as his conscience reminded him.

Well, no—it wasn't, really. After all, she had rejected his suit—spurned him, in fact. He felt a certain kinship with this maiden, who had sought her true love and been disappointed by him.

He shook the thought from him. It was unworthy of a knight. "It may be that he has not turned to another," he said. "It may be that he remains true to you."

"Oh, can you truly think so?" She stepped back from him a pace, looking up, eyes brightening with hope.

"It may be," Alain said solemnly, "though it may be as we suspect, too. Only by returning to your father's house shall we discover the truth. Come, tell us—where is your home?"

"Yonder, sir." She pointed down the roadway. "In the West, a day's ride."

"So far as that?" Geoffrey crowded his horse up near them. "You have come so long a way by yourself, unescorted, through half the night, alone?"

"Aye." She looked up at him, shuddering. "I did fear; I did start at every noise. I thought every moment to see a band of outlaws step forth from the greenwood, to assail me."

There was every chance that exactly that would have happened, Geoffrey knew, and that her purse would have been the least of which they would have reft her—if, by good luck, he and Alain had not sent the local gang packing. "But by good fortune, they were all abed, and you came here untouched, to wait for the dawn. You hid till daylight, did you not?"

She nodded.

Geoffrey looked at her, court-bred and dainty, her delicate gown soiled at the hem, and knew that any woodsman worth his salt could have found her trail and tracked her down. It had been luck, good luck only, that no bandit had done exactly that.

"The owl's hooting never had so much quality of menace as it did last night," she said.

"Then 'tis only by great good fortune that you have come thus far in safety." Alain looked down at her sternly. "You must return to your father's house forthwith—but you must not ride alone. Come, mount! We shall accompany you!"

"I could not ask that of you." But even as she said it, gladness suffused her face. "Assuredly, you are bound to other destinations."

Alain saw those huge eyes glowing up at him, and knew that he could not do anything else. "No true knight could turn down a request from a damsel in distress," he told her. "We shall ride with you—and we shall not hear a word to the contrary."

Nor was she apt to give it, Geoffrey thought—but he did not say so. After all, he would never turn down an opportunity to escort so voluptuous a lady, either.

"I hesitate to ask it of you." She bowed her head, looking up at him through long lashes. "Surely you must be bound on a mission of great importance."

"You may say that." Alain smiled. "We are two knights-errant, wandering where we will to discover damsels in distress, so that we may give them aid and succor. I could not think of any mission more important. Could you, Sir Geoffrey?"

"Oh, nay, assuredly not, Sir Alain!" Geoffrey fought to keep both sarcasm and amusement from his voice. At least one of them was sincere.

"Then 'tis said; 'tis done." Alain stepped away from the lady, albeit reluctantly, and stepped over to the palfrey. He untied it and led it out from under the willow leaves. "Come, my lady, mount!" He dropped the horse's reins, set his hands to her waist, and lifted her up to the saddle, amazed that she felt so light. She gasped with surprise and fright, clinging to his arms, then smiled tremulously as she found herself on horseback again. She hooked a knee about the horn of the sidesaddle, arranged her skirts, and beamed down upon him. "Bless you, sir!"

She looked up at Geoffrey, and for a second, he was hit with the full force of that enchanting gaze, that adorable, piquant face, those full ruby lips . . . "I shall praise you in my prayers every night! How can I thank you for your mercy, to a poor, lost damsel and, aye, a foolish one. How foolish, how credulous, to believe what I have believed!"

And Geoffrey found himself reassuring her, just as Alain had done. "Your trust does you credit, even though it was betrayed—for surely, what woman would think that her own sister would play her false? What man could think less than highly of a woman who would ride to meet her lover? Assuredly, my lady, we must accompany you!"

And, as he pulled his horse into step beside hers, he realized the truth of what he had said. Thank heavens she was an innocent, for that face, that voice, that form gave her a power over men that was absolutely incredible.

Somehow, it never occurred to either of them that she might not really be so innocent, and might know exactly how much power she had. Even more should they have believed that she knew how to use that power, too.

They rode back onto the forest road, turning their horses

away to the west, Geoffrey and Alain vying, with witticisms and flattery, to raise her spirits. They succeeded admirably—within half an hour her eyes were alight with mirth, and her laughter rang like music in their ears.

The bandits were on their way, and Cordelia resolutely forgot about them. Yes, she had put those dark, reckless eyes, broad shoulders, and sensuous lips firmly out of her mind, and she knew she had, because she thought of them every now and then, just to make sure. Her mind clear, she went soaring off on her broomstick to track down her brother and her suitor, cursing the delay under her breath—with far too much vehemence.

It didn't take her long to find the village in which Alain and Geoffrey had spent the night. She searched the minds of the villagers quickly and lightly, injecting a thought of the two heroes who had come through the town, and reading the memories that rose in response. Her eyes widened as she learned of the appearance of the ogre, and of the battle. She was even more surprised to learn that it was Alain who had slain the monster, not her brother—or, at least, that Geoffrey had given him full credit for the deed. She wondered, for a moment, if her brother had lied, then decided that he probably had not. Not that Geoffrey was above lying, mind you, or at least prevaricating—it was merely that, in this instance, there was more for him to gain by truth, at least in terms of his goals for Alain. Geoffrey was not the sort to lie unless it was to give him a military advantage, anyway, and never in matters of honor or glory. Chivalry, to him, was sacrosanct. *How silly*, she thought, but was astounded when she found no memory of their leaving; everyone in the village seemed to have waked to find them gone—except . . .

Except the village priest, who had risen early for Matins, and seen them ride into the forest . . .

Cordelia arrowed off toward the trees.

CHAPTER
~8~

Cordelia sped high above the treetops, a speck in the sky, listening for thoughts from her brother and . . . yes, suitor. But flying takes time, and broomsticks move considerably more slowly than jet planes. The sun was dropping toward the western horizon before Cordelia finally "heard" Alain's mind with her own. Not Geoffrey's, of course—he habitually kept his mind closed, his thoughts guarded, and he took considerably more concentration to read, if he did not choke off all contact. But Alain . . .

Alain was besotted.

Cordelia sat rigid for a moment, wide-eyed, horrified, all attention riveted to Alain's words reverberating in her mind, gallant and flattering. Why, he had never spoken to her like this! Through his ears, she heard the musical, bell-like tones of the female voice answering him. She sat frozen, unable to think, unable to spare the slightest thought for anything else . . .

She was falling.

She was plunging toward the earth, broomstick in a nosedive, falling out of the sky! She truly had become distracted, not even sparing a thought for telekinesis! Anger flowed; at herself, for such carelessness; at Alain, for his fickleness; at Geoffrey, for having led him into this; but most of all, at that scarlet hussy who dared to steal the affections of her man! Never mind that the girl probably knew nothing of Cordelia, or Alain's proposal—she was loathsome anyway!

But Cordelia was not about to be outdone, nor to see her prize stolen from her. She would match the hussy on her own ground, and win! She brought the broom out of its nosedive and sped above the treetops, scolding herself for having let Alain get away. Surely there must have been some way to say no and insist on a proper courtship, without packing him off to the arms of such a vampire as this!

And that, without ever having met the girl.

There they were, on the roadway, visible for a moment between the leaves! But neither of the boys noticed her in the slightest, and the girl certainly didn't. Just as well, Cordelia thought, and sped ahead of them until the road curved close to the river in an open meadow. Cordelia decided that they would not pass by so ideal a camping place with the sun already low. She landed in the woods a short distance from the edge of the clearing, leaned her broom against a tree, and waited.

They came riding into the meadow through the shadows of trees stretched long across the grass—a golden young knight and a dark young knight, with a blonde beauty between them, laughing and chatting as they came out of the woods, both men seeming mightily pleased with themselves. Cordelia lingered a few minutes longer under the shelter of the leaves. Both of them were looking quite lively; their color was heightened, their eyes sparkled. So did the woman's; she looked down with frequent blushes—very coy, very demure, very calculating! Cordelia hated her on sight, not only for her golden tresses and baby-doll face—after all, the poor child could scarcely be eighteen!—but also for her deliberate manipulation of the men. Couldn't the fools see what she was doing?

No. Of course not. They were enjoying it too much.

What was worse, Cordelia found herself feeling dowdy for the first time in her life—at least, in comparison to this paragon of pulchritude.

Oh, but what a scheming creature she was! The high neckline seemed demure and innocent—but the clinging fabric showed her for what she was, in every sense. Shameless, brazen! Cordelia must learn how she achieved the effect. The blushes, the coquettish glances, looking up at Alain with spaniel eyes, every movement planned, every modulation of her laugh, and no doubt, the choice of every word, though Cordelia could not hear them. She fumed inside, but also felt a sinking despair. How could she possibly compete with such an accomplished man-eater?

And she had to admit, after all, that the woman had been blessed with uncommonly good looks.

For a moment, her heart quailed, but only for a moment. Then she saw the men dismounting, vying with one another to see who would help the lady from her perch. Laughing, she chose Alain—of course!—and his hands closed about her waist, lifting her down. Of course, she slid a little too hard, a little too far, and fetched up against his chest. For a moment, he froze, still holding her toes off the ground, then put her down with a little, forced laugh. She laughed, too, then turned away to blush—each movement exactly timed, head bent at exactly the right angle. Cordelia seethed, but she had to admire the sheer artistry of the wench.

Well, she would learn to outdo the minx at her own game!

No, not her own, Cordelia reflected—if she tried to compete with the woman on her own terms, she was lost. Honesty and innocence were Cordelia's strong suit—being forthright without being forward. She must somehow make those qualities into advantages—and she would!

She set forth from the trees, strolling closer, waiting for them to notice her. It was the woman who looked up first, then looked again, surprised, staring. The men noticed and broke off their laughing, looking up. Geoffrey stared, as startled as though he had seen a mouse walking about on the bottom of a river, and Cordelia had the immense satisfaction of seeing Alain turn pale. Then he blushed beet-red and turned away—as well he might, Cordelia thought grimly.

But she smiled as boldly as she could and stepped forward. "Well, brother! At last I have found you!"

"Indeed!" Geoffrey smiled. "You are well met, sister. But wherefore did you seek me?"

He knew very well who she was seeking! "I have wearied of my duties at home, and have come to see that, if you may go adventuring, so may I."

"A woman, adventuring?" The vixen stared, scandalized. "It is not seemly!"

Well, she should know, if anyone should. "Quite so," Cordelia agreed. "A woman alone may not—but in her brother's company, there is surely nothing improper."

She had the satisfaction of seeing the look of dismay flit across the hussy's features, though it was quickly masked. It was even more gratifying to see the look of delight that crossed Alain's face, even though it was hidden so quickly as to leave Cordelia wondering if she had really seen it. She felt a stab of remorse—how badly had she hurt him, that he dared not show pleasure in her company?

"Well, this will be pleasing." Geoffrey smiled, amused. "And timely: we are about to concoct supper. Surely you will join us—must she not, companions?"

"Oh, surely she must," said the vampire, all syrupy sweetness. Alain mumbled something that sounded vaguely affirmative and looked away. He certainly should, Cordelia thought, with a flame of white-hot anger—but she suppressed it with a self-control that was new to her; she had more important things to fry than Alain's conscience. She advanced toward them, doing her best to simulate the movement of a cat on the prowl. "Do you gentleman fetch some game for us, and we shall set about building a fire for it. We shall see what we may do to spark a blaze among kindling—shall we not, damsel?"

"Indeed!" For a second, the minx looked startled. Then she smiled in amused anticipation.

Geoffrey cast a dubious glance from one to the other, then shrugged. He, protect Cordelia from another woman?

As well to think of protecting a lynx from a kitten! Besides, he had a notion of what was about to follow. "Well enough, then. Milady, this is my sister, the Lady Cordelia." He almost said "Gallowglass," then thought better of it—an instinct to caution, Heaven knew why. But they were, after all, supposed to be incognito. "Cordelia, this is the Lady Delilah de Fevre."

"Delighted," Delilah purred.

"The pleasure will be all mine," Cordelia assured her, carefully not specifying what she would take pleasure in.

"Come, Alain, let us seek out game!" Geoffrey turned his horse back toward the woods. With a dubious backward glance, Alain rode after him.

The clearing was quiet for a moment, only birdsong and breeze, as the two women regarded one another, both with slight smiles. Cordelia only wished that she really felt as confident as she looked. Well, anger would have to serve in place of confidence, and she surely had enough of that at the moment! "Perchance we may come to know one another," she said. "Come, let us chat, whiles we gather firewood and tinder."

"Gladly, if you will show me what it is," Delilah said. "I would not know what to seek, for my servants have always done such chores."

Cordelia held down her indignation and forced a saccharine smile. " 'Tis the curse of we who are well bred," she agreed, "that we cannot care for ourselves when the need arises."

"The need has arisen for you, then?" Delilah said sweetly. "And you know that it will arise again?"

"Perchance," Cordelia said between her teeth, "and then, perchance not. It was my mother's teaching that every woman should know how to fend for herself if she must, that she not be dependent upon a man's whims and cruelties."

"Your mother was no doubt wise," Lady Delilah purred. "Had she cause to know?"

That stung worse—because, of course, Gwen *had* had cause to learn how to take care of herself, until Cordelia's father Rod came into Gwen's life. Cordelia was a little hazy on the details, knowing only the story of how they met, courted, and wed, with very little about how Gwen had occupied her time before Rod had come unto her life; she knew only that they had not married until Gwen was twenty-nine—very late for a medieval woman. "My father did not think so," she said sweetly. "Did thine?"

A frown creased the smooth perfection of Delilah's brow. "My what?"

"Your father," Cordelia explained. She sighed, as though striving for patience in explaining something elementary to a five-year-old. "Did your father find need for your mother to be dependent upon him?"

"Surely she did rely on him, and he proved ever reliable," Delilah said, amused. "In truth, I thought she fended for herself most excellently in that."

Cordelia frowned. "How so?"

"Why," said Delilah, "the lady who fends for herself, and has no true need of a husband, will not have one."

Cordelia stared at her, frozen for a moment, fuming—but she kept the fumes inside, forced them into a curdled smile, and said, "She who does not need a man for living will have naught but the best of men—and only for love, true love."

"Ah! True love!" Delilah looked away toward the trees. "How each of us does long for it! But what if it comes not, Lady Cordelia? How then shall we fare?"

"As well as we wish," Cordelia snapped.

"Oh, nay!" Delilah turned huge, demure eyes upon her. "We shall do as well as we may."

Alain, Cordelia saw, was as well as Delilah had decided she might do. A change of subject was obviously in order. She turned away, stooping to pick up a twig here, a stick there. "How came you here, maiden, to the company of my brother and his friend?" She put perhaps a little more emphasis than was necessary on the word "maiden."

"Alas!" Delilah lamented. "I came at the behest of him whom I love—but he betrayed me, and did not come."

That snatched Cordelia's poise away from her. She stared, aghast. "Truly he did not mislead you so!"

"Aye," Delilah sighed. "I fear I am ever too trusting."

Cordelia knew, with dead certainty, that "trusting" was one thing Delilah was not—except, perhaps, trusting in her own ability to manipulate a man. "Did you not fear the outlaws of the forest?"

"Oh, aye!" Delilah touched her eyelid, where a tear had presumably formed. "I feared they might hurt me sore— yet not so sorely as my lord has hurt me." She looked away—and sure enough, fat tears trembled in her eyes, then rolled free. For a moment, Cordelia almost embraced her in a rush of sympathy—but it was replaced with a rush of anger. So the female serpent could actually weep on demand! Her admiration for the woman's artistry rose one notch higher, even as her opinion of the woman's honesty dropped even lower.

Still, she strove to sound sympathetic. "The night must have been long indeed."

Delilah said, "Any night is long, when one's love is not near one."

Cordelia had been wondering about Delilah's right to the title "maiden," but she was fast becoming sure. "I would not know," she said sweetly.

Delilah gave her a sudden, searching stare. "Nay," she said, nicely seasoned with scorn. "I think you would not."

Cordelia felt her cheeks flaming—why, she did not know; to be a virgin was something to be quite proud of. How dare this flaunting flirt make it sound like a deficiency!

"How came you here?" asked Delilah. "I see you have no horse."

Cordelia did some quick mental jockeying, trying to decide whether she was better served by Delilah's ignorance, or her probable awe of esper powers. Discretion won out, and she said, "I do not believe a beast should be tethered, but should be free to roam as he will, till I have need of him."

"Then he must be well trained indeed, to come at your call."

Cordelia wondered at the tone of mockery in Delilah's voice, or why it stung. "I shall whistle him up when I wish," she assured the wench.

Delilah sighed in a parody of longing. "I have never learned to whistle."

"Then you have not had the bittersweet fortune of having brothers," Cordelia said, with a sardonic smile.

"I have not," Delilah said, all wide-eyed innocence. "Does that make a lass less hungry to be wed?" And, before Cordelia could answer, "You must forgive my asking. I am too young to know. I am but eighteen."

Eighteen what? But Cordelia did not say it out loud. "You shall know all that a woman needs within a year or so," Cordelia assured her, thinking all the while that Delilah already knew far more than a genuine lady should.

"I trust I shall," Delilah sighed. "What is this 'kindling' that you spoke of?"

Geoffrey hailed them from the edge of the wood.

"Small sticks and twigs." Cordelia displayed her skirtful of bits of wood. "We shall let the gentlemen fetch logs— but do you quickly catch up some tinder, for they are come with dinner."

"What is 'tinder'?"

"Dried grass and leaves!" Cordelia stooped impatiently to catch up several handfuls as she walked toward the riverbank.

Geoffrey rode down toward the river. Cordelia went to him, with Delilah trailing behind—which was fortunate, for she could not see how Cordelia's cheeks flamed with anger and humiliation. For some obscure reason, Cordelia felt she had come off the loser in that battle of wits—and was sure it had been a battle, though most of Delilah's comments had seemed entirely innocent.

It was doubly strange that she should feel the loser, since she had certainly given as good as she received, when the comments had been barbed.

Hadn't she?

"Well!" Geoffrey surveyed the heap of kindling that Cordelia dumped onto the bare clay by the water—then the cascade of dead leaves and dried cattails that suddenly fell on top of them. Cordelia looked up, startled, and met Delilah's sweetest smile. The cat had snatched them up by

the handful as they had come back to meet the boys!
" 'Tis a good beginning," Geoffrey pronounced.

" 'Twill do to kindle a blaze." Cordelia knelt, brushing grasses from her skirt.

Alain came up with a six-inch rock in each hand, set them by the tinder, and, glancing furtively at Cordelia, mumbled something about needing to fetch more, got up, and went away. She gazed after him for a moment, frowning. Admittedly he should be remorseful, repentant—but how was she ever going to win him back, if he would not talk to her?

"Here is your flame." Geoffrey had dismounted and knelt by the tinder now, drawing his dagger and taking a piece of flint from his pouch. He struck them against one another with an expert touch, several times, until a fat spark fell into the tinder. He struck another, and another. Cordelia breathed on them gently, and they began to flame. Out of the corner of her eye, she realized that Delilah was still standing, looking down in contempt at the hoyden who could get down on her knees in the grass and kindle a fire as well as any boy. Cordelia turned and smiled sweetly up at her. "It is given to women to be the keepers of the hearth."

"Indeed." Delilah's eyes sparked. "But for a lady, the hearth is watched, while servants build it up."

Fortunately, Alain arrived before the two of them could go any further, with two more rocks to set by the flames. Cordelia looked up, about to say something about their not being overlarge, but saw how closed his face was, the furtive glances that he flicked at her, and decided it was not the time to say anything that was at all critical.

There was a rustle of cloth beside her. Cordelia glanced out of the corner of her eye to see Delilah folding herself gracefully to sit by the fire, adjusting her skirts to cover her legs in complete modesty—that is, if you disregarded the cut of her bodice. Apparently, she had realized that everybody else was sitting or kneeling. Cordelia smiled to herself as she took kindling from her little pile and fed it to the flames, building them up little by little, letting it grow. "What have you found for us to eat, gentlemen?"

"A hare." Alain proudly held out a spitted blob of pink meat that bore about as much resemblance to a rabbit as a toad to a toadstool. He was obviously very proud of having shot, skinned, and cleaned it himself, but Delilah shrank back with an exclamation of frightened disgust, as a delicate maiden would when coming face-to-face with the world's realities for the first time.

Alain was instantly all contrition. "I pray you, look away, milady. I had forgot that you would never have seen raw meat as it came from the hide."

"Nay, I never have." Delilah turned away, trembling. "I doubt if I shall be able to eat of it now."

Alain stepped over to her side. "Come, come! When 'tis done, you shall not recognize it at all!" He reached out to her, then drew his hand back. "I would not offer a murderer's hands to you . . ."

She blinked up at him, and forced a smile. "Nay, surely not. You mean only my welfare, I know, to see that I am fed. Forgive me that my stomach is too delicate for such a sight." She relaxed into his arms, laying her head on his shoulder. Alain wiped clean hands on his hose before he put his arms around her.

"Sister," Geoffrey murmured in Cordelia's ear, "what is that grinding noise?"

"Only my teeth," she grated back. "Can he not see through her, Geoffrey?"

"Why, no," whispered Geoffrey, surprised, "and neither can I, though her skin is perfectly clear."

"So is her behavior! She is positively transparent!" Cordelia made the comment a lash. "I would have thought that my much-experienced brother would not be so easily deceived."

"Better, or worse?" Geoffrey smiled, amused. "Few of us are born with defenses against a pretty face or form. Be patient, sister. If she truly is as you imagine her to be, no doubt we shall discover it."

" 'Beauty is as beauty does,' do you mean?" Cordelia's tone was scathing. "Many a man has discovered nothing of the sort, 'til the priest has pronounced the words."

Then, with sudden despair: "What am I to do, Geoffrey? I have no tricks, no skill in dissembling! How shall I save him from her?"

"Do you care about him?" Geoffrey seemed quite surprised. Then he frowned. "Or is it only that you fear that something belonging to you will be taken?"

The echo of their mother's words irritated Cordelia. "Nay, 'tis more than that." But the image of Forrest came up unbidden before her inner eye.

Geoffrey was not intent on reading her mind at the moment, so he missed the picture, but he caught the hesitation, the uncertainty. "When you are sure, Cordelia, you shall prosper. But I pray you, do nothing extreme until we know whether or not she is the monster you think her to be, or is truly as sweet and kind as she seems."

"Read her mind, brother," Cordelia said, exasperated.

"I have tried." Geoffrey's brow knit, puzzled. "There is only a sort of swirling there."

"What—say you that she has no mind?"

"Oh, nay! She is there, surely enough. We do not deal with a witch-moss construct." Geoffrey deliberately mistook her meaning. "Still, her thoughts cannot be read, though she seems to make no effort to block them."

"Truly?" Cordelia glanced up in time to see Delilah push herself a little away from Alain, blushing, eyes downcast, then looking up and smiling, as though thanking him for his concern.

It was like a stab to Cordelia's own heart, that he did not even think of her enough to realize that she might be hurt by seeing him be solicitous to her rival. Either he was so smitten that he did not even remember that Cordelia had reason to object—or he was truly only being chivalrous.

Kindness to a stray kitten? And, in his own mind, nothing that she should object to?

She didn't believe that for a minute.

They chatted as the roast turned on its spit, Cordelia wondering at the back of her mind what Delilah was going to do when it came time to eat. She toyed with the notion of conjuring up knife, fork, and plate, but remembered that this was the boys' affair, not hers. She sat back, hiding a wicked smile, to see what her brother and her besotted beau would do.

She found herself wishing that he was besotted with her.

Then she remembered that he had been, but she had turned him down.

Well, no—the arrogance with which he had approached her had not been besotted, by any means. But she remembered a younger Alain, of only a year before, whose gaze had followed her everywhere she went, and the Alain of five years before that, who had followed her about so persistently that she had scolded him for being a pest.

She regretted that bitterly now. Had that scolding broken her spell over him? Or was it still there, but he, in obedience to her sharp tongue, was no longer allowing it to show?

Watching him closely now, she would have to say that he wasn't besotted with Delilah, really—only very attentive. Too attentive. Far too attentive. And not at all so to Cordelia—though he seemed to be avoiding her out of guilt rather than indifference.

Still, what was Cordelia to do? Feign a swoon? Certainly he would not believe that she needed comforting or protecting! For a moment, a tide of self-pity swept her. For the first time in her life, she found herself wishing that she were not so confounded capable.

Geoffrey solved the tableware problem with slabs of journey bread—flat, round cakes eight inches across. Lady Delilah, however, did not even have a dagger—of course. Alain solved the problem by cutting her meat for her, presenting it on the improvised trencher as though on a silver platter.

"Oh, sirs, you should not trouble yourselves!" Delilah protested.

" 'Tis no trouble at all, my lady, I assure you." Then, as an afterthought, it seemed to Cordelia, Alain turned and, for the first time, addressed her. "Cordelia, may I serve you in like fashion?"

She would have cheerfully served him instead—on toast. But she kept the lid on the seething and smiled sweetly. "Why, surely, Alain. I thank you." She bit back a scathing comment about being second, and probably always being second in his affections. Hot tears stung at her eyes, but she blinked them away. It was silly indeed to think that; Delilah was surely a passing fancy, no more.

Surely . . .

"I thank you." She held out her makeshift trencher with strings of steaming rabbit meat on it. Alain took it, cut the meat, then handed it back to her, inclining his head gravely, and offered his knife, hilt first. "Take it, I pray you, so you need not soil your fingers."

Delilah froze, a bit of meat halfway to her mouth, her eyes turning cold.

Cordelia was surprised to find herself blushing with gratitude—or was it relief? "Gramercy." She was on the point of refusing the knife—after all, she had a smaller one of her own—but realized she had better not; he might take it as a refusal of himself, too. "I shall endeavor to finish with it quickly, so that you may once again have the use of it."

"An excellent notion!" Geoffrey proffered his own knife, hilt first. "Will you take my point, my lady?"

"Why, thank you, sir." Delilah bestowed a very sweet smile on Geoffrey and took his knife.

Cordelia reflected on other potential uses for the blade as she stabbed the bits of meat and popped them into her mouth. "It is well done, in truth. You are an excellent chef, Alain."

"I learned something in the kitchens, from time to time." Alain smiled, relieved at having found a neutral topic—and wondering why Geoffrey was suddenly coughing so violently.

"I am sure you have," Cordelia said, with a touch of sarcasm.

Alain blushed and looked away.

Oh, no! Cordelia thought. *I have set him off now!* And she set herself to being pleasant, with renewed determination. What ailed the man, anyhow? If he felt so guilty at paying attentions to Delilah, why didn't he simply stop?

She chatted about the weather and about events in the palace, while Delilah found occasion after occasion for a subtle compliment, drawing Alain into telling her more and more about himself.

Cordelia did her best to change the topic, but not too much. "And how have you fared, knights-errant? I see you have saved a damsel in distress. What of the monster that did guard her?"

She was surprised, and chagrined, when Delilah broke into peals of laughter, and the gentlemen grinned in answer.

"We seem to have saved her only from abandonment," Geoffrey explained, "though it may be she would have had more fell creatures than that preying upon her, if we had not come when we did. Still, in your name and for your glory, Alain slew an ogre."

"An ogre?" Cordelia turned, eyes huge. She remembered hearing the villagers thinking of the event, but recognized a chance when she saw one. "How is this, Alain? Does he mock me?"

"He does not, I assure you," Alain said, with grave courtesy. "It was indeed an ogre, though your brother will not admit to his part in its defeat."

"An ogre! Oh! How brave of you, sir!" Delilah exclaimed, clasping her hands at her breast. "But how dangerous! Thank heavens you are returned alive!"

Definitely overdoing it, Cordelia thought—but apparently, Alain couldn't see that. He swelled visibly at her praise. "It was a poor thing, in its way," he said modestly.

"A poor thing! Oh, aye, nine feet tall, with four arms!" Geoffrey scoffed.

"Well, true," Alain allowed. "But it had very little brain."

"Though a great deal of brawn," Geoffrey reminded him, "and it does not require so very much brain to swing a club half the size of a man."

Cordelia stared at Alain. "And you rode against it with naught but your sword?"

"I did indeed." Alain looked rather happy about it. "I will own, though, that I did take a wound of him."

Delilah gasped again.

"Though 'tis naught that a little time will not heal," Alain said quickly.

"How gallant of you, sir!" Delilah caroled—but Cordelia was suddenly all business.

"Let me see." Cordelia stepped around the fire and began to unbutton Alain's doublet.

"Why, Cordelia!" he said, eyes wide.

"Really, damsel!" Delilah huffed.

"Oh, be still!" Cordelia snapped. "If he is hurt, I must know it. Where, Alain?"

"Why, you are a forward wench indeed!" Delilah gasped.

"A wench when it pleases me, but for now, I am a nurse!" She folded the doublet open—and stared a moment.

My heavens, the man had a massive chest! When had he grown all those muscles? She felt the strange feelings beginning to churn within her again, and turned her attention to the rough dressing held to his side by a bandage that was wrapped around and around his abdomen. "That was only a scratch, you say?"

"In truth, it was." Geoffrey frowned. "Do you fault my doctoring, sister?"

"Was it you who did this?" Cordelia looked up. "How deep was the cut? Was any organ harmed?"

Delilah turned pale.

"Nay, only muscle tissue, and not much of that; it scarce passed beyond the layer of fat. No large blood vessels cut, either, but only a seepage from many capillaries."

Delilah turned away, a hand to her mouth.

"Peace, peace!" Alain tried to recover his doublet with a glance at Delilah. " 'Tis naught, Cordelia, truly!"

Cordelia probed the wound gently, and when Alain only gasped lightly, she grudgingly said, "It seems well enough." She frowned up into his eyes. "My touch does not pain you?"

For a moment, his face turned fatuous. "Not in the slightest," he breathed. " 'Tis as the petals of a flower that brush against me."

Cordelia stared at him in complete amazement.

A slight smile touched Alain's face. "If such touch as that be pain, may I live in torment all my days!"

Now, finally, Cordelia blushed, and turned away.

CHAPTER
~9~

"Why, Alain," Cordelia said, "you have never spoken so before."

"Aye. I have been a chowderheaded fool," Alain said, with self-disgust verging on anger.

Delilah looked up indignantly, and Geoffrey decided it was time he took a hand—a hand he had been wanting to take for quite some time now. He stood up and stepped over to Delilah, reaching down. "My lady, will you walk? While we hunted for dinner, I found a small garden by the riverside. It must have been planted by Nature herself, but it is so sweet a sight that it must needs be the perfect setting for such beauty as yours." He smiled, looking deeply into her eyes. "Will you not come see it?"

Delilah looked startled, then cast an apprehensive glance at Alain—a glance that gained an edge.

"I am sure they will be safe by themselves," Geoffrey said, then leaned to murmur, "as you will be quite safe with me—if you wish to be."

Delilah turned back to him, startled—and for a moment, he saw the naked desire in her eyes, so hot that it led him suddenly to doubt that she was quite the virtuous maiden she seemed. But he could also see the calculation behind her eyes, as she glanced at Alain with a scornful smile. That smile turned to one of amusement, not altogether pleasant, as she turned back to Geoffrey. "Do you promise, sir?"

"Aye, surely—that you shall be safe as you please."

Passion flashed in her eyes again, but was quickly hidden. "Then I shall come." She rose in one lithe, sinuous motion, taking his hand. "I thank you, sir. Surely this garden will be at its most beautiful by moonlight."

"Alas!" Geoffrey tucked her hand into the crook of his arm and turned her away toward the trees. "The moon does not rise for some minutes yet."

"Then we shall await it." She turned back with a vindictive smile for Alain—but he wasn't looking, and the smile disappeared. "We shall return anon," she informed the couple. "Fare well in our absence."

"Farewell indeed." Cordelia tried to hide her elation—and silently thought a beam of thanks at her brother. He smiled and winked, since Delilah still had her back to him. Cordelia tried to remind herself how thoroughly she disapproved of Geoffrey's womanizing—but at the moment, it didn't seem at all bad.

Alain looked up, startled at Delilah's words, then glanced quickly at Geoffrey, who only gave him a sly wink. Not altogether reassured, he glanced at Delilah—but she was already turning away to go with Geoffrey, and when she looked up at him, her smile was dazzling. Alain stared after her, wondering whether he should feel wounded or relieved. He decided on relieved, and turned back to Cordelia, dismissing Delilah from his mind—and was rather surprised at the ease with which he did it.

He caught Cordelia watching him with a look that clearly said he was being weighed in the balance. "She is quite attractive—in fact, a beauty."

"She is," Alain said judiciously, "but will she remain in my mind when she is gone from my sight?"

"A most excellent question." Cordelia's answer was somewhat tart. "Will she, indeed?"

"I think not." Alain tilted his head to the side, regarding her. "But then, I have been spoiled, Cordelia."

"I know." Inside, Cordelia could have screamed at herself for the sniping remark—but it was too old a habit; it would take her some time to break it.

To her surprise, though, Alain only smiled, amused. "No, I do not mean only as a Prince, having had all defer to me, and having been given . . . almost all I wish."

Almost? She wondered what he had been denied, then realized that one thing had certainly been herself. She blushed, looking down.

"I mean spoiled in regard to loveliness," Alain said. "Now and again during my childhood, I have been exposed to true beauty; I have had it before me more often than not. It may be that I have become inured to the charms of beauty alone."

He was speaking of herself, she realized, and suddenly felt rather dizzy. Where had Alain learned to make such pretty speeches? And were they only that, pretty speeches? Or did he really mean what he said?

Alarmed, he moved closer, taking her arm, resting it on his, chafing her hand. "Are you unwell, Cordelia? Or have I given offense?"

"Nay. I am . . . well." But the support of his arm felt very good indeed. Suddenly, she realized that if she were a little *more* unwell, he might put his arm around her. "It—is simply that it has been a long day, and . . ." She let herself go limp.

Alain's arm tightened about her, holding her up. "Mayhap I should let you sleep."

Somehow, that sent alarm bells ringing through her. She wanted him close, yes, but not too close. "Nay. Only . . . hold me . . . for a small space."

"Why, that I shall," he said softly.

She let herself relax into the curve of his arm, leaning against his chest. She was surprised to discover how hard it was. "I . . . I must thank you, Alain, for your . . . gift."

He looked at her, puzzled.

"Some dozen men in rags of green and brown," she explained.

"The outlaw band!" His face cleared. "Did you truly find it pleasing, my lady, or was it another piece of gaucherie?"

"Well . . . it did make the day . . . quite interesting," she admitted. "I found myself beset with curiosity as to what I should do with them. But it was simple enough—I sent them on to Sir Maris. And I own that I did feel honored, and quite complimented that you had sent me such a tribute."

"I scolded myself for it when it was too late, and they were out upon the road," Alain said sadly. " 'Tis no great gift to a lady to have a dozen filthy, ugly knaves attending upon her."

"Oh, nay! It is the kind of gift that most I wish!" She looked up at him, eyes wide, and very, very earnest. "To restrain the brutal, the predatory, and to protect the weak! Giving me signs that you have done these things, Alain, is the most that I could ask of any man!"

Alain beamed down at her, reflecting that most other women would have been far more pleased by the gift of a diamond bracelet or a ruby tiara. He had no doubt at all the Cordelia meant what she had said. "How . . ." His voice sank almost to a whisper. "How if I could heal the sick as a king's touch is supposed to do? Would that be a gift to you? Or only my duty to my subjects?"

"Your duty to your subjects would be your gift to me!" She moved within his arm, a little away from him, so that she could look directly up into his eyes. "Truly the greatest gift that any woman can have is knowing that she has made a man a better man! But, Alain . . ." She lowered her gaze. "I should not accept such presents—or any presents of any sort, for . . ." She looked back up at him again, forcing herself to be honest. ". . . I cannot be sure that, were you to ask again, I would be willing to wed you."

Alain gazed down at her, his victory turning to ashes in

his mouth—until he remembered her words: "I cannot be sure . . ." Hope flickered in his eyes again, and he said, "Then there may be yet some chance?"

"Oh . . . aye . . ." She looked down again. "There may be some chance . . . But I would have you know, Alain, that it is only this night that you have begun to talk to me as yourself, Alain, not the Crown Prince. How can I know whether or not I love you yet, when we have only now met?"

"Well," Alain said softly, cradling her closer in his arm, "I will be very glad with that, Cordelia. Come, let us learn to know one another—truly, if we can."

They sat by the river, his arm about her, talking of inconsequentialities, talking of grave matters, talking of themselves and of each other, as the moon slowly rose.

But the moon had not yet risen when Geoffrey led Delilah to the little fairy garden. It rose where a little stream trickled into the river—tall, feather-soft columns in a semicircle, backing smaller flowers and ferns: anemones, poppies, spirea. They were only varying shades of gray in the starlight, of course, but the stream reflected glimmers back at many points, and the soft susurrus of the leaves of the willow that overarched the whole of the tiny garden made it seem like an undersea grotto—partly magical, and entirely alluring.

"Oh! How wonderful!" Delilah reached out to caress the slender stalks. "Scarcely have I ever seen anything so lovely!"

"We should leave a bowl of milk." Geoffrey knelt beside her. "Such a wondrous place cannot have grown by nature, and who but the elves could have tended it?"

"Fairies, say rather." Delilah looked up at him with excitement in her eyes—not of wonder, Geoffrey realized, but of anticipation, almost as though she were a hunter tracking quarry—eager, eyes dancing with mischief. "For what have you brought me to this place, sir?"

"Why," said Geoffrey, "to admire beauty."

"Then admire! Admire all you wish!" In a smooth, continuous motion, she rose to her feet, skirts belling around her as she pirouetted. "Gaze your fill—but you shall not touch!" And she fled, laughing.

Geoffrey rose, grinning; he knew the game, and understood it. He was on his feet, stalking her.

With a gay laugh, she disappeared among the trees.

He echoed her laugh with a deeper tone of his own, and followed.

In and out among the trees they darted, playing at nymph and faun. Her laughter was not the pure, innocent trilling of a maiden, but the mocking taunts of a woman of experience.

Geoffrey's blood flowed hotter for hearing it, and he followed hard and close.

Several times he lunged out, grasping for a handful of cloth, but she whirled aside at the last second, and the fabric slid out from between his fingers.

Finally, she tired—or tired of the game. She tripped, and stumbled back against a huge old oak. Geoffrey was on her in a second, one hand slapping the trunk to either side of her, boxing her between his arms, his face only a few inches from hers, both of them laughing with delight—but not sheer delight. No, delight and anticipation, as his lips came closer . . .

At the last second, she caught her breath and ducked out under his arm, fleeing again, but not quite so fast as she should have, and he caught her wrist. She pulled against it, but not too hard. "Oh, sir, leave off! Let me flee!"

"Why, I shall let you do whatever you please." Geoffrey stepped lightly around, circling her into the crook of his arm and pressing her close. "But what do you truly desire?"

"Why sir, for shame!" She lowered her gaze, but only as far as his doublet. She reached up as though to pluck a piece of lint from it—but her fingers ended by fumbling with the fastenings. "Have you no shame?"

"Shame?" Geoffrey wrinkled his brow, puzzled. "What is that?"

"It is something that you do not have, but should," she reproved him.

"It does come undone, you know," he said.

"Do you?" She rolled her eyes up to look at him through long lashes. "Ah, sir! You might prove *my* undoing!"

He loosed the fastener and began the next. "Why, so I shall. Have you never heard that you should do as you are done by?" He reached around to the nape of her neck and let his fingers trail down her back. She gasped, with a wriggle, then laughed. "You are deceived, sir! I have no fastenings of any kind; this dress is all of one piece."

"Why, then." His fingers traced under the curve of her breast, to the lacings of her kirtle. "I shall have to undo here, instead."

She laughed, twirling away, but he held onto the lace, and the bow came undone.

"Sir! How dare you!" She put her hands to the kirtle, pulling it tight, even though it had scarcely opened at all.

Geoffrey let the end of the lace slip of out of his fingers. "What would you have me do?"

"Why, whatever you will." She tilted her chin up. "But my sights are set higher than yourself."

"That takes not overmuch doing," Geoffrey countered, "for my sights are set low—very low indeed."

"Nay, nay!" She stepped away with a wicked glance. "I pursue one of higher station than your own."

Geoffrey was still for a second, then gave her a wicked grin. "Why, think you I am but a squire?"

"Why, are you more?" she returned. "And is not your friend a knight?"

"Am I not knight enough for you?" he countered. "Or enough for a night?"

"I think perhaps you might be." Her voice was low and throaty, and she stepped close to him, so close that he could have sworn he had felt the touch of her body, though there was still an inch of space between them—and for a second, her eyes burned with the heat of desire.

Then she whirled away again, and when she turned back

to regard him from a distance of five feet, her eyes had cooled to the chill of icebergs, and she gave him her most haughty look. "I think you are not all that you seem."

"My friend, though, is?"

She shrugged elaborately. "I *think* that he is more. Certainly I shall discover it."

"Will you truly?" Geoffrey grinned. "And will you discover how much of *me* is substance?"

She gave him a cool, appraising stare, then flashed a wicked smile. "If it pleases me—for surely, I know that *I* would please *you*."

Then she turned and fled again.

He followed her, running fast, dodging in and out among the trees. There was no laughter this time, only hot breath panting in their throats, until finally he reached out and caught her by the sleeve. She spun about, tripped, and fell to the ground. He dropped down by her side, fingers trailing fire across her cheek, down her neck, and across the swelling curve of her breast, breathing hard. "Ah, lass, pray do as you please! Fulfill your desires, and care not how base they may be! Know that I am a man for all you might wish!"

"Aye, well might you be," she sighed, and her breath was perfume, perfumed smoke from a fire where incense burns. "Yet still shall I withhold, till I have taught another man delights of which he shall never have his fill!"

"He shall cleave unto you always?" Geoffrey raised an eyebrow.

"In truth! Then may you court me to the end, to the finish! But for now, sir, I pray you—leave off!"

It cost him dearly, it required a huge effort—but Geoffrey had sworn to himself, very early, that he would never pursue a woman farther than she wished. He forced himself away with a sigh, reflecting that if she had really wanted him to continue, it was her own hard luck that she had bade him hold. She would have to pursue him more fervently, and be more open and more sincere in her flirtations, if she wished a different ending to the game. "As you wish, then. Come, sit beside me for a moment or two. I promise I shall touch naught but your hand."

"Why then should I sit beside you?" But slowly, she sat up, her eyes wary, weighing him, gauging him, not understanding, not believing.

"Why," he said softly, "to look at this fairy grotto in the moonlight. Only see!"

She sat up beside him, staring, then clasped her hands and gasped in delight.

They had come full circle, had returned to the elfin grotto—and surely, it was no surprise to her. The moon had risen while they played at nymph and faun. The garden glittered in the moonlight like the agglomeration of turrets and spires that form a fairy palace.

She stared at it, spellbound, but as conscious of his hand tickling fire across her own as she was of the magical garden. He was true to his word—he touched no more than he had said he would—but the way in which he did it made her bitterly regret the course that she had chosen. She promised herself that, when she had captured Alain, she would visit upon Geoffrey every ounce of pleasure of which he dreamed, and more, far more, until it was torment. She would use him, she would drain him, then revive him to use him again—but only at her pleasure.

When they returned to the campfire, they had assumed demeanors that were properly chaste and sober. Alain and Cordelia, though not quite so demure, seemed rather content with each other's company.

Alain, for his part, wondered whether Delilah's eyes were really glittering in the moonlight. Delilah, in turn, exulted within to see that Cordelia and Alain were not talking to one another. She had given her rival her chance, and, as Delilah had expected, Cordelia had made a hash of it. She sat down by the fireside with a sigh that was perfectly balanced between boredom and gloating satisfaction.

Cordelia looked up with a spark in her eye. "Was the garden so pretty, then?"

"By moonlight," Delilah purred, "one would have thought it was a mermaid's grotto beneath the waves."

Cordelia felt a burning anger within her. What had the cat been doing with her brother? What had she done *to* him?

From the look of him, though, she might have asked him the reverse: what had *he* been doing with *her*? However, there was still an edged and whetted hunger to him, a devil-may-care, reckless, barbed delight about him. She did not have to wonder long about what they had been doing, but only how far the game had gone. Not too far, or Geoffrey would not still look famished—but somehow, the notion was not reassuring.

"Where shall we fare tomorrow?" she asked.

Delilah turned her head, locking gazes with Cordelia; she had not missed the "we." "The gentlemen shall escort me to my home," she purred, "or so they have promised."

"And so we shall do," Alain said stoutly. "We could not let so gentle a lady wend her way unescorted."

"Oh, aye!" Cordelia said, with a smile of her own. "I shall join you."

"And what shall you ride, then?" Delilah asked gaily. "For I see you have no horse! Perchance you shall ride a broomstick!"

"Perchance." Cordelia's tone flowed like honey. "Though perhaps I should leave it for you."

Delilah threw her head back with a tinkling cascade of laughter. "Do not trouble yourself—for I have an excellent palfrey."

"Why, then," said Cordelia, "I shall have to find a stallion."

Cordelia waited until the others were asleep, then rose and moved quietly off into the wood, but only a few paces. She directed a thought at her sleeping mother, asking her to send her father's great black robot-horse, Fess—with a sidesaddle.

Gwen agreed, and so did Rod, easily. Cordelia couldn't tell they were only a mile away.

● ● ●

The sound of movement waked her. She opened her eyes, lying still to avoid surprises. She frowned, feeling muzzy-headed, and pressed a hand to her temple, but it would not drive the shreds of dream away. A patched and ragged dream, surely . . .

Alain lay to one side of her—good. She muttered and turned over as though she were still asleep, then peeked through her lashes and saw Delilah, eyes closed, breathing deeply and evenly.

You need not pretend, sister. Only I await you.

As well you might, Cordelia returned. *To be sure, none has the advantage of you.*

There is some truth in that, Geoffrey admitted.

Cordelia sat up, slowly, carefully, pressing a hand to her head again. *I had the strangest dream . . .*

I too. Let us go.

He was sitting on his heels across the campfire from her, but now he rose silently, stepped around the coals, holding out his hand. She took it and rose to her feet, then stepped away from Alain and Delilah. Brother and sister wrapped their cloaks about them, for the morning was chill. They moved silently away from the sleepers and in among the trees, but not so far they could not watch the campsite.

"Tell me your dream first," Geoffrey said.

" 'Twas a dream of this Lady Delilah," Cordelia said, watching his face—but he only nodded. No look of guilt, no look of keen interest—no look of surprise. Heartened, Cordelia went on. "I dreamt that in the deep of the night, she did come into these trees and meet with several men."

Again, Geoffrey nodded, and did not look surprised.

Cordelia took a deep breath. "She did give them orders—orders, Geoffrey! She did command! And not a one of them disputed!"

Geoffrey still nodded, very intent.

"She did command them to prepare her home for her. She spoke of a manor house and staff, but she bade them dress as servants, and named one to impersonate her father. Nay, it did seem that she had already given such orders, for these commands were only in the nature of asking if all was in readiness—and they told her nay, but nearly." She watched her brother out of the corner of her eye. "What would you say to that?"

"I would say," Geoffrey replied slowly, "that it was the product of spleen, envy and jealousy that one woman might have for another—had I not had the same dream. Not only *like* yours, mind you, but the *same*."

Cordelia stared at him in surprise.

"Aye," said Geoffrey. "And what would you say to that?"

Cordelia turned away, walking very slowly. "I would say 'tis not the sort of dream I would have thought a randy young man like yourself would have dreamt, of a beautiful woman."

"Cordelia!"

Cordelia shrugged impatiently. "A spade is a spade, brother, and a lecher is a lecher. I will own I had some intent to speak to you of that anon—and aye, I have seen the covetous looks you cast upon the Lady Delilah, so I was not so surprised as I might have been, to learn that you had dreamed of her. But such a dream as this is not the sort I had expected."

"Nay, I am sure it is not," Geoffrey said, with a sardonic smile.

"How is this, brother?" Cordelia spread her hands. "How is it we have both dreamed the same dream, even though it is quite inappropriate to yourself?"

"Why, you know as well as I," Geoffrey countered. "What could it be, but truth?"

"Truth of what sort?" Cordelia frowned. "Can it be she is a telepath, a projective, and does not know it?"

"That, or one who does know it, but felt no need to shield her thoughts from sleepers." Geoffrey frowned. "In either case, it would seem that our Delilah is not what she seems."

Cordelia gave a harsh little laugh. " 'Tis no great news

to me, brother. I have seen the looks she gives you when she thinks Alain does not see."

"And that you do not see, either?"

"Oh, no! She cares not if *I* see. Indeed, she would prefer that I did." Cordelia's lips thinned. "No doubt she thinks that I believe you to be my puppy, and will be quite wroth with her for seeking to steal your affections. But I know you well enough to doubt that could happen."

Geoffrey looked up, offended. "Be not so certain, sister! I, too, may fall in love."

"You may," Cordelia said acidly, "but not with such a thing as that. Nay, Geoffrey, speak truly: I know you have felt lust for her, but has there been the tiniest shred of love?"

Geoffrey relaxed in an easy grin. "Oh, nay! I know what she seeks, and may well find—but no more, I assure you." Then he sobered, frowning. "But if she orders men to make a false home for her, what is she truly?"

"A commander," Cordelia said slowly, "though I think she is not a lady born."

Geoffrey nodded slowly. "I have that feeling, too," he said. "I cannot say why, for she counterfeits well. No doubt 'tis a host of small signs that I am not aware of consciously—but they are there nonetheless, and I read them without knowing that I do. She is not nobly born."

"Yet she may be a telepath." Cordelia looked up at him, feeling a sudden pang. "Oh, Geoffrey, my brother, be wary, I pray you! For I do fear for your safety!"

For a moment, he looked grim. Then he gave a soft laugh, and gave her a brotherly squeeze. "Do not fear for me, big sister. I have learned in a hard school, and have been taught by experts."

But Cordelia did not return his laughter. The statement had an odd echo; it reminded her of something she had once heard their older brother Magnus say, shortly before he left home. She tried to give Geoffrey a glare, but her heart wasn't in it, and she gave him a reluctant smile instead. His own answered her. She sighed and looked back at the campsite. "Do you watch these two, brother, while I step aside a moment."

"Surely, sister. And what shall I do if they arise and walk?"

"Be sure they do not walk toward one another," she answered drily, then turned away to step in among the leaves.

In a few seconds, she was surrounded by the rustling susurrus of greenery, and projected her thoughts. *Fess! Are you near?*

A shadow moved from under the trees, and the great black horse stepped forward, nodding. *I am, Cordelia. What do you wish of me?*

"Oh, Fess, it is so good to see you!" Cordelia rushed forward, throwing her arms around his neck—but carefully; that was hard metal beneath the horsehair, not flesh. He was the companion of her childhood, the dream horse that many young girls imagine. She had been six before she fully understood that he was not really a living creature, like herself—but she had always thought of him as her friend and, in the depths of her being, still believed him to be a living, animate consciousness.

And, suddenly, she found that she was relaxing, letting the pressure and stress of the last few days evaporate, trembling as she clung to the great horse. Fess sensed it through sensors imbedded in his artificial horsehair. "What troubles you, Cordelia? Perhaps it were best that you tell me."

She lifted a tear-streaked face. "Alain had come a-courting—except that he did not court, he commanded me to marry him! Dearly though I had dreamed of that moment all my life, I could not bear to have it come in so undreamlike a fashion!"

"I know of this," Fess said, his tone thoughtful, "and of his quest with Geoffrey, though I confess I do not truly understand it."

"Ohhhhhhh . . . Geoffrey!" Cordelia stamped her foot. "He has taken it upon himself to turn my callow swain into a proper lover, to teach him the right and proper way of courting a maid—and corrupting him betimes, I doubt not!"

"Only Geoffrey?" Fess was picking up undertones that she hadn't intended.

"There is also a witch of alluring enchantments," Cordelia said, seething. "She has preyed upon their kindness—and, aye, their randy lust—and prevailed upon them to escort her to her home, each mounted upon a horse. I have only my broomstick. Fess, will you carry me?"

"Surely," Fess told her. "I would not miss this for the world."

Cordelia reflected sourly that everybody but herself seemed to find the whole episode monstrously entertaining.

They breakfasted on quail and pheasant, then saddled their horses (of course, Alain insisted on saddling Delilah's mount). Geoffrey had only a raised eyebrow when the great black horse strode into the clearing. Alain looked up, then looked again sharply. He turned to Cordelia with a look that was an amused accusation.

But Delilah stared, taken aback.

She recovered her poise quickly, though. "Truly, so great a stallion would be beyond my feeble horsemanship. I marvel that you can ride him, Lady Cordelia."

"I do prefer stallions," Cordelia said.

"To ride, of course," Delilah said, with an insinuation that made Cordelia blush, though she didn't understand why. She covered by reaching up for pommel and cantle, setting her foot in the stirrup, and swinging up to hook a knee around the horn of the sidesaddle.

"How athletic," Delilah purred. "Surely I could never do such wonders. I have no skill in this. Alain, would you help me to mount?"

"Gladly, Lady Delilah." Alain gave her a small, courtly bow, then set both hands about her waist and lifted her up to the saddle. Delilah squeaked, and if Alain's hands lingered a little longer than was strictly necessary, who was there to blame him?

Only Cordelia.

So it came about that they rode toward Delilah's home—a witch, a warlock, a Prince, and another whom Cordelia thought to be more truly a witch than herself.

CHAPTER
~10~

Smoke exploded in the roadway in front of the four. The real horses shied with whinnies of alarm, and the riders fought to hold them down. Alain grasped the bridle of Delilah's palfrey before his own mount was fully under control, and managed to calm both.

Fess, of course, stood solid as iron, observing the situation with interest.

The smoke blew away to reveal a woman, quite young but unbelievably ugly, leaning on a staff. She had a huge, curving nose, lantern jaw, small eyes like a swine's, and a sickly pale complexion. Worse, her face had five large warts, and her hair was dun-colored, sparse, and stringy. She was clothed in a murky gray robe, her hood thrown back, with six hulking men in livery of the same color behind her. Each wore a small shield on his arm and brandished a sword.

Cordelia stared, as amazed as she was revolted. Surely such ugliness could not be real—especially in one so young!

"Avaunt, damsel!" the ugly woman cried. "You escaped my clutches yesterday, but you shall not escape them now!"

"Sister!" Delilah gasped, alarmed. Then joy lit her face, and she cried, "Lord Roland would not have you, then!"

"He would not, even for all our father's lands and fortune." The witch's eyes narrowed. "Mayhap my dowry would move him, though, if he knew you were dead, no longer to beguile him. I shall see that you are!"

"Nay, sister, I beg you!" Delilah cried, shying away.

The hag went on inexorably. "Then, when all the lands have come to me, and Roland, too, I shall bring down the King and Queen with my magic, and rule as sovereign over a dukedom in my own right, with no hindrance from the Crown!"

Cordelia could only stare, unable to escape the feeling that she was watching a stage play.

The hag raised a knife, poised for throwing, and Delilah screamed.

"You shall not!" Alain shouldered his horse between Delilah's palfrey and the hag. His eyes blazed with anger, and he surely had cause, for it was his own mother and father whom the hag had threatened, as well as Delilah. "Bid your men lay down their swords, or they shall die by mine!"

The witch threw back her head with a high, wild cackle. "One man, against six?"

"Nay." Geoffrey smiled, drawing his sword and urging his horse up alongside Alain's. "It will be two against six. The odds are, I will admit, unequal. If you could find four more men, we might call them even."

Cordelia noticed that he didn't mention his sister. Good—it was always wise to keep a secret weapon in reserve.

Of course, knowing Geoffrey, he probably didn't think he needed one—and what was really galling was that he was probably right.

"Out upon them, men of mine!" the hag shrilled. " 'Tis for me to slay my sister!"

The thugs answered with a shout and charged forward.

They were all big men, six feet or more, broad-shouldered and muscular—but Geoffrey gave a shout of glee and rode into them. They stepped aside adroitly and slashed at him as he went by, but he caught the blows of the two on his right on his sword and lashed out with a kick that knocked the left-hand man's hilt from his grasp. He howled and fell back, clutching his hand.

The right-hand men turned as Geoffrey swerved around them, then leaped to pull him from the saddle. Geoffrey slammed a punch into one's jaw, using his hilt as brass knuckles. The man shouted with pain as he fell back; then his eyes rolled up, and he lay still. His mate was doubled over from a kick in the belly, making strangling noises.

Meanwhile, Alain had spurred to meet the other three, who charged him, shouting, swords waving over their heads. He swung his horse dancing aside a split second before they reached him; they went barrelling past, trying to slow, to stop themselves, thrown off balance for a minute.

That was long enough. Alain slashed downward, knocking one man's blade out of his hand. The man shouted with pain and leaped backwards, swinging his shield up to protect his head. Alain turned to his next assailant.

But while the boys were occupied with the henchmen, the hag rushed at her sister, waving her staff and shrieking something unintelligible, pointing at something overhead, something invisible, but whatever it was, Delilah reeled in her saddle, crying out in pain and terror.

Alain looked up in alarm, shouted, and charged the hag. She whirled on him with a scream and threw something invisible—but her aim was off; she hit the shield of one of her own men, and an explosion erupted right underneath the nose of Alain's steed. The horse reared, whinnying, terrified; Alain shouted and fought to control the beast.

Fireballs? Cordelia thought dizzily. It was not how a true witch would throw a fireball—it would come streaming from her fingers.

Yes, Fess's thought answered hers, *and a true witch does not use lycopodite; I catch the telltale aroma of modern explosive.* He was, of course, equipped with sensors of every type, including the olfactory—in his case, a chemical analyzer.

And, suddenly, Cordelia realized the name of the game.

The hag was a fake; her magic was that of technology—which meant that she was a Futurian agent. She was there to create a situation from which Alain could rescue Delilah, which would bring all his protective feelings to the fore. Then she would hail him as her savior. A very romantic situation indeed—and one which just might result in his falling in love with her. It would certainly give her the motive she needed for showing her gratitude, in ways which would send her head spinning.

Well, Cordelia could certainly take care of that. A fake witch was no match for the real thing.

Cordelia glared at a rock by the side of the path, and it shot up off the ground to clip the "witch" on the shoulder. She cried out in fright, spinning away, then turned in fury. "I do not know how you did that, sister, but you shall die for it! Avaunt!" She charged at Delilah again, but this time with the staff poised as a lance, to knock her from the saddle.

"You shall not," Cordelia cried, and Fess stepped in to come between Delilah and her "sibling."

But Delilah cried, "Oh, spare me, sister!" and threw her arms wide. Her left fist backhanded Cordelia in the stomach with all the power of a trained fighter. Cordelia doubled over, gagging, realizing that it had been no accident . . .

But Fess was still dancing to head off the witch, who leaped aside with a shout of victory—and her staff cracked into Cordelia's head. Dimly, she heard Alain shouting her name as she reeled in the saddle, the world swimming about her. The day seemed to darken, and she knew she was going to lose consciousness . . .

Be of good heart, my lady. A new and strange voice echoed inside her head. *Hold to wakefulness; she shall not prevail.*

Then there was a renewed clamor of swords ringing. Cordelia lifted her head as her vision cleared . . .

And saw Forrest, the bandit chieftain, standing between herself and the hag, parrying her blows with his quarterstaff, knocking her rod from her hand. She screamed, falling back, crying, "Aid me, men of mine! A rescue, a rescue!"

Two of the men stumbled toward her, but they were

bare-handed, swords gone, only their shields left. The other four lay unconscious on the ground.

Alain rode down on them, eyes narrowed, not disposed toward clemency.

The hag screamed and stumbled away toward the trees, her men backing quickly behind her—but Forrest followed in hard and fast, battering on the shield of the right-hand man, while Alain followed closely at the left, slashing with his sword.

Dizzily, Cordelia wondered where her brother was—and her vision cleared just in time to see the look of outrage on Delilah's face.

Forrest, Cordelia guessed, had not been part of her plan.

The hag turned and fled with a scream of despair. Her men stumbled after her.

Alain gave a shout of triumph, swinging his sword high, kicking his horse into a gallop.

Delilah let out a scream of terror and slumped in her saddle.

Geoffrey was at her side in a second, and Alain whirled about, wide-eyed in alarm, then turned his horse and galloped back to her side.

The witch and her henchmen disappeared in among the trees.

Alain and Geoffrey were each chafing one of Delilah's hands.

The fallen men began to crawl toward the trees at the side of the road.

"There, now, lady, 'tis done!"

"There, they shall not harm you!"

"Come, you must revive!"

"Geoffrey, have you a dram of brandy in your saddlebag?"

"Aye, here, and more!"

Cordelia stared at the two of them in outrage, feeling very much ignored and forgotten, reflecting bitterly that there were grave disadvantages in being able to take care of yourself. She was quite sure that Delilah could, too—and she was certainly proving it now!

"My lady, are you well?"

She looked down in surprise.

It was Forrest who had remembered her after all, and had stepped up beside her saddle. Cordelia looked down at him, instantly grateful . . .

And saw his eyes glowing up at her, glowing with a gleam that only desire can bring; desire, and perhaps something more . . .

Cordelia's smile of gratitude faltered; she felt as though his eyes were growing larger, larger, and for a moment, his face seemed to be all she saw. She felt a strange tingling beginning deep inside her, radiating outward to envelop her back, legs, and scalp like an aura. "Yes," she gasped, but her voice cracked, and she had to wait a moment to regain control of herself. Then she forced a smile which quickly turned real. "Yes, I am well, thanks to you, brave Forrest. But how came you here?"

Before he could answer, Alain remembered his courtesies and turned to the bandit. "I thank you for assistance, sir."

"Aye, most great thanks for your assistance," Delilah purred, far too sweetly. Her eyes glinted.

Forrest turned to her, his lips parting, no doubt for a retort. Then he saw her face, and froze.

So did Delilah, for a moment, her eyes widening.

Alain, Cordelia, and Geoffrey all sat staring; even they could feel the sudden tension in the air, for the long, long minutes that the two stared at one another.

Then Delilah turned away with a look of scorn. "Why, he is nothing but a woods-runner, an outlaw!"

"But a woods-runner on your side, Lady! Or, more aptly . . ." Forrest turned quickly back to Cordelia. ". . . on *your* side."

"Outlaw?" Alain frowned. "Hold! I know you, do I not?" Then, before Forrest could answer: "Indeed I do! You are the bandit chieftain whom I defeated and sent to my lady!" He turned to Cordelia. "Lady Cordelia, how is it you have let this man go free?"

"I did not." She frowned, puzzled, but kept her eyes on Forrest. "I sent him, with his whole band, to Sir Maris. How is it the seneschal has dispatched you, Forrest?"

"Forrest?" Alain stared. "You know his name?"

"Indeed," she said indignantly—perhaps the more indignantly because Alain had been fighting for another woman. "I required his name and rank of him."

"Sir Maris bade me go, and trouble good folk no more," Forrest explained. "He said nothing of bad folk."

Alain smiled, amused. "So you have seen your way clear to the troubling of such as these?" He nodded after the witch and her cronies.

"Aye, though I follow good folk." Forrest gazed up at Cordelia, his smile so warm that she felt it with an almost physical pressure.

Alain's eyes sparked with jealousy. He moved his horse closer to Cordelia's. "Surely milady is indeed 'good folk'— the best of the best, and the fairest of the fair—far too good for so incorrigible a rascal as yourself to attend upon her!"

"If I am incorrigible, do not incorrige me." Forrest was still gazing up into Cordelia's eyes. "Will you bid me go?"

"No-o-o-o," Cordelia said, as though the words were being dragged out of her. Then, quickly: "This pathway through the forest seems to be hazardous; there is no saying what dangers lurk upon it."

"Well, I can say." Forrest grinned. "I have been through this wood before—and through it, and through it! You speak truly, my lady—there are dangers by the score: monsters, wild beasts of all sorts; wolves and bears are the least of them. There are ogres, wild men, all manner of dangers! Nay, even with two such doughty knights to guard you, you cannot have too many defenders."

"Nor I," said Delilah, with an air of hauteur.

"Nor yourself either, milady." The gaze Forrest had given Cordelia had been warm, but the look he gave Delilah was a sunburst. "Any fair ladies who travel this wood do need protecting—and the fairer they are, the more they need warding."

"By that token," Geoffrey said, with an edge to his tone, "the Lady Delilah would need an army."

Forrest turned to him in surprise. "And what of the Lady Cordelia, sir?"

"Oh, Cordelia?" Geoffrey made a dismissive gesture. "She is my sister."

"I see." Forrest's lips quirked with humor. "And a sister, of course, can never be beautiful to her brother." He turned back to Cordelia, his gaze boring into hers. "But I assure you, my lady, I am *not* your brother."

"No; I should have recognized you if you were." Cordelia strove to sound cool and disinterested, but it was no use. He knew exactly how interested she was.

"Come! Must we stand here all day chaffering?" Delilah shook her bridle till the rings jingled. "Or shall we not move onward toward my father's house?"

"Aye, most assuredly!" Alain turned back to Forrest and said severely, "Thank you for your help, good fellow. Now be off."

"Nay, I shall be on. As to calling me 'fellow' ..." Forrest's face hardened as he looked up at Alain. "I am as well born as you, I warrant, and was knighted. It is true that I have fallen on evil days, and I may have been less than honorable as a consequence, but that does not lessen my quality."

Alain's mouth quirked in wry amusement. "As well born as I, sir? To be sure, any lapse in chivalry does show you to be of lesser quality than your birth."

"If that is so," Forrest returned, his voice hardening, "there are many men in Gramarye who are of lower quality than that to which they were born, yet wear duke's coronets and sit in great houses."

Alain lost his smile.

Cordelia decided the tension was growing too thick. She clucked to Fess, and he moved between the two men, so that she broke their gaze. "Come, gentlemen! Let us not stand in idle chatter; the Lady Delilah hath the right of it in that." She stressed the word "that." "Let us go."

"To her father's house?" the outlaw asked in surprise.

"Indeed," Cordelia answered.

"Aye," Alain said severely. "We have given our word that we will escort the lady to her home—though I doubt that you would understand the importance of honoring one's word, sir!"

Now it was Forrest's gaze that darkened, and Cordelia said quickly, "Alain! That was unchivalrous of you, sir!" Then, to both of them, "Do what you will—*I am going.*"

She kicked her heels against Fess's sides, and the great black horse moved off with alacrity. The two men looked up, startled; then Alain kicked his horse and rode to come up beside her, and Forrest ran.

Cordelia reined in Fess, and the two caught up, pacing along on either side of her. She made sure that Fess was going slowly enough so that Forrest wouldn't be pressed too hard.

"Nay, you must not leave me behind, fair lady!" Forrest protested. "For this Forrest would be dark indeed without you!"

She turned to him, tilting up her chin, and said, in her coolest tone, "Black-haired, sir, and black-bearded; how dark can you *not* be?"

The outlaw stared at her a moment, then grinned, showing white teeth. His lips, she noticed, were very red, and fuller than most men's. "Even as you say it, my lady—but darker tenfold for want of your smile."

"Though any man would seem dark," said Alain, "near the light of your beauty, lovely Cordelia."

She turned, gratified. "Why, thank you, Alain. Where have you learned such pretty manners of speech?"

"Why, from my heart," he said, gazing into her eyes. For a moment, *her* heart fluttered, and she found herself wondering if he really did mean it.

No. Surely. It was only the competition with Forrest that had caused him to say it—though she seemed to remember a few compliments of the night before . . .

Still . . .

Alain had always hated to lose, she remembered that well enough from their childhoods, though he had learned how to pretend a better grace as he grew older . . .

"The leaf that flutters from the tree cannot be lighter than your step!"

"The summer's sky cannot be more clear than your eyes!"

"The cherry's blossom must pale when set against your cheek!"

"Nay, for those blossoms *are* your cheeks!"

Cordelia looked from one to the other, soaking up the compliments as they settled about her. She knew better than to trust either of them, or to think that they really meant it—but she might as well enjoy it while it lasted. She decided that there was definitely something to be said for competition.

Behind her, her brother was looking decidedly grumpy. "What do they see in her? Surely she cannot have grown into a beauty in the space of one day!"

"Oh, it is only as Alain has said," Delilah answered, disgusted. "A brother can never see his sister's beauty." She turned toward him, a wicked notion coming into her mind.

"Perhaps that means that only brothers can see truly." Geoffrey looked at her for a moment, trying to make up his mind whether or not to be offended. Then he decided to give Cordelia a little of her own medicine. "You have never had a brother?" he asked.

"Nay—only my sister." A shadow crossed her face.

Geoffrey spoke quickly to erase the thought. "Then I must fill his place, and see you as you truly are."

For a moment, she seemed discomfited, even alarmed; but it was only a flicker. Her eyelids drooped, and a slow, lazy smile curved her lips. "Come, sir! Did you not see me truly last night?"

"What, by moonlight?" Geoffrey breathed. "Or by starlight? Nay! Surely only the light of the sun shows us as we truly are."

"Indeed." She lost the smile and tilted her chin up, gazing at him in disdain. "And what has the light of the sun shown, sir?"

"Why," said Geoffrey, "a dozen tiny features that I could not see by night—how red your lips are, how rosy your cheeks! Though your complexion, I note, is as flawless as ever it was—even the alabaster that it seemed by night! And surely the stars, that had fallen from the skies in despair of matching your eyes, knew truth, for you outshine them all!"

Delilah gave a laugh of delight. "A very pretty speech, sir! Nay, I think I will listen to some more—if you have any in your repertoire."

Cordelia glanced back, frowning—just in time to see Geoffrey kissing Delilah's hand, and to hear her laugh again. "La, sir! Pretty speeches are not enough!"

Then, more softly, so that Cordelia could not hear, "What actions can you show me?"

"Why, what you will." Geoffrey looked up with a slow smile that turned into a grin. "Name the deed you fancy, lady, and I shall do it."

Delilah cocked her head to the side, evaluating him. "I think that I shall wait to say it. Until I do, sir, you shall lie low."

"As low as you wish," Geoffrey said, his voice husky. "But where shall we lie? Sooth, we must wait for night!"

Delilah's eyes sparked with anger, but her mouth curved in amusement, then in derision. "You shall show me nothing, sir, if you must wait for night—for then there will be nothing that shows."

"Ay de mi!" Geoffrey leaned closer. "Must I wait? For you tell me that if I do, I shall have nothing!"

"Why, then," she breathed, "do not."

He covered her mouth with his own, both leaning from their saddles to bridge the gap, only their lips touching.

Cordelia glanced back again at the sudden silence, and stared in indignation, then whipped about, eyes front, face burning.

"Why, how have I offended, beautiful lady?" Alain cried, wounded.

Cordelia thawed a little, turning toward him, and bestowed a smile upon him. "Why, in no way, sir, and neither has Forrest. I am only indignant when I remember the verse,

> " 'By all the promises that e'er men broke,
>   In number more than women spoke.' "

"Then blame me not, for I have made no promises." Alain's voice softened, and he leaned closer. "I have only asked them, and they have not been given."

Cordelia stared at him a moment. Her own lips curved, and she said, "Then do not ask again until you are sure they will be granted."

"And when shall that be?" he breathed.

"When will the sun fall from the sky?"

They looked up, startled; then Alain's face darkened at what he thought was Forrest's impertinence—and perhaps it was, but the outlaw was gazing up through the leafy canopy at the sky. "There cannot be so much of daylight left. Where shall we camp?"

"There is no need." Alain's voice was stern. "Lady Delilah has said we shall come to her father's house ere darkness falls." He turned back to Delilah. "Shall we not, milady?"

Delilah broke off from the kiss, though not quite as quickly as she might have, considering how surprised she looked. Alain stiffened, and Cordelia's heart twisted.

"Shall we not what, sir?" Delilah tucked at her hair, though it didn't need the attention.

"Come to your father's house ere nightfall." Alain's tone was stiffly polite. "Shall we not?"

"Nightfall?" Delilah looked up through the leaves at the sun rays. "By suppertime, or not long after, I should say. Indeed, there is no need to hurry."

"That is well." Alain turned back to face front, seeming relieved. "Then let us tell tales as we go along—or shall we sing?"

Geoffrey shrugged. "Sing, if you will—but let it be a tune that we all know."

"Why, so I shall." Alain thought for a moment, then began to sing in a clear, rich tenor.

> *"Alas, my love, you do me wrong,*
> *To cast me off discourteously . . ."*

Geoffrey joined in with the baritone line, and the two girls began to sing a descant. Forrest's voice underscored

them all with a warm, resonant bass—resonating within
Cordelia, giving her shivers. She glanced down at Forrest;
he glanced back at her. Some electric current seemed to
pass between them. Cordelia shivered, and turned her gaze
resolutely back to the front. Perhaps Alain was the safest
for her, after all. But did she truly wish to be safe?

The tall stone pillars seemed to rear up very suddenly,
for they were right in the middle of the woodland. Huge
iron gates hung from them. Behind them sat a serf in tunic
and hose. Cordelia stared for a moment, startled, then
glanced to either side. The woods were so thick, the roadside trees so intertwined with bramble and thorn, that what
she had mistaken for a thicket was really a very artfully
constructed fence. It would not deter an armored knight, of
course, but it would protect the people within from the ca-
sual trespasser or poacher, and from most wild animals.

"Willem!" Delilah carolled. "How fare you?"

The porter jerked awake out of a doze and stared as
though at an apparition. "My lady Delilah!" He leaped
from his seat. "Is it truly you?"

"Yes, Willem. I am returned to you, thanks to the protection of these good folk. How fares my father?"

"In anxiety and woe, my lady. He wrings his hands and
cries out every hour, that his men can be of no worth if
they have not found your trail. Ah, praise Heaven you are
come! For it has been a grievous time for all of us!"

"Why, then, I am filled with regret." Delilah bowed her
head. "But I am filled with gladness to be come home
again. Send word to my father."

"Aye, milady, as you say!" Willem unlatched the gate
and swung it wide. The party rode in, Forrest at its head.
Willem latched the gate behind them. "I shall run with the
news, milady!" He sped away.

The party followed more slowly, riding up along a
gently winding track that was overhung with graceful ma-
ples and oaks—not planted in neat rows, Cordelia saw;
rather, the roadway had been picked out between them.
Somehow, the idea struck a chord of rightness within her.

"I have told a gardener, my lady, and he bears the word!" Willem paused by them to duck his head in a bow before he ran back to his post.

Through the trees, Cordelia could see hedges, flowers, and a closely cropped lawn. The gardeners were busy indeed. Then the road took a final turn—and there, perhaps a quarter of a mile away, was a huge old house of stucco, half-timbered, its leaded panes glinting in the sun. Cordelia caught her breath; set in a border of flowers and ornamental shrubs, it was really quite lovely. She hated to admit it, but Delilah had a beautiful home.

As they neared the house, a gray-haired, gray-bearded man came hurrying out to the steps, his servants streaming behind him. They stood waiting, and cheered as the company rode up, reining in their horses.

"Delilah!" the old man cried in a deep and resonant basso. "Come to my arms, my child! Oh, thou hast worried me so horribly!" He ran down the steps, reaching up; she hopped down into his arms, and he crushed her to his breast, then held her back to look at her, beaming. "I was so filled with anxiety, so horribly afraid that some harm might have befallen thee, that thou wouldst never come home!"

"Alas! I feared, too, Father!" She threw herself into his arms again, embracing him.

Alain looked on, smiling fondly—but Cordelia glanced at Geoffrey, and found him glancing at her, too, one eyebrow raised in skepticism. Cordelia gave a tiny nod; it did seem rather artificial. She decided that she would have to marry Alain, if for no better reason than to protect him from people who would take advantage of his good nature.

She scolded herself for the thought a moment later, of course.

The old man held Delilah away again, looking down gravely. "It was very wrong of thee, my dear, to worry thy father so, and to put thyself in such peril."

"I—I know, my father." Delilah lowered her gaze. "But Roland had sent word that I should meet him 'neath a certain willow, deep within the wood, at dawn ... or so I thought ..."

"Young Roland?" Her father frowned. "Why, he came to call upon thee the very day thou hadst left—but thou wert not here!"

"No." Delilah looked up, very obviously nerving herself to speak. "The word that had been brought to me was false, my father. I learned that, but too late—for I sat me down beneath the willow where he bade me meet him, and he never came . . . he never . . ." She gulped; tears began to flow again.

"There, there!" The old man whisked a handkerchief from his cuff and dabbed at her cheeks. "Assuredly, he could not come, for he did not know thou hadst gone, nor where! When we told him thou wert fled, he was as distraught as I!" Her father frowned. "Who brought thee this false news of him, my dear?"

Delilah lowered her gaze again, biting her lip.

"Nay, thou must needs tell me!" her father said sternly.

But she looked away, very reluctant indeed. "I cannot, my father. It would be . . . wrong."

"Wrong? To tell me the name of one who hath betrayed thee so? Come, child! Speak truly!"

But she shook her head, eyes still downcast.

Cordelia decided somebody was going to have to say something; she could see the storm clouds gathering in the old man's brow—and apparently, both her brother and her suitor were too concerned with honor to speak a word. Forrest, of course, did not know—he had not been there the night before to hear this tale. "It was her sister."

The old man looked up, staring, appalled. Then he looked down again, scowling, anger gathering. "Is this true, Delilah?"

Delilah said nothing, only bit her lip and gave a quick nod.

"But it was her sister who waylaid you upon the road!" Forrest exclaimed. "Sir, I came in time to help them beat her off, she and her henchmen, so I know whereof I speak."

The old man lifted his head. "How now, sir! What henchmen are these?"

Forrest shrugged. "Big, hard-faced men in garb of murky gray, with targets on their arms and swords in their

hands. Hardened men, by the look of them, but no match
for two young knights and . . ." He grinned. ". . . a forest
outlaw who came upon them unawares."

" 'Tis even so," Geoffrey said at last.

"I cannot believe it!" the old man said, the color draining
from his face. He looked down at Delilah, at the misery in
her eyes, and groaned. "But I see I must. Nay, we shall have
thy sister out, and hear the truth from her own lips."

Tears trembled on Delilah's lids.

"I think, good sir," Geoffrey said softly, "you are not
like to see your other daughter again. She shall know what
has passed here, and shall stay far from home."

"Nay, never say so!" The father looked up, distraught.
"Am I to be bereft of one daughter, no matter what I do?"

Geoffrey and Cordelia exchanged glances, and Cordelia
said slowly, "There may be a way. I doubt it, sir, but there
may be. Let us sleep upon the issue, and see what we may
do."

"Why, surely, then!" But he frowned at them, puzzled.
"Be sure that I shall be grateful for whatever thought you
may give it."

He looked back at Delilah again. "Who are these good
folk who have escorted thee here, my dear? May I not
know their names?"

"As much as they have let *me* know, Father," she said,
"for these gentlemen have told me that they ride bound by
a vow not to name themselves fully to any but each other,
until some purpose of theirs is accomplished."

"Which, of course, must also remain a secret." The old
man nodded. "You are knights-errant, then?"

"We are." Alain inclined his head, looking faintly puzzled.
Cordelia could understand why. The old man was
clearly of the gentry—a squire at least, more probably a
knight himself, even of the petty aristocracy. It was very
unlikely that the Crown Prince would not have met him,
for he had been introduced to every nobleman in Gramarye at one time or another. Of course, there were always a
few who never came to Court, but kept themselves buried
in the country, managing their estates. . . . Still, the home

was not a castle, nor even a moated grange or battle-tower; and although there was every sign of comfort, there was no appearance of such luxury as befitted a great lord.

"Forgive my lack of manners." Delilah turned to them, one hand on her father's arm. "Gentlemen and lady, may I present my father, Sir Julian LeFevre. Father, Sir Alain . . . Sir Geoffrey . . . his sister, the Lady Cordelia . . . and Sir Forrest Elmsford."

Each of the young men inclined their heads. Cordelia couldn't drop a curtsy, being still mounted, but she smiled warmly.

"You are welcome, welcome, and with all the thanks I can bestow!" Sir Julian cried, throwing his arms wide. "Step down, step down! My grooms shall see to thy horses. Come in, come into my house! You must bathe, you must dine! You must allow me to show my thanks! Nay, you must stay a day, two days, three, that I may lavish my hospitality upon you in gratitude."

"The road has been long." Geoffrey and Alain exchanged glances. "A bath would be welcome, and some little rest."

Alain turned to Cordelia, inclining his head. "If you wish it, my lady?"

"Surely," Cordelia said quickly. She wasn't about to take a chance that the boys would stay at Delilah's house without her. "I, too, would be most grateful for some respite."

Alain turned back to Sir Julian with a smile. "I thank you, sir. We accept your hospitality."

"I rejoice!" the old man cried. "Come in, come in!"

CHAPTER
~11~

Hostlers took the horses to the stables. Fess's words echoed in both the Gallowglasses' minds: *Farewell, Cordelia; be wary, Geoffrey. These people are not what they seem. If you have the slightest need of me, call.*

We shall, Fess, Cordelia promised.

Delilah and Forrest both wondered why Cordelia and her brother were so quiet for a few seconds. They could not sense the exchange, since Fess's remarks had been made in the encrypted mode of telepathy that the Gallowglasses had invented for the use of their family alone.

Servants showed them to their rooms. They looked about them as they were led through the house—at the graceful double stairway, and the leaded panes of tinted glass that adorned the landing, filling the whole entry hall with light.

Up the stairway they went, to the chambers above. The ceilings were ten feet high, the hallways broad, and the rooms spacious. It was scarcely a castle or a palace, but it was a good and very big house, with real glass in the windows and featherbeds in the bedrooms—both great luxuries, in a medieval society.

Since Fess had taught the Gallowglass children history, Cordelia recognized the architecture as being post-Medieval—Tudor, at least. It did not concern her terribly—she knew that her planet's original colonists had redefined Medieval society to incorporate whatever suited them. A Renaissance manor house was only a century or two too late, after all.

Cordelia was delighted with the chamber—it was huge, light, airy, and decorated with the sort of frills and pastels that reminded her of her own room at home. She went to the windows to see how much of a view she had, and was delighted to see an acre or so of carefully tended garden, bright with flowers, and cut into several smaller gardens by high hedges.

"Shall I draw your bath, milady?" the maid asked.

"Not quite yet," Cordelia answered. "I must explore this delightful garden that I see below me! Will you show me to it?"

The maid did, and Cordelia went out, looking about her, feeling refreshed by the mere sight of such gay flowerbeds amidst luxurious lawns. She bent to smell a rose—and as she straightened, she saw Forrest watching her.

"Like will to like," he said.

She blushed and looked away, hoping he spoke only of herself and the flower, knowing he hinted at more. "You have me at a disadvantage, sir."

"The best way." He stepped up, proffering his arm. "Come, shall we discover what wonders this garden holds?"

He was almost courtly about it, his manner reminding her that he was gently born and well bred, no matter what he had become. Almost against her will, she slipped her arm through his, knowing it was dangerous but finding that gave spice to the stroll, making it almost an adventure.

They strolled between beds of glorious flowers. "Truly

a riot of color," Forrest said. "Do you not find them attractive, my lady?"

"Indeed I do," she sighed. "He who laid out such beds must have been truly inspired."

"But why should it have been 'he'?" Forrest asked. "Might not a woman prove as proficient at laying out beds as a man?"

She wondered again if he meant more than he said. "I should think a woman's taste in color and form should be equal to any man's," she agreed.

"Nay, far more." He halted, and she realized that they stood in a corner of the hedge, screened from view of the house—and he stepped closer, his face coming nearer. "A woman's taste should be far superior to a man's," he breathed.

Transfixed, she stared at him—and he lowered his face, touching his lips to hers.

It was almost as though sparks spangled across her mouth, seeming to sting even as they tasted amazingly sweet. For a moment, her eyes fluttered closed, savoring the delicate, exciting sensation . . .

Then she felt the tip of his tongue touch her lips, and a stew of emotions boiled up within her: longing and revulsion, yearning and fright. A tickling began deep within her and spread . . .

No more! She stepped back, with a gasp of surprise.

"Oh, nay!" he pleaded. "A moment more, only a second longer . . ."

Somehow, the plea frightened her, and she darted away from him, pausing ten feet away, hands clasped at her waist, striving for composure . . .

Forrest laughed, and leaped after her.

Cordelia gave a cry of alarm and ran.

Forrest gave a joyful shout and chased.

It was the joy in his voice that banished her fears, his laughter that made it a game. Breathless, she nonetheless found herself laughing, too, as she dodged behind a tree, then peeked out to see if he still followed—and found herself staring straight into his face.

She ducked back behind the tree, out the other side, found him there before her, ducked back twice more, then ran, laughing. Crowing with delight, he followed.

In and out among the hedges, under arches of roses they fled, he chasing, she fleeing with a high, wild excitement singing through her. Finally her steps began to slow, and he reached out and caught her. She turned to fight him off with joyful squeals, but tripped over a root and fell backwards. Unfortunately, she caught at Forrest for support, and instead of holding her up, he fell with her—and landed on top.

He caught himself on his forearms, so there was no impact—none but the softest, of his body against hers, sending wild currents of heat all through her. She panted, her bosom heaving, staring up into his eyes, only inches away. "Oh, sir, you must let me rise!"

"Must I?" He grinned, his face coming nearer, his voice husky. "Wherefore?"

"If you are a gentleman, you must!"

"Oh, then, I pray I may not be a gentleman!" he breathed, and kissed her.

She stiffened, galvanized beneath him, as the unfamiliar welter of emotions churned up within her—but she was truly frightened to realize that she wanted him to go on. And on, and on. She wrenched her head aside with a little cry, protesting in earnest. "Nay, sir, you must let me up! Would you force a lady against her will?"

"If I must, I must," he sighed, but she wasn't sure how he meant it. "Come, then, milady, I shall do as you ask— but you must pay a ransom."

"What ransom is that?" She regarded him warily.

"One more kiss," he breathed, and lowered his lips again.

She was taut for a moment more, then reminded herself that he would let her go after only one more, and let herself relax a little, let the wonderful, frightening feelings well up within her . . .

Then his fingers touched her breast.

She lay rigid a moment, her whole consciousness focussed on that one touch, turning now to a caress, trailing fire through the cloth across her skin, the maelstrom of feelings boiling up toward it, threatening to engulf her . . .

The fright was too great. She broke away from his lips with a gasp, then slapped his cheek with all the force she could muster—which was not very much, given her position.

But it sufficed to startle him; he drew back just enough for her to struggle free. She leaped to her feet and backed away, pressing her skirts smooth and crying, "For shame, sir! You have taken far more than the ransom you stated!"

"I have, I will own," he said, all contrition. " 'Tis only that you are so irresistible to me, that I crave more and more of you. I implore you, sweet lady, do not disdain me for naught but love's labors."

"Love's labors will be lost, unless they be less free," she replied tartly, and hurried away, face flaming.

At the opposite edge of the garden, Alain plodded moodily along. He, too, had felt the need for a walk before bathing, but to his eyes, the beauty of the garden seemed dimmed. He was rapidly coming to the conclusion that Cordelia was lost to him, if he could not learn to be more romantic—and he did not think he could, for truly, he was not romantic by nature. All he could do would be to learn to be false. As he was, all he had on his side was sincerity, and what use was that?

A bunch of roses caught his eye—white, and near them, a bush of pink ones. Behind them glowed blossoms of deep red. Alain gazed at them moodily, reflecting how much they seemed to be like Cordelia, and himself . . .

He stiffened, struck with inspiration. He had only sincerity to recommend him, had he? Well, mayhap sincerity could be romantic, in its way! Kneeling, he plucked a few of each color of rose, then hurried back toward the house, face glowing, hoping to come upon Cordelia.

He found her almost on the threshold. She, too, seemed to have been for a stroll, and surely, it seemed to have been good for her. She seemed filled with energy, and her cheeks were rosy.

"Alain!" She saw him, and brought up short. "What do you here?"

"Only strolling in the garden," he explained, "feeling the need to let my limbs cool ere I heat them in water."

Her eyes fastened on the bouquet. "Whence came those?"

"I found them in the garden." He pressed them into her hands. "I could not help but pluck them for you, sweet Cordelia, for they remind me so much of yourself—at least, the white blooms do, for they are so pure, like yourself. The red, alas, are steeped in passion, as I am when I gaze at you—and the pink are, I hope, the love I feel for you: my passion allayed by your purity."

Cordelia felt her heart melting, so touched was she by his clumsy tenderness. She leaned forward to give him a quick peck on the cheek, but even as she did, she remembered Forrest's kiss, and felt leaden guilt within her. She turned away, ashamed.

"Ah, once more I have offended!" he cried. "Say, fair Cordelia, what have I done?"

"Only what is right," she answered, trying not to let her anger at herself turn into anger at him. She turned back, managing a flirtatious smile. "If only you had done it sooner! And if only you would do it more often, my Prince, you might yet save me from a drastic fate!"

"What fate could that be?" he asked in total innocence.

Exasperated, she almost told him—but instead, she snapped, "Spinsterhood!" Then she spun on her heel and sped through the door, leaving Alain to gape after her, not understanding at all.

Cordelia splashed water on her face, then turned away to find a beautiful afternoon dress of green and yellow laid out on the bed for her. She stared, amazed, then took it up reluctantly. Surely it could not be Delilah's! The lady was too small for any of her clothing to fit Cordelia. Her sister's, perhaps? Certainly the style, though outdated, was not old enough for the dress to have belonged to her mother. Cordelia wavered for a moment, but the gown was very pretty, and her own russet travelling dress was rather dusty. With a sudden decision, she unfastened the dress, letting it drop to the floor, then wriggled out of her shift, took the washcloth, and gave herself a quick sponge bath. When she was done, she waved her arms and hands, fanning herself, to dry, and slipped into the clean shift that had been laid out for her. She delighted at its smoothness—not silk, perhaps, but very fine linen. And yes, it did fit.

Then she took up the green-and-yellow gown and slipped it over her head. She fastened the kirtle around her waist and wished for a cheval glass to regard herself in, but of course there was none; her brother would have to do in its place. She projected a thought on their family's encrypted mode:

Geoffrey.

Aye, Cordelia. He answered so quickly that she might have thought he was waiting for her call.

Let us walk in the garden. Her tone was peremptory.

Geoffrey didn't disagree for a moment, though. *In truth, a stroll among the flowers should be most pleasant. Let us walk, sweet sister.*

Lightfooted, she stepped out through the door and ran to the garden, feeling much more presentable.

Geoffrey was there, though he too had changed garments. Strange that they had clothing to fit him so well—although, coming closer, Cordelia could see that his doublet was of an old-fashioned cut. No doubt it was one that had belonged to Sir Julian in his youth.

"Why, Geoffrey," she began, to compliment him, but before she could, he grinned broadly.

"Cordelia! Why, how lovely! I would never have thought green and yellow to be your colors, but they are most becoming!"

"Why, thank you, sir." Suddenly, Cordelia felt even better. She smoothed her gown, feeling more than a match for anything Delilah might bring on.

Then she became solemn; it was time to compare notes. "There is one chamber in this house that is shielded from thought, brother."

"There is indeed," Geoffrey agreed. "Either there is some telepath who is given full-time to its warding, or . . ."

Cordelia nodded. "There is a machine of some sort hidden within it that cloaks it from all human thought."

"Let us assume it to be the latter," Geoffrey said, "and that our hosts know something of advanced technology. But why would they give themselves away in this fashion? They must know that any telepath who chances upon them will know at once what they do!"

"Even so," Cordelia said, "as surely Delilah must have known that we should know her for a witch, simply for the excellence with which she has shielded her mind."

Geoffrey lifted his head suddenly. "The shielding is gone."

Cordelia tested the room with her own mind, and nodded. "Mayhap it is only an esper who wards there."

Geoffrey asked, "You were not greatly surprised to learn that Delilah was a witch, were you?"

"Nay, surely," Cordelia smiled. "And it did not take telepathy to read my mind in *that* regard, brother."

"Well, then, we deal with witchfolk," Geoffrey said.

"Do we deal with aught more?"

"If the dream we shared last night was true," Geoffrey said slowly, "we deal with a woman who has command of men, though she would have it seem that she does not, and who could order this house prepared for her use simply to deceive us."

Cordelia nodded. "But such a house, Geoffrey! Have you ever seen its like?"

"A few," Geoffrey said slowly. "They are rare, but they do exist."

"Nonetheless, there is something about it that strikes me as anomalous."

"Anomalous indeed," Geoffrey agreed. "There is too much of good planning here, of the well-coordinated. We must consider, sister, that we deal with our old enemies from the future, who may move against us in some such way as they have before. Of course, I suppose this *could* be the work of a native telepath . . ."

"Not so," Cordelia said, "if the telepath knew no more of machines, or the universe outside our world, than the folk who are born here. She could not have expected that two who have such knowledge might visit."

Geoffrey gave her a cynical smile. "Come, sister! Do you truly think we have deceived her any more than she has deceived us?"

That gave Cordelia pause. "No," she said slowly, "from what you have said thus far, she must know, must she not? Are we not therefore in peril?"

"We must believe so," said Geoffrey, "if we are not to be taken by surprise."

Cordelia felt a touch of fear. "Then we must be on our guard night and day, brother."

"You may take the day," he said at once. "I shall take the night."

"To be on *guard*, Geoffrey." Cordelia glared at him. "I have seen the way in which you look upon the Lady Delilah."

Geoffrey shrugged carelessly. "I can be on guard whiles I do other things, Cordelia."

"Oh, surely," she said, with a withering glance. "Yet bear in mind, brother—you are only human."

Geoffrey grinned. "Well, that is so—there are some weaknesses built into us."

Neither of them said a word about leaving. In fact, Cordelia felt a stab of fear, and was amazed to realize that she was more frightened for Alain than for herself.

"Truly," Geoffrey said, "you do not think they would dare attempt to assassinate the heir to the throne?"

Cordelia shrugged impatiently. "We do very poorly at disguising ourselves, do we not, brother? For who is there in this land who does not know of the High Warlock and the names of his children? Nay, especially among witchfolk, who does not know of us?"

"True," Geoffrey agreed, "and who does not know that

the Crown Prince is named Alain, nor that he is the friend of the children of the High Warlock? Nay, you have the right of it, sister—we must be prepared for anything, even murder. Yet there is this." He spread his hands. "Why have they not already struck?"

"There is that," Cordelia said slowly. "We may yet have some time. Still, brother, ought we not leave tomorrow, or as soon as we may?"

"We should leave now, but Alain would never agree to it," Geoffrey said. "He would see it as a breach of courtesy."

Cordelia wondered if that was the only reason.

"No, we must stay at least the night—and study the situation. It may be that we can strike a blow now that will save us a hundred in the future. We can always call for help, if we need it—but let us first see what this pleasant nest of traitors does intend."

"Aye," said Cordelia. "But guard the Prince, my brother. Ward him well. Although perhaps I should do that—and stay close by him."

"Oh, you need not," said Geoffrey quickly.

Cordelia smiled. "Why, brother—could you fear for my honor?"

Geoffrey took a second, and answered as delicately as he could. "Let us say, my sister, that I know how fragile a thing honor may be, and I would not wish to lay more stress on it than needs be. But come—our host will be expecting us for dinner soon enough, and we must not disappoint him."

"As you say, brother." Cordelia took Geoffrey's arm, and they went back toward the manor house arm in arm.

They went in through the tall windowed doors that opened onto the terrace. Sir Julian looked up as they came in. "Ah, well met! I thought you had tired of my company so soon!"

Cordelia smiled. "Surely not, my lord." She accepted a glass of wine from a servant and looked about her at the Great Hall. The trestle tables were set up as they would have been in a castle, though with many fewer places. The head table stood on a dais only a few inches high. Behind it, painted on the plaster and beams, was a huge coat of arms. Cordelia gave it a glance, memorizing it for later analysis; she did not easily remember any such tokens as these.

The rest of the hall was plastered too, between the old oaken beams. There was a tapestry centered in the long wall across from the windows, and another at the end.

The original colonists of Gramarye had reconstructed the Middle Ages not as they really were, but as they should have been. Accordingly, they had kept costumes and customs from the Seventh Century, and mixed them in with all the succeeding centuries through the Fifteenth. But when it came to the amenities and courtesies, they had been more much eclectic; the range spanned through the Nineteenth Century and into the early Twentieth. On Gramarye, there were elements of gracious living that had never been there in the real Middle Ages of Terra—and this gathering for wine before dinner was certainly one of them.

So, for that matter, was the manor house itself.

They had come late; Delilah had already managed to work Alain off to the side of the conversational grouping.

Seeing Delilah, Cordelia felt dowdy all over again, for the hussy was attired in a demure gown of pink and cream, considerably looser than her riding dress, only hinting at the lush contours beneath. It complemented her blonde hair so well that Cordelia automatically felt dimmed by comparison. But she lifted her chin; she would not be outdone!

Even as Cordelia watched, though, the vixen took another step toward the far corner. Alain perforce stepped with her, to hear what she was saying. He began to respond gravely, but Cordelia could tell, from the color of his face, that her suggestion had not been entirely decorous. Her flirtations had become even broader than on their journey.

Cordelia leaned over to Geoffrey and murmured, "Brother, would you see if you can distract the Lady Delilah from my inconstant suitor?"

Geoffrey looked up, then smiled. "He is constant, Cordelia, or he would not be blushing. Naetheless, I am certainly more than delighted to do as you ask." He stepped away.

But Cordelia stopped him with a hand on his forearm. He turned back, eyebrows raised in polite inquiry.

"Only flirtation, mind," Cordelia said sternly.

Geoffrey grinned. "I make no promises." Then he was gone, moving over to join Alain and Delilah. She looked up with a flash of annoyance, which turned very quickly into a sensuous stare which she even more quickly broke, turning to Alain with a silvery laugh.

Cordelia turned half away from them, satisfied; Delilah certainly would not be able to keep her mind on Alain now. She reflected that a brother with overabundant hormones could have his uses.

For herself, she must not appear to be watching too closely . . .

"Lady Cordelia! How beautiful you are!"

She turned, warmed by the sincerity in the voice—then caught her breath.

Forrest stood beside her, resplendent in a doublet of the same cut and period as Geoffrey's, hose clinging to his legs to show his magnificent calves and thighs to advantage. Cordelia scolded herself; she should not be noticing his legs so, even if they *were* remarkably well turned. Or the feeling of his lips on her hand, though they were amazingly soft, amazingly sensuous . . .

He looked up, gazing into her eyes, and she managed to find enough voice to say, "You sound surprised, sir. Is it so rare that I am . . . presentable?"

"Nay, not in the slightest!" He grinned, white teeth flashing. "You are rare indeed, my lady! Surely there cannot be another like you!"

"Oh, is there not?" Cordelia began to feel a bit better. "And to how many damsels have you said that, sir?"

"Never, milady, not to a single other woman!" Forrest

reflected that he had also never been given so good a cue line. "I have never seen you in those colors before. Surely they bring out highlights in the glorious auburn of your hair that I would never have known, though 'tis so great a pleasure to see your hair unbound in the sun's rays that come through this window."

Cordelia blushed. "You extol my charms too much, sir."

"I speak honestly." He stepped a little closer. "Would you have me prevaricate?"

He was so very near, the aroma of him so masculine, so compelling . . . and the strange feelings had begun within her again . . . "I would have you speak only as a gentleman should, sir!"

"Alas! Must I be a gentleman, then?"

"You must be as you were born!"

They both looked up, startled.

Alain stood by them, looking stern, wearing a russet doublet, again of the antique cut, and fawn-colored hose. Cordelia could not help but notice that his legs, too, looked very well, perhaps even better than Forrest's . . .

"Why, so I must!" Forrest turned to Alain with a dangerous glint in his eye. "But who are you to tell me what I must and must not do, sir?"

Alain began to answer, but caught himself in the nick of time.

Forrest noticed the pause, and lifted an eyebrow.

"Only a knight," Alain said, still stern, "but as such, 'tis my duty to remind you of your duty to knighthood."

"Am I still a knight, then?" Forrest cocked his head to the side. "I, who have broken the law?"

"You are still a knight!" Alain snapped, more sternly than ever. "You are a knight, who can redeem himself, and behave as a knight should once more."

Cordelia stepped a little closer to him. Yes, sometimes Alain was insufferable, overbearing, and his holier-than-thou attitude did grate upon her now and then—but she felt safer next to him, somehow. The troubling feelings inside her were so much less in his presence . . .

She glanced up at Forrest, and knew a moment's longing. If only he were as proper a man, as morally sound and steady a man, as Alain!

Though if he were, she wondered, would he be so attractive?

Then Sir Julian was offering her his arm, and leading her to the head table. "Surely you will allow your host the benefit of your beauty and charm, my dear, if only for the space of this dinner."

"I shall be honored, my lord." But even as she said it, Cordelia wondered if this was a ploy to get her away from Alain, so that Delilah might work on him at her leisure. A glance out of the corner of her eye showed her that she had no need to worry, though—the lady was sandwiched between Geoffrey and Alain, and Geoffrey was definitely occupying most of her attention. Alain was looking none too pleased about it, but he glanced up at Cordelia longingly.

She found it very reassuring.

She turned back to Sir Julian. "I thank you, my lord."

"Then sit! Sit! And we will dine!" Sir Julian sat down, and immediately, the servants began laying in front of them the huge slices of bread that served as plates. Behind them came another server, laying thick slices of beef on the trenchers.

Sir Julian picked up his knife and began to cut at the meat—the signal to begin.

Cordelia found it slightly disturbing that he did not start with a blessing over the meal, but she had no choice other than to abide by the custom of the house.

"I must honor you, my daughter's rescuers!" Sir Julian said, lifting a cup. "Honor you with a toast tonight, and a ball tomorrow night!"

"Ball?" Cordelia stared, appalled.

"Indeed. I have sent word to my neighbors, bidding them come rejoice with me." He laid a hand over hers. "You must not be upset, lady. We are rude folk here in the country, taking any opportunity that offers to celebrate Life—and if our dress is not elegant, why, we make up for it with exuberance."

"My sister has left many beautiful dresses behind her," Delilah said, all sweetness. "I shall bid my maid show them to you."

Cordelia was certain that Delilah's maid would not show her anything that was too lovely.

"Or if you wish," the lord said, "I have bolts of wonderful cloth, yards of laces. Only say what you wish, and a seamstress shall labor all this night and all tomorrow, to make a gown that will delight you."

"Indeed she shall," Delilah said. "My own seamstress, if you wish it, my dear."

Cordelia had a brief vision of the kind of dress Delilah's seamstress would make for her, and smiled sweetly. "How good of you, Lady Delilah! It will not be necessary, though. However, my lord . . ." She turned back to Lord Julian. "I would see your cloths and your laces. It may be that I myself can craft a dress to my taste."

"Yourself?" The Lady Delilah tittered behind her hand. "Why, I had thought you a lady high-born, Cordelia— surely not one who plies needle and thread in her own right!"

"Why, my dear, do you not embroider?" Cordelia asked, all innocence.

Delilah stared at her, paling. "Aye, most assuredly, and most excellently!"

"Why, then, so do I," Cordelia said, "and my mother was quick to teach me the crafting of a gown—for, she said, I must know how 'tis done, if I wish to make sure my seamstress does it well." She turned back to Lord Julian. "Yes, my lord, I shall see your cloths."

CHAPTER
~12~

The cloth, at least, was every bit as beautiful as Sir Julian had promised. She chose an emerald green lawn, almost as fine as silk, for the gown itself, then selected yard after yard of intricate lace to adorn it. She was tempted to take some long strips of embroidery they showed her, but decided that she would not be able to compete with Delilah in ornamentation; indeed, she remembered her mother's dictum, that when a woman resorts to an abundance of decorations, it is because she does not believe in her own beauty.

Unfortunately, Cordelia did not.

Still, she would never admit that. The lace would have to do—the lace, and the wonderful cloth that showed her hair and eyes to such advantage.

Petticoats and kirtles the maid was glad to bring her, presumably from the sister's store. Cordelia did not even stop to think of the wonderful coincidence that they should be almost exactly the same size.

Then she sat down with pen and paper to make a rough sketch by candlelight—but the more she sketched, the more excited she became, till finally, she heard a clock somewhere tolling midnight, and told herself sternly that she must desist; she would have to have a good night's sleep, or she would be incapable of doing anything tomorrow, certainly not be able to be as charming as she must be at the ball.

And so to bed.

At last, Cordelia was able to lie down to sleep, dressed in a nightgown that she had found laid out on her bed. She nestled into the softness of the featherbed, luxuriating in it after a night on pine boughs. She burrowed deeper, letting her mind roam free, letting images arise and fade of their own accord—but the images were not of lovely gowns, or even nightmares of the extravagant dresses Delilah might wear to the ball tomorrow night, but of Alain . . . and then Forrest . . . then Alain again, then Forrest, then the two of them side by side, then Forrest alone, looming over her, his eyes bright, his lips moist . . . She was only a little afraid of the feelings that the picture of him aroused, almost unafraid at all, considering that he was not really there. There was something about his gaze, his stare, and (be honest!) his body, his muscular build, that raised those tingling, tickling feelings inside her, and she admitted to herself at last that it was a longing she felt, that perhaps she was beginning to be able to understand the desire that seemed to drive Geoffrey.

But there was something that repelled her about Forrest, too—the very recklessness that made him appealing was also threatening, in its way. She found herself wishing that she could marry Alain for security and friendship, but still have Forrest for romance . . . romance, and the pleasures of his attentions . . .

She sat bolt upright in bed, staring into the darkness, realizing what she had been wishing for, blushing furiously in the privacy of night. Then, completely ashamed of herself, she burst into tears and buried her face in her pillow.

The campfire was a spot of cheer in a very dark night. It was chill indeed, very odd for August. Rod and Gwen shared his cloak, staring at the flames.

"I don't like this," Rod said. "The three of them could be at the mercy of whoever owns that manor house. How long has it been here, anyway?"

"By appearances, a hundred years, at least," Gwen answered.

"By appearances," Rod agreed. "But people can build things to look old."

"Indeed." Gwen was thinking of some of the wonders of modern technology she had seen in her brief sojourn off-planet.

A squat shadow detached itself from the darkness under the trees and came toward them.

Rod looked up. "Any news, Brom?"

The dwarf sat down on a rock by the fire, holding his hands out toward the flames. "I have sent elves to keep watch throughout the house. If anything untoward occurs, we will know of it within minutes."

"How long do the local elves say the house has been here?"

"Only these last two years—nay, some months less. A crew of strangers came to build it. They cleared the land here in the center of the forest, where none might see them. The tools with which they cut down the forest were magical, say the elves, and the job was done in a day."

Rod pricked up his ears; he knew the sound of high technology. "Anything about beams of fire?"

"Summat of the sort. They builded the whole of the house in a month, again with sorcerous machines, and gave it the appearance of age, though it was new."

Rod nodded. "Do they have any idea who lives there?"

"A lady and her retainers," Brom answered. "A most beautiful lady, slender, not very tall." He shrugged. "That is all they can say. Her face doth seem to change from time to time, as does the color of her hair. She doth bear herself as one well born, but they do sense a maliciousness about her."

"Anything definitely bad to say about her?"

"Not from without—and they have had no wish to enter inside that house. Not that it houseth fearsome deeds, mind you, nor doth it repel them in any wise—'tis that it hath no interest for them. They have other fish to fry."

"No interest?" Rod stared. "Elves, with no curiosity?"

Gwen frowned. "That doth sound little like any elf I've ever known. Indeed, a brownie's natural curiosity would send him prying into every corner. Or are these elves only, and no brownies among them?"

"What difference?" Rod said. "Elves are just as curious as brownies. Not so inclined to go indoors, I'll admit, but still . . ."

"There do be brownies among them, and they too have no interest in the house," Brom verified.

"It doth smack of enchantment," Gwen said, "of witchpower, and mighty, too."

"Even so," Brom agreed. "It doth bespeak one who hath laid spells of disinterest on all who come nigh."

"Is there danger to Cordelia, or to Geoffrey?" Gwen asked.

"Or even to Alain?" Rod finished.

"There is no sign of danger yet, to any one of them," Brom said. "There is hazard only in that they are amidst strangers who are themselves unknown in their desires or goals. But there is no present danger in evidence. Be sure that if there is, the elves will warn them—and, if need be, protect them with their own magics."

"But if there are witches in that house," said Gwen, "elfin magics may not suffice."

Rod shivered.

"They will bear word to us, will they not?" Gwen asked.

"Be sure that they shall," Brom promised her. "Be very sure of that."

Morning came lustrous, cool and moist—like herself, Delilah thought. She stretched luxuriously, treasuring the feeling of rest, of satiation of sleep, knowing that Cordelia was probably red-eyed and weary, her hair in disarray and her mouth stuffed with pins, trying vainly to cobble together some sort of dress. It made breakfast in bed so much more tasty.

Her modiste, of course, had been up all night, and was still busy with a fabric-bonder, computer, design program, and a ROM library of medieval style plates.

Delilah rose for her first fitting.

Cordelia had risen an hour earlier, her heart singing as she gazed at the cloth and lace. Then she noticed the breakfast tray by her bed, still steaming. So that was what had waked her—the servant. She felt an instant's panic, but found her sketches still carefully hidden away in her boots—in her enemy's house, there would be spies everywhere.

Boots! Yes, she would have to make slippers, too.

Then she donned the riding dress, pleased to notice that the dust had been brushed from it. Clad once again in her working clothes, Cordelia buckled down.

Delilah came out of her bedroom into the sitting room of her suite as her modiste was finishing running the hem through the molecular bonder. "Nice timing, Chief." She held up the completed dress.

Even Delilah couldn't withhold an exclamation of delight. It was a daring confection of a dress, all pink and gold, that would set off her peaches-and-cream complexion and blonde tresses to perfection. "Quickly! I must see it!" She slipped into her petticoats and stood impatiently while the modiste fastened the gown around her. No need to trouble with a brassiere—the Middle Ages had not had them, and any reasonably civilized planet in the Third Millennium had them built into the garments with tiny electronic devices that enhanced buoyancy and line.

Of course, Delilah thought smugly, she did not really need enhancing—but it never hurt to fire a broadside.

The modiste finished the last fastening—primitive, but they had to be something that *could* have existed in the Middle Ages, whether they truly had or not—and Delilah whirled away to stand in front of the doorway to her bedroom. The modiste pressed a button, an electronic circuit closed—and the surface of the doorway swirled into silvery reflectance. Delilah gazed at her reflection in the electronic mirror with smug satisfaction, posing side view, back view, three-quarter profile. That snob, Cordelia Gallowglass, could never match such a gown, not even with the most talented seamstress on Gramarye! She was, after all, limited to medieval technology, and certainly, mere needle and thread were so far from the devices available to Delilah's modiste that Cordelia could not have produced even an indifferent dress. But she would have tried—oh, yes! She would have stayed up all night and would stay up all day! Her hands would be raw with pinpricks, her skin pale with fatigue, and her eyes red. She would be snappish and insecure with weariness.

Even if her dress were presentable, though, it could never come within a mile of Delilah's for allure. But then, she thought with complacency, Cordelia could never have matched her for voluptuousness in any case. Delilah was, after all, a projective telepath, and a very talented and very skilled one at that—but the greatest of all her talents was the projection of sexual desire.

Cordelia was digging into her task with verve and glee. Never had she had such beautiful fabrics to work with! It seemed such a self-indulgence, when there were peasant women on her own estates who had only the one blouse and skirt, and those patched. No matter how her parents urged her, she had never been able to bring herself to indulge in outright luxuries.

Here, however, there was the best of reasons. She had to save her poor Alain from the clutches of that poisonous female, Delilah—and had to save him personally.

She had draped the cloth, marked it, then laid it out and chalked the patterns with not a moment's hesitation, following the diagrams in her mind's eye. Then she cut it—staring at the lines, thinking of the separation of molecules, watching the cloth separate itself along the lines she had drawn. Twice she made a mistake; twice she held fabric together, stared at it, and thought of the linen molecules moving, faster and faster until the cloth was whole again, each separate thread having bonded itself to its other half so that it was no longer cut, but as sound as new.

She was as talented in telekinesis as Delilah was in projection.

Now she held the sections of cut cloth together, staring at the edges, watching the threads flow together so well that you could see no seam at all. Molecule bonded to molecule, far tighter than any thread could bind. The unfinished edges folded themselves over, bonded, and made themselves into hems.

By noon, it was done, and she slipped it on for the first fit. She went to the window, opening the casement and letting out a trilling whistle. The aural call was only there to help her concentrate; really, it was her mind that reached out and summoned . . .

A robin flew down, perching on the tree branch outside her window. It stared at her, then cocked its head inquisitively. Cordelia stepped back, reading the bird's mind. The robin saw her, and she read her own image from its mind, viewing herself through its eye, stepping back until she could see all of herself.

She gasped with delight.

She saw a fairy-tale princess complete in every detail— except the headdress, of course; she had yet to make that.

However, it was a dress such as a fairy-tale princess would have thought scandalous. The neckline was daringly low, and it fitted her torso as though it had grown there. Even as she gazed, she thought of a slight rearrangement of electrical charges, and the skirt and petticoat moved toward her legs, clinging. She walked toward the window opening a few steps, and the static charge molded the cloth to her limbs—not completely, for the petticoats muffled the outline considerably, but enough to more than hint at her contours. She viewed them with a critical eye, and decided that her contours might not be so insufficient, after all—and there had been enough boys who had sought to

touch them on some of her outings. Not so lush as Delilah's curves, perhaps—assuming that Delilah's were real—
but more perfectly proportioned.

She turned, walking away from the bird, gazing at the
back of her reflection, at the neckline, scooped low enough
to show her shoulder blades, cloth clinging to hint at the
smooth curves of hips. She looked back over her shoulder,
lowering her eyelids, giving her best imitation of Delilah's
alluring smile, and tried rolling her hips as she walked.

Yes, it did seem to work.

She blushed as she thought of herself actually putting on
a performance of that sort before Alain. She would not
dare! And even if she did, surely he would not dare to ap-
preciate it!

But the thought did excite her.

Still, the dress was a trifle too loose here and there. She
thought at the cloth, and the seam turned inward, the darts
tightening until it fit her—well, perhaps not quite like a
glove above the waist, but certainly like a flower below.

And, too, it did need some adornment. She blew a kiss
at the bird, dismissing it, slipped out of the dress, lifted the
lace, measured it off against the cloth, and bonded it so
that it filled in the scoop of the neckline, the dip behind
her shoulders. Her mother had told her that what was
imagined was more effective than what was shown; it was
only necessary to give the gentlemen something for their
imaginations to work on.

Cordelia certainly didn't intend to give them anything
more.

When she was done, she summoned another bird—a
bluebird this time—to look at her while she read its mind,
and caught her breath with delight. It was quite the most
lovely gown she had ever seen, even if she did say so herself. She dismissed the bird with a gay wave, slipped out
of the dress and, in her chemise, took up the buckram, the
lawn, and the veil, and began to make the headdress.

Somewhere in the middle of all these labors, she caught
a sudden, stray thought—a servant approaching her door.
Quickly, she dumped the dress into her lap topsy-turvy and

pulled a thread through a needle, then scrubbed fingers through her hair to make it tousled, disarrayed.

A knock came.

Cordelia called, "Open!"

The door opened, and the serving-wench stepped in, holding a tray in one hand. "My lady, you have not come to dine."

"Oh, I cannot!" Cordelia did her best to sound frazzled. "See how deeply in the toils I am!"

The wench came closer, large-eyed. "Surely, my lady, the seamstress could aid thee . . ."

"Mayhap, but I am loath to ask. Oh, I will be done in time, I am sure of it! Nay, but set the wine and bread there, on the little table—I think there is room. I shall take it when I have a moment."

"Even as you say, my lady." The maid curtsied, round-eyed, then stepped out, closing the door behind her. Cordelia caught the impression of smug satisfaction, and answered it with a vindictive smile, glaring at the door. So they thought they would have her beaten, did they? Well, all to the better. Let Delilah think Cordelia was in a state and could not possibly have a decent gown. Nothing would strengthen her so much as Delilah's overconfidence.

She was done by early afternoon. The bread, cheese, meat, and wine were quite good. She ate lightly, not wanting to feel sluggish when she waked.

Because, of course, she wanted to be fresh for the evening's festivities. She lay down to nap, closing her eyes as she sought out a finch, leaving a stern command within its mind to come trill beneath her window in an hour. She left the same command within her own mind—only to wake, not to trill—hid the lovely gown in the wardrobe, locked the door, and lay down to sleep, satisfied.

After all, she did want to look her best.

She woke at four, added one last touch—a cloak, of a contrasting material; only a great circle of cloth that she could throw over herself to hide the gown. When the knock on the door came, she quickly threw the cloak over her shoulders and called, "Enter!"

It was a servant, with a can of steaming water. Cordelia bade her put it by the hearth, and the maid did, then left, with many curious glances about the room.

"Oh, I had almost forgot!" The maid turned back in the doorway and came to bring Cordelia a domino mask. "It is to be a masked ball, my lady."

Cordelia thrilled with delight, but tried to sound worn and exhausted. "Thank you, good soul."

"As you wish, my lady." The maid gave a little curtsy, then left, closing the door behind her.

Alain stared, paling. "I could never behave so!"

He was watching the "neighbors" flirt with one another as they bowed and chatted and danced. None had been introduced as other than the character they were dressed as, most of them from the romances, some from old myths. But they were all very outgoing, and the dances were rather earthy.

"Of course you can," Geoffrey assured him. "It is a masked ball, Alain. None shall know who you are."

"Well . . . there is truth in that," Alain said thoughtfully, then looked up sharply. "But hold! I have heard of these masked balls. Is there not something about unmasking at midnight?"

"Well, aye," Geoffrey allowed, "so, if you are careful to leave before midnight, no one will discover your identity."

Alain's gaze wandered over the glittering company, golden in the light of myriad candles. "Well . . . true . . . 'twould be a pity to miss the last of the ball . . ."

"Yet mayhap would be worth it." Geoffrey took a sip of his wine. "Bear in mind, though, that you need not decide until it is nigh the hour of midnight. If you feel that you would do something . . . exhilarating, something . . . that is not truly evil, mind you, but only a little wicked, or no, not even wicked, but . . . daring . . . why, if you have done it, you leave before midnight!" He clinked his glass against Alain's. "If you have not, you stay for the unmasking! Drink up!"

Alain sipped the wine absently, his mind clearly elsewhere. Then he looked up, suddenly remembering what he had been thinking before. "Hold! I should not drink wine so early! 'Twill make me drunk, will it not?"

"What—one goblet of wine?" Geoffrey gave a deprecating laugh. "Do not give it a thought."

But *he* had. He had given Alain's wine quite a lot of thought. It was now thirty percent alcohol.

Geoffrey knew Alain of old, of course, and knew that the Prince had grown up drinking wine, as did most noble children on Gramarye. He would not become drunk, Geoffrey knew, but perhaps rather ... uninhibited ...

The musicians had tuned their instruments and begun to play. Cordelia stood in the shadow at the top of the staircase, shrouded in her cloak, eyes wide as she stared at the guests, feeling a strange nervousness, a strange apprehension. How many of them were truly neighbors, and how many Delilah's minions?

How could she hope to outshine Delilah on her own territory?

But my heavens, there were a lot of people!

Admittedly, their garb was old-fashioned by the standards of Runnymede—but nothing was ever really out of style on Gramarye. They were certainly jovial enough, laughing and talking as the servants passed among them with goblets of wine. The entire Great Hall was already filled with company—at least half dowagers and their husbands.

But the other half were young. Probably most of them were married, but they were young and vibrant nonetheless. They milled about, making quite a roar. Like waves upon the beach, they were about to engulf her.

"Surely you are not timid, Lady Cordelia!"

Cordelia looked up, alarmed.

It was Delilah, parading down the stairs in a gown so lovely that it made Cordelia gasp. Mask or not, there was no mistaking her—the cascade of golden hair was artfully arranged and equally artfully displayed, as was a generous expanse of bosom. The heart-shaped face, the voluptuous curves—all were enhanced by the splendor of her pink-and-gold gown.

Cordelia felt a bitter stab of jealousy.

"Why, what a mouse you are!" Delilah said. "Will you start at every shadow? Come, how can you possibly not delight in such an evening as this?"

"I . . . I will endeavor to." Cordelia summoned what remained of her self-possession and drew herself up.

"I rejoice to hear it. Do you go before me, for I have no wish to dim your luster."

Cordelia's eyes narrowed behind her mask. "Surely, Lady Delilah, no gown can compare with yours tonight. Nay, do you precede me. 'Tis your house, after all, and 'tis your due."

"I thank you, my dear. I shall." Delilah nodded with a pinfeather smile and stepped to the head of the stairs.

She motioned, and her maid hissed down to the major-domo. He looked up; his eyes widened a moment; then he turned to the crowd and bawled out, "The Lady Helen of Troy!"

Of course, Cordelia thought.

As one, the crowd turned to look, and the musicians struck up a soft march.

Delilah paraded down the stairs.

For a moment, the crowd was silent, staring.

Then, as one, they broke into applause.

Cordelia tried to remind herself that most of them must be in Delilah's pay—but still, the jealousy burned within her. The hussy!

Well, Cordelia would answer in her own style.

The applause turned into congratulatory conversation as Delilah reached the foot of the stairs. The young men were pressing forward to kiss her hands; the ladies were "oh"ing and "ah"ing and congratulating her on so wonderful a costume, then turning away to mutter savagely with one another.

Cordelia knew her hour had come. Her heart thumped so painfully that she thought it would tear through her dress. Still, she handed a note to the footman on the stairs, who handed it down to the majordomo.

When Delilah had moved far enough away from the stairs, the majordomo raised his voice and cried, in his clarion tones, "The Lady Elaine of Shallot!"

It had seemed like a good idea, at the time—a silent rebuke to Alain. Now, Cordelia wasn't so sure.

The crowd quieted a little as they turned to look at the new arrival.

Cordelia held her breath, straightened, and stepped onto the first step.

The crowd was totally silent, a sea of faces staring up at her.

Cordelia nearly died inside. She descended another step, another. There she stopped and whirled the cloak from her shoulders.

All eyes were on her, stunned.

She began to walk again, but faltered in her step, holding on to the handrail for dear life. Had she committed some immense faux pas? Was she truly in enemy territory in more ways than one?

Well, then, she would show them of what she was made! She lifted her chin high and took another step.

Suddenly, the crowd burst into applause, cheering—most of it masculine.

It slammed at her ears. Her eyes widened behind the mask in amazement. Could they truly be applauding her?

They certainly could. The young men were pressing to the fore, with the older men not far behind them. She came down the stairs slowly, the applause and cheering ringing in her ears.

As she stepped onto the last step, some of the young gallants pressed forward to seize her hands and kiss her fingers. She looked down at them, amazed, then lifted her eyes . . .

And saw Delilah's glare of hatred.

She knew she was truly a success.

CHAPTER
~13~

The look on Delilah's face was all Cordelia needed. Obviously, her gown was far more beautiful than even she had supposed.

She still did not realize that she was a very beautiful woman in her own right—as beautiful as Delilah, really, though less voluptuous. The severity of the gown enhanced her classical features, and the warmth of the color set off the fairness of her complexion marvelously, bringing out the golden highlights in her auburn hair.

Her nervousness fled, to be replaced by gloating. She smiled like the cat who had lapped up the cream, graciously extending her hands to her eager admirers, stepping down into the middle of the throng, blowing kisses to one and all, feeling a secret, shameful thrill as they bowed low over her hand—and her decolletage.

"You are the sun, milady!"

"Then beware that I should shine on you, milord," she returned, "for I might burn you."

"Indeed you might," he gasped, and another man said, "Ah! Would that I should be so roasted!"

"I should make it hot enough for you, be sure," she said.

"But I should prefer to see you by the light of the moon," said another gallant, looking deeply into her eyes.

" 'Ware, sir," she said. "You may lie."

"I could hope for no sweeter fate," he promised her—exactly the response she had hoped for. She felt a secret, scandalous delight, and let her laugh cascade down low to end in a throaty chuckle. The man's eyes burned into hers, but another man caught her other hand. She turned, and looked directly into . . .

Forrest's eyes.

Eyes that seemed to devour her, to swallow her up, and he was breathing, "My lady, surely there could never have been such beauty as yours!"

"Why, sir," she said, her breath catching in her throat, "you have known me these days! And you have never told me so before!" The strange, tickling feelings inside that his presence always seemed to evoke were there again—but she must have been becoming accustomed to them, for somehow, she wasn't at all frightened. No, she found these feelings no longer so novel, but much more exhilarating, delightful, and only wanted more of them.

She stepped a little closer to him, and he breathed, "Sun and moon alike you are, and they both shine upon me in your presence."

"But I have no presents to give you, sir." She stepped a little closer.

"Your own fair self is a wealth of gifts that would honor a king," he returned, stepping closer too, his arm slipping about her waist. "Will you dance?"

"Aye—I think that I shall," she said, letting her eyelids droop and turning her head a little, so that she was eyeing him sidelong.

He laughed, low and in his throat, but catching his breath as he did so, and stepped away from the disappointed gallants, who rumbled their outrage as he swept Cordelia out onto the floor.

They flowed smoothly into the motions of the age-old

peasant dance, body to body, hip to hip, for only a few moments as their feet moved in unison—then apart, clapping, back to back, and his shoulders brushed hers, his hips brushed hers, then back to the front again for a few steps more, then, arm in arm, for a few paces side by side, their gazes locked, gazing deeply into one another's eyes. She felt herself turning warm inside, felt her knees weakening, but that was fair enough, because he turned then and, catching her about the waist, caught her right hand in his left, and pressed her against him as they flowed through the steps of the dance, and she could let herself weaken, let her limbs go limp, for he was holding her up . . .

Halfway across the floor, Alain followed their every move. "Can she truly be as wanton as she appears, Geoffrey?"

"One can never say, my friend," Geoffrey answered. "Women often go to great lengths to seem to be something that they are not."

"But why should they do such a thing?" Alain demanded.

"Why," Geoffrey said, "to hold our interest by making themselves mysterious—or simply because they wish to, because it gives them pleasure."

Alain's eyes returned to the lady in green. "She surely seems to take delight in it! And you say that she may be truly virtuous, and only enjoys the pretense of wantonness?"

"Oh, quite surely! There is not a woman alive who does not wish to be desired, to be beautiful and the center of all attention, simply because of her beauty and her grace—and her sexual allure. No, my friend, every woman has the right to be as attractive as she can be and wishes to be, without having to fear men's advances becoming improper."

But though the words were fair, his expression was one of subdued shock as he watched his sister move about the floor with the forest outlaw—and when the dance brought them together, moving as though they were one.

Alain's gaze still wandered. "Where is Cordelia, though? This whole ball is empty, lackluster, if she is not here."

Geoffrey looked up, startled. Certainly so flimsy a mask did not really make Alain unable to recognize Cordelia!

Of course, it could—if he did not *want* to recognize her.

Geoffrey chewed that thought over for a moment, then said, "She will come anon, I am sure. For the nonce, my friend, seek you a dance with yon lady in green and lace."

Alain turned to him, staring, scandalized. "Why should I do any such thing?"

"Why," Geoffrey said slowly, "because a dance with her would be a delight to any man—and will teach your body ways of holding a woman and moving with her that would delight Cordelia, and draw her to you."

Alain looked suddenly very much on his guard. "Do you truly think so?"

"Most truly, I assure you." Geoffrey plucked a goblet from a passing tray and presented it to Alain. "Here, my friend. You have not drunk wine for half an hour. Do so, I pray you—for what is gaiety and mirth if it has no spirit? Therefore, drink you spirits!"

"I would scarcely call wine 'spirits,'" Alain said, accepting the cup.

"Oh, but I would," Geoffrey said, his eyes on the cup as the Prince drank. "I would, most certainly."

The dance ended, and Cordelia was immediately besieged by a dozen would-be partners.

"I shall never come to her," Alain said, dismayed—and, perhaps, relieved.

"But I shall," Geoffrey assured him, "and when the dance ends, we shall be nearest to you, be sure. Drink your wine, my friend—it will sweeten your breath for her." And he moved away to join the throng of Cordelia's admirers.

Cordelia, fortunately, was taking her time about accepting a partner, laughing and parrying flirtatious sallies. Geoffrey managed to elbow his way to the front of the rank just as the musicians began to play again. "My lady," he said, with an edge to his voice, "I *must* have this dance."

She looked up, startled—and before she could recover, he had taken her hand and her waist and was beginning to move into the steps of the dance. She accepted the fait accompli, but glared daggers at him—and as soon as they were away from other people, hissed, "How dare you intrude, brother!"

"How dare I not?" Geoffrey returned. "Surely a brother must guard a sister, guard all of her—especially when she is showing more of herself than she ever has before!"

Cordelia smiled, amused. "You, brother? Offended by decolletage? When you seem to seek out the lowest that you can find?"

"In other women, aye," he said stiffly. "In other women, 'tis pleasant, 'tis right in its way—but not in a sister."

She laughed scornfully. "For shame, Geoffrey! Do you not realize that every woman you have ever pursued may have been someone's sister?"

"Well . . . perhaps." Actually, he never had. "But they do not care for her nor cherish her as much as I!"

"There has been scant evidence of caring or cherishing, 'til now."

"Cordelia!" he exclaimed, wounded. "This whole quest is because I seek to protect you and gain you your heart's desire!"

She gazed into his eyes, and saw that he meant what he said. He cared for her very deeply. "For that, I thank you, brother," she said warmly. "Yet am I, therefore, not to be allowed to enjoy the pleasures of dancing and flirtation—only because I have a brother who cares?"

"Indeed! Leave that to them who have none that care for them—and therefore care naught for themselves!"

"Oh, Geoffrey, you are so prudish so suddenly!" Cordelia said impatiently. "Do not tell me you disapprove of such behavior—for surely you enjoy it well enough in the women you pursue!"

"Well . . . aye . . . but they are not my sisters!"

"Pooh, brother! If you will not be a model of virtue, wherefore should I?"

Geoffrey bit back the retort, and Cordelia enjoyed watching the flush of anger rise to his face. She laughed, with a light, ringing quality, as silver as Delilah's, and said, "Still, brother, I shall have mercy. For this dance, at least, I shall be all propriety."

And she was.

When the dance ended, Geoffrey dropped her hand, stepping back with a slight bow. Cordelia curtsied, inclining her head—and looked up to find herself facing a cavalier in gold and scarlet, with a long, flowing scarlet cloak and golden hair above the dark severity of a domino mask. Her heart stopped for a moment, at his handsomeness.

"May I have this dance, my lady?" His voice was low and sensuous.

"Surely, my lord," Cordelia murmured—and he stepped up, arm in arm, before the music had even started, leaving a dozen disappointed would-be partners behind.

Then, as the music started, he slipped his hand about her waist, taking her right hand in his, holding it high. He did not touch her body with his, did everything that was decorous—but the reckless look in his eye, the gaze he gave her, the flashing whiteness of his teeth as he grinned, the paces of the dance, she found dizzying, giddy. All decorum, mind you—but there was a sensuality to his movements, a beckoning, a yearning for closeness, that she would never have suspected in a man. A tingling began, deep within her, spreading through her; she began to feel warm—and was shocked to realize she was responding to this stranger even as she had responded to Forrest.

That scared her.

He swept her away, and finally their bodies met, hips pressing against one another. Cordelia felt a shiver that ran through her from head to toe. The golden stranger seemed to sense it, too. He grinned, and his eyes grew hot, then almost worshipful, burning into hers. She stared, transfixed.

Then, thank heavens, the moves of the dance called for them to break apart and stroll sedately side by side—but she felt her hips churning as she went, and knew she was not being as sedate as she might. She looked up at the tall, handsome stranger, wondering who he was, immensely tempted to peek into his mind and discover . . .

But, no. *Let us enjoy the moment for what it is,* she thought. *Seize the day.*

Then they came together again, and he was murmuring, in a voice low and husky, certainly one that she could not recognize: "My lady, you are the most beautiful, the most luscious fruit that ever has adorned the Tree of Life! Nay, if we were not so closely hemmed by other people, I could not resist seeking to nibble, and taste."

She giggled, feeling the emotions well up within her, her joints loosening, and beamed up at him. Greatly daring, she said, "Why do you withhold, sir? Are you so ashamed of what you would do that the simple presence of other people will halt you?"

"Nay, surely," he breathed, his face coming closer to hers, and closer . . . Then his lips were on hers, light as a feather, but growing heavier. The kiss deepened; she gasped, but that drew him deeper. For a moment, the kiss was all their existence, and everything else went whirling away, and she was dizzy, very, but she could feel his body pressing against hers.

Then, finally, he pulled away, chest heaving, gasping for breath, and there was a wildness and an awe in his eyes; she had never seen a man look at her that way before, not even Forrest. She felt vulnerable, beset—but she also felt waves of pleasure rocking her, felt the lingering taste of his lips on hers, and knew that she wanted that sensation again, more than anything.

Suddenly she could hear the music anew, and stepped back. "Sir! We have missed the measure!"

"Oh, we must not do that!" he said, his voice husky, and slid his hand beneath her palm, his forearm under hers, and they moved on down between the ranks of the other dancers, who stared at them gaping. They turned and strolled back, as all the company did; then turned and were together again, whirling through a timeless moment, his eyes her universe.

Is this love? she thought, almost frantically. *Could* this be love?

Then, for some unaccountable reason, he had stopped, and she was unutterably sad that he had. "Why, sir," she began, but he stood a little farther away from her, lifting her hand to his lips.

"The music is done, sweetest, most beautiful of dancers," he breathed, "and though I would be selfish to the utmost, holding you in my arms and dancing through the night, I would not do it without your leave."

"Do not give him leave, my lady, I pray you!"

"Nay, lovely damsel! You could not be so cruel as to deny me yet again!"

"Dance with me, lovely damsel, with me!"

They whirled her away, they came between her and the scarlet-and-gold man. She chose the most handsome among them, but he seemed to pale into insignificance next to her cavalier. But she danced with him, feeling her limbs become firm again, and the residual emotion from that last dance made her laugh and flirt. The evening restored itself to normality.

She was not sure if she regretted it or not.

She glanced about to find the golden young man again, but could not.

Actually, he was standing beside her brother, shielded by a curtain in a nook.

"Well! You did seem to enjoy that dance, my friend—while you did it," Geoffrey said, somewhat acerbically.

"What a goddess!" Alain breathed. "What an angel, what a fairy! As light as thistledown, and her kiss . . ." He laid a hand on Geoffrey's shoulder. "Forgive me, my friend, for I have wronged your sister. I know now that my heart is elsewhere."

"Elsewhere!" Geoffrey looked up, amused. He could tell Alain now. "Have you no sense at all, you great ninny? That *is* my sister!"

"What!" Alain stared at him.

Then he blushed furiously. "You mean I have treated the Lady Cordelia as . . . as . . ."

"As a woman." Geoffrey gave him a steely glare. "You have treated her as she wants to be treated—as something feminine, desirable. Oh, it is true that she wishes to be loved for her mind, my friend—but it is also true that she wishes to be loved for her body, nay, for all of herself. I assure you that evenings of scholarly discourse are only *part* of what she wants from a man."

But Alain wasn't listening. He was gazing at the dancer who fluttered on the far side of the hall, and breathing, "It *is* Cordelia! Oh, Geoffrey, I have never truly known her before!"

An idea sprang from the fertile soil of Geoffrey's imagination, for this was a campaign, in its way. "Then enjoy her favors while you can, my Prince—for after this night's festivities, she may choose a man other than yourself."

Alain stared at him, appalled.

"Oh, she well may, I assure you! There are few traits so well sung as the fickleness of women. Nay, enjoy the dance with her, as strongly as you can—for if anything will move her to accept your suit, it is that above all else."

"What?!!? *My* enjoyment would move *her*? But how could that . . . how could . . ." Alain swallowed and looked out across the floor. "That a woman might deign to marry me . . . because *I* enjoyed *her*?"

"That would be part of it, at least." Finally Geoffrey could not contain his impatience any longer. "Why, Alain—do you think she would marry you because you did *not* enjoy her?"

"Oh . . . her company . . . yes," Alain said. "But . . ."

"Company is more than sitting by the fireside in converse, friend," Geoffrey said, and gave him a little push. "Go! Dance with her again, when you may! And when you cannot, seize a chance to dance with the Lady Delilah, too."

"But . . . why should I do *that*?" Alain turned back, wide-eyed.

"*Trust* me, friend," Geoffrey said, trying to hide his exasperation. "If you wish to win the Lady Cordelia, dance with Delilah. Then dance with Cordelia again, and if you have more questions, ask me in the morning."

Alain shook his head, not understanding a bit of it. He turned away to do as his mentor had bidden.

The music ended, but he was too slow. Cordelia was dancing again by the time he came near her, dancing with that tall, dark lout of a bandit, Forrest! Who else could it be, with that wealth of dark hair and beard? The mask hid him scarcely at all, although a doublet did go far to disguise him, Alain had to admit—he was so seldom decently dressed. He could not help but wonder if Cordelia would find the man attractive, now that he was properly clothed.

An unworthy thought. He put it from him and turned to join the crowd that hovered around Delilah.

Cordelia, as a matter of fact, *had* recognized Forrest, and was already deep in his embrace, feeling the world spin about her as Forrest whirled her around the floor, devouring her eyes with his own, murmuring extravagant compliments which she was sorely tempted to believe.

"I would know you, Lady Cordelia, through and through. Surely you are the lady of my dreams, Lady Elaine of Shallot! I could never have my fill of you!"

Even as he said it, she could feel the probe, the presence of his mind hovering about her own, seeking entry. Instantly, her own shields were up, and tight. She relaxed outwardly, though, dissembling, trying to hide the fact that she was now on her guard. She laughed. "You may only know me without, sir, for surely the exterior must be enough for two who may not become intimate."

"May I not, then?" He stared at her, wounded. "Wherefore not?"

"Why," she said, "because you have been a thief, and have not yet done a deed that redeems you—and because I have only known you for two days—nay, less! We must come to know one another slowly, Sir Bandit, from the outside in—and you have only begun to know my exterior, as yet."

"I wish to," he breathed, pressing close, and his body seemed to fill every hollow of her own. "I wish to know every inch of your exterior, to kiss every iota of it." His lips touched hers, his tongue tickling, probing, exploring. Dimly, she was aware that they still moved in the paces of the dance—but only dimly, for those movements were churning up the tingling, the rush of feeling within her. Her limbs had turned to water, and only his arm bore her up.

Then the cymbals rebuked her, and she stepped away, as the dance dictated, with a surge of self-disgust. How could she be in love with two men at once, and not even know who one of them was? And what of Alain, who had pledged her his troth, however clumsily, but was devoted to her, and remained so?

"You are troubled, sweet one." Forrest touched the little wrinkle between her eyebrows. "Let it pass. Tomorrow is time enough to think of the world again. Tonight there will be time to think of other men. For this moment, for these few, brief minutes of the dance, think only of me."

Well, when he put it that way, what did she have to lose? Just for this one dance, she decided to do as he asked, to let herself think only of Forrest.

And she did.

But when the dance ended, and she found herself in the arms of a youngster whom she did not know, who prattled merrily to her, she saw the golden cavalier across the room, dancing with the Lady Delilah—or Helen of Troy, as she pretended to be tonight; but her movements were anything but regal. Slowly churning as she went through the dance, every gesture an invitation, her body pliant in his arms—and certainly, from where Cordelia watched, he seemed to be paying very close attention to Delilah. Not kissing her, perhaps, not holding her as closely as she was trying to be held—but he did seem to be mesmerized. She felt a stab of jealousy, felt indignant, but quashed the feeling quickly. He was not her property, after all . . .

Unless she chose to claim him.

Cordelia decided that she would. She had promised nothing to Forrest, after all—or at least, had promised only to think of nothing but him while they danced. She had, and it had been delicious—but there were other flavors to taste.

At the end of the next dance, she kept her eye on her gold-and-scarlet quarry, contriving to end her steps near him as he stepped back from Delilah with a bow, and the tidal wave of young gallants surged between him and the vixen. He looked up, saw Cordelia, and was at her side instantly, claiming her. "You must dance with me, sweet one. I have waited this night in longing."

She molded herself to his arms and began to move to the measure of the dance that had not yet begun. "You have not waited in loneliness, sir. I have seen what excellent company you have kept."

"I will not deny having sampled other pleasures on this Tree of Life," he breathed, "but none could be half so sweet as yourself."

"Oh! Must you compare me with others, then, to know my virtues?"

"I must not." He moved closer, his body not quite touching hers, but she felt her flesh burning as though he had. Her body prickled in anticipation of his touch.

"If you must leave me alone," the cavalier mourned, "I have no choice but to make the time pass as quickly as I can speed it—but with ever a yearning to have you in my arms again."

Almost, she might have believed him; almost, she found that she did, as the dance caught them up again, and they moved together, then apart, then together in perfect unison, closer and closer until they kissed again. This time, somehow, she found herself unable to resist, unable to break away, only meeting his lips with her own in a kiss that went deeper and deeper, caught up somehow in a timeless moment in which the world around them ceased to exist, in which there was nothing but their mouths, their bodies, their minds, touching and longing to touch more deeply.

Then cymbals clashed, and they stepped apart. He glared up at the musicians, but she was glad of the respite, gasping, amazed how shaken she was, not only by the surge of her own desire, but by the realization that the last embrace had not been one of lips and bodies alone, but one of minds as well. Whoever this gallant young stranger was, he was a telepath of some degree, for he had reached out and enwrapped her mind with a psionic touch, enfolded her in his own churning emotions, blending them with hers, stirring hers up even higher than they had boiled by themselves. Breasts heaving, she looked up into his face. Somehow, she was sure he had not read her thoughts—but her emotions he most surely had, and had mingled his own with hers, his desire fueling her own, leading her up toward . . .

She broke off the thought, shivering. How could she ever be content with any other man again, how could any other ever bring her so close to ecstasy as he had this night?

And she did not even know who he was!

But the dance was done, and other young men were pressing in between them, separating them, a gulf of young bodies opening to divide them. With relief, she turned to the youngest and stepped into the measure, bodies well apart, gradually regaining her composure.

She had recovered nearly all when the dance ended, and she found her brother slipping his arm about hers and moving away from the other young men as the music began again. "I believe you could do with a bit of rest, my sister."

"I certainly could," she said with relief. "Thank you, brother."

"My pleasure, I'm sure. We shall have to at least begin the dance, though, or you will have a dozen young boobies claiming your hand."

The music began, and they moved in time to its strains—but Geoffrey steered them closer and closer to the tall windowed doors that opened onto the terrace. There he stopped, offering his arm, even as she had taught him to, years before. She took it with a pang of nostalgia and affection, and they stepped out onto the flagstones.

She breathed in the cool air with a shuddering gasp. "It has been—a very exciting night . . . my brother." She looked up at him. "But where is Alain?"

Geoffrey smiled, with a glint in his eye. "Why, you have danced with him twice this evening."

"Twice?" She stopped still, staring up at him in shock. Then her mind reeled, reviewing all the men she had danced with that evening. No, she could not possibly say which one had been Alain; they had all been too gallant, too heroic; none looked like him in the slightest. "Nay, tell me which one he was, brother!"

"I most certainly shall not!" Geoffrey drew himself up, offended. "It is half the delight of the game, sister, not to know with whom one dances. After all, how else are we to discover our feelings?"

Cordelia frowned up at him. "Why, how do you mean?" she said dangerously.

He gazed down at her, dropping his lofty manner, letting himself be serious for the moment. "How are you to know whether you are truly in love with Alain, if you do not let yourself enjoy the dance with any other man?"

"Who said I was in love with Alain?" Cordelia snapped, hands on her hips. "Indeed, I seem to recall telling you that I was not!"

"And if you are not," Geoffrey said gently, "surely you should be sure of it, so that you can continue to refuse his suit."

Cordelia turned away. "I did not say I would refuse his suit—only that I did not love him."

"Being Queen is not worth a loveless marriage."

Cordelia stiffened. "I could be a good Queen to him. I could be a good wife."

"But if you did not love him," Geoffrey murmured, "you would cheat him, as surely as he would cheat you."

"Be still!" she blazed, turning on him. "What do you know of it? You, who are not married, and who claim never to have been in love!"

"But I have heard what love is," he said. "I can imagine it, and long for it. Aye, even I, who am so busy changing partners that I scarce have time to tread the measure."

Cordelia looked up, eyes wide in sudden panic. "But if I might discover that I truly love someone else, might he not discover the same?"

"He might," Geoffrey said gently, "and it is far better for him to learn that now, than after you are wed."

Cordelia turned away, thinking of the gold-and-scarlet

young man, thinking of Forrest. "Yes," she said, her voice very low, "I suppose that is so. Tell me—is Alain enjoying the evening?"

"He is," Geoffrey said, carefully noncommittal.

"Does he flirt with other ladies?"

"He does."

"More than one?"

"Aye, more." Geoffrey smiled, guessing which "one" she meant. "And quite successfully, I might add."

She could hear his pride in his student, and turned on him. "Geoffrey, why could you not have left me to my own affairs? My life is my own; I did not need your meddling!"

"Perhaps," he said softly, and looked straight into her eyes. "Could it be, sister, that you have found that you, too, are enjoying this ball? The dancing, the flirtation?"

"Should I not?" She thrust her chin up. "Have I not the right to enjoy being a woman, to enjoy my youth?"

"Every right," he said softly, with total conviction, "and I rejoice to see it at last. Nay, you have also the right to be in love. I could wish you no greater joy, sister. I hope that you shall be."

Cordelia stared at him, shaken by his sincerity.

Then she turned away. "Let us return to the dance, brother. I think I am quite refreshed now."

"Ready for more dancing?" Geoffrey grinned, the seriousness dropping from him like an ill-fitting garment, like a dark cloak. "Aye, sister, so am I."

She paused at the doors. "Geoffrey . . ."

"Aye, sister?"

"The man in scarlet and gold . . . the tall one, with blond hair . . ."

"I have seen him." His voice was carefully neutral.

"Spy upon him for me this evening, will you not? And see if he reaches out to other women with his mind, to touch theirs as he dances with them."

Geoffrey frowned. "A strange request—but surely, sweet sister, I could deny you nothing."

"As long as it was something you had planned to give me already?" Cordelia smiled, remembering the puppy he had given her for her tenth birthday. "Surely, brother. Shall we dance?"

They went in through the door.

Her eyes immediately sought out the tall young man in gold and scarlet. She could see him dancing with an older woman, bantering and laughing. She felt something twisting within her. Had he only been being polite, then?

She turned away, and her gaze sought out Forrest.

She could only stare in shock.

He was dancing with Delilah, the two of them molded so tightly together that they seemed almost to be one entity. His gaze never left her face, or hers his, and even this far removed, there was an almost palpable energy about them, a tension that seemed to crackle all the way across the room.

Cordelia turned away, shaken. Was he, then, a man for all women, and she no more important to him than any other?

Then suddenly, the dance was ended, and the gold-and-scarlet young man was there, elbowing his way through a crowd of her admirers, taking her hand, saying words that pressed her into dancing. The other young men clamored for her attention, but she let herself move into his embrace, into the movements of the dance, let his lips touch hers, his mind reach out to mingle with hers—not thoughts, no, but emotions, his exultation at having her once again in his arms, his joy at the feel of her body against his, giving her a thrill of pleasure such as she had never known before this night.

Therefore, she insisted on dancing once again with Forrest, and as she did, she watched the gold-and-scarlet young man across the hall, dancing with Delilah, hearing his laughter clearly, saw that they were chatting, saw Delilah's flirtatious glances becoming more and more sensuous. The young man only laughed, though, and swung her about, with every appearance of enjoying the dance for its own sake—but without the slightest sign of seeking to enjoy Delilah's favors.

So she danced once more with the gold-and-scarlet cavalier that night, and once more with Forrest. Both times she began with her defenses up, but the music and the movements swayed her, to make her yield to the moment. Somehow she had the feeling she might never know such pleasure again in all her life, so she revelled in the delight of the moment, almost desperately.

Then, suddenly, a great brazen gong was chiming, and a brazen voice with it, booming, "Twelve strokes! Twelve strokes! Midnight! Midnight!"

It was the majordomo, his stentorian tones blending with those of the gong. " 'Tis midnight, and the hour for unmasking! Let truth be known! Let faces be bared, names be declared!"

All the guests clustered together at the center of the hall, giggling and chuckling in anticipation, wondering who would be revealed as whom.

"Let us first introduce our guests!" The august king in purple robes and pasteboard crown, who had been announced as the fabled Charlemagne, stepped up onto the dais at the end of the hall. "You have heard, my friends and neighbors, the occasion for our celebration—my daughter's safe return, thanks to the rescue and protection of two stalwart knights, a gentleman of the greenwood, and a most enchanting lady who did chaperone my daughter. Let me call them now, summon them forth, so that we all may thank them! Sir Geoffrey!"

Geoffrey stepped up beside him on the dais and took off his mask. There was applause all through the hall, and cheering.

"Sir Forrest Elmsford!"

Forrest stepped up beside Geoffrey, unmasking. In the crowd, several ladies were murmuring and "oooh"ing outright.

"Sir Alain!" Sir Julian cried.

No one stepped up.

"Is Sir Alain not here?" demanded Sir Julian. "Seek him out, some of you!" And while the young men turned to the hunt with a cheer, Sir Julian called, "The Lady Cordelia! Step up beside us, and unmask!"

Most of the young men turned back to watch—every

woman was a source of fascination, until they knew who "Lady Elaine" was.

Cordelia stepped up onto the dais, and the young men ripped loose a cheer—but as she lifted her hand to her mask, she saw the scarlet-and-gold young man moving toward the doorway.

What! Didn't he even care to learn who she was?

It seemed he did; he was frozen in place, staring at her. Their gazes met; she lifted her mask.

The young men cheered again. The gold-and-scarlet cavalier stared, then moved toward the doorway again.

Cordelia pointed, her arm a spear. "Stop him!"

The young men shouted, all too glad to obey her whim—but it was Delilah who laid hold of him first, catching his arm and dragging him back. The young man still struggled, seeming to be almost in a panic, but she worked her way hand-over-hand up his arm to the shoulder, undulating as she came.

"Have we found him, then?" Sir Julian called. "Sir Alain! Unmask, young sir!"

The gold-and-scarlet cavalier froze, and Delilah lifted his mask.

It was Alain!

He stood frozen, staring at Cordelia, aghast.

She stood frozen too, staring at him and feeling as though the floor had dropped out beneath her. Alain? She had been flirting with *Alain*?

Alain, being so gallant, so passionate—Alain, with kisses of fire!?! Alain, with his mind touching hers?

Her Alain, flirting so deeply with a strange woman, one whom he had known only as the most beautiful at the ball? Flirting so earnestly, his desire fuelling him with such ardor that his mind had reached out to enfold hers?

Alain, an empath?

She dropped her gaze in confusion, unsure whether to rejoice or to curse, and Alain stood frozen, his face drained of all color.

CHAPTER
~14~

"How could he! How could he?" Cordelia paced back and forth, wringing her hands. "How could he pledge his troth to me, but pay court to a stranger whom he did not even know? How could he do it!"

"Why, with my encouragement," Geoffrey said, leaning back and toying with his wine goblet.

"Your encouragement!" Cordelia turned on him. "Sir! Will you cease to meddle?"

"In this case, no." Geoffrey chose his words carefully.

Cordelia glared at him, taking in the unbuttoned doublet, the chessboard in front of him, the bottle on the table at the side. It seemed odd to her that he should play chess against himself—it was more the sort of thing she would have suspected her little brother Gregory of doing—but still, he did. She noticed the other glass beside the bottle, but dismissed it, being preoccupied with her own difficulties. Surely he only wanted it in case the first glass broke.

He was sitting there grinning at her in his insolence and his arrogance, and she would have liked to scratch his eyes out—but then, she had felt that way about him before. He was, after all, her brother. "How dare you meddle in my romance!"

Geoffrey looked down into his wine goblet, reflecting that for her to use the word "romance" in relation to Alain was a definite improvement. "Let us not put too fine a point on it, sister." He looked up. "Alain has never been a terribly exciting man. In fact, one might almost say he is stuffy."

"Well . . . there is that," Cordelia agreed. "But tonight, he was not!"

"No, not tonight." Geoffrey looked straight into her eyes.

Cordelia stared at him a moment, feeling the blood rush to her face. Then she said, "So that is why you encouraged him."

"Of course, that is why." Geoffrey twirled the glass's stem between his thumb and his forefinger. "And it would seem to me that it succeeded quite well, sister mine. Was he not more enjoyable? Almost, one might say . . . exciting?"

Cordelia turned away, remembering the touch of the gold-and-scarlet stranger, of his lips on hers, of his arm about her, of his mind . . . She shivered, wrapping her arms tightly about herself. "But he did not know it was me! He thought that I was . . . some strange wench. He cared not!"

"Oh, be not such a goose," Geoffrey said crossly. "He knew it was you."

"What!" Cordelia spun around. "How could he know!"

"Why, the simplest way imaginable," Geoffrey replied. "I told him."

Cordelia stared at him in outrage, growing redder and redder. Then she exploded. *"Will you cease to meddle?"* She stalked over to her brother, pounding at him with little fists.

Geoffrey laughed, holding up his arm to fend her off. "Nay, sister, nay, I prithee! Think not of the havoc I have wrought, but only that I had most excellent intentions."

"And we all know which road is paved with those!"

Cordelia relented, seething; her fists did no good against him, anyway. "At least tell me—what of your spying? Did he make advances to any other woman?"

"We-e-e-e-ell . . ."

"The truth, turtle of turpitude!" Cordelia stormed. "Do not plague me, do not torment!"

"I shall not," he sighed. "Oh, Alain had a great deal of fun flirting with other ladies—but only by words, and the occasional touch of a hand. He certainly never sought to kiss one, and never held another close."

Cordelia quieted surprisingly there, staring into his eyes. "Was there . . . ardor?"

"No, not a bit," Geoffrey assured her. "Only a sense of play, a sense of fun. It is the first time I have seen that in Alain. Not even when we were children did he seem to have fun at his games. He was always so deadly serious that he must win, or die." He shook his head. "I cannot understand it."

This, from a man who would rather die than lose, Cordelia knew—but you *did* expect it from Geoffrey, and she had to admit that he had always had a great deal of fun at his games.

She turned away. "Why has he not told us he is an esper?"

"Why, because he does not know it!" Geoffrey said. "Nay, do not look evilly at me! If he cannot hear thoughts, but only feel emotions, how should he know that he has any talent at all? Oh, aye, he may feel what others feel— but any person can be empathetic, if he truly cares about others. Any person who is at all sensitive to others can read the host of unspoken signals in their bearing and demeanor. How should Alain have known that he could do more, that he could actually read their feelings, as you and I read thoughts?"

"Or make another feel his?" Cordelia's voice was very small.

"Ah, that is a greater gift," Geoffrey said softly. "But surely, he could not know that he had done *that*." He paused a second, watching her face, then said, "*Can* he?"

Cordelia was still a moment, then gave a very short nod.

"Well, well, well," Geoffrey breathed. "Mayhap there is hope for our clay-footed suitor yet." He watched his sister for a minute, but she said nothing, only stood with eyes downcast. Geoffrey smiled. "Even so, he would not know that he can sway a person to him, wrapping her in his feelings, whirling both up into . . ." He broke off, seeing her shiver again. "And it may be that he cannot project emotions unless he feels them very strongly. Indeed, he may not realize that he does it at all—for all he knows, 'tis what everyone feels. So if he has the talent, sister, he probably knows it not."

"How is this?" Cordelia cried. "As he usually is, as he has always appeared, I do not find him at all appealing— but I have found him very much so tonight! Never before has he appeared so handsome, so gallant! Never before has he reached out to touch me with his mind!"

"Never before has he danced with you," Geoffrey murmured.

"Oh, he has, in the Christmas reels—but always with only the set, formal steps, never with such ardor! Indeed, he did become, as you say, exciting. Was it simply because he wore a mask?"

"A mask," Geoffrey said judiciously, "and because I insisted that he drink three glasses of wine."

Cordelia frowned. "Surely three glasses of wine are not enough to . . . Oh!"

"Yes," Geoffrey confirmed. "I boosted the alcohol content considerably."

"Alas!" Cordelia looked down into the depths of Geoffrey's wineglass. "Is he only to be a man of romance when he is drunk, then?"

"The wine could not bring it out if it were not there to be brought." Geoffrey looked down into his glass, too. "Be honest. Alain is ordinarily tremendously dull—not a bit of fun, and deadly serious, and far too concerned with his moral rectitude."

Cordelia reflected that a bit more such concern could do

her brother a world of good—but she had to admit it was rather overpowering, in Alain.

Geoffrey looked up at her. "I attribute it to his having been reared with far too great a sense of his own importance as Heir Apparent, and too much insistence on developing his sense of responsibility. No doubt it will make him an excellent king ..."

"Yes," Cordelia said sadly, "but a very boring person."

"And," Geoffrey said, very, very softly, "a stultifying husband." He clucked his tongue. "Beware, sister—or you may lose him to Delilah."

"Oh, I do not wish that! Not that at all!" Cordelia cried, distraught. "Not for my sake alone, no, but for his also!"

"If he could only become fun ... ?" Geoffrey suggested.

"Exciting," Cordelia agreed. "But if he becomes romantic only when he is half drunk? Oh, no, Geoffrey! I cannot have that!" She turned away, chafing her hands. "Yet I would not see him the victim of Delilah, for I know what a vampire that woman must be!"

Geoffrey tilted his head to the side, considering her. "Is that the only reason you do not wish to see him united with the lady?"

Cordelia blushed, embarrassed. "I do not know. Oh, Geoffrey, do not ask me! I do not know!" And she fled in confusion, away out the door.

Geoffrey sighed, gazing down into his wine. Then he shrugged, drank what was left in the glass, and reached out for the decanter. His gaze lighted on the other goblet, and a gleam came into his eye. He lifted the bottle and poured, but only a small amount.

Cordelia fled back to her bedroom and sent out her own clarion call. *Mother! Awaken, I pray you! I have need of you!* Then, a little less stridently, *Mother! Mo-o-o-o-ther!*

The answer came, as though Gwen were still swimming up through layers of sleep to consciousness. *Yes, daughter. What troubles thee?* There was no irritation, no resentment. Weariness, yes—but also alertness, and concern, lest her child be hurt.

Mother, I am so confused! I must talk with you!

I listen. Gwen was already more wakeful.

Nay, not in this fashion. Cordelia wrung her hands. *Face to face. I must be with you, be in your presence! I know it is a hard thing to ask, but—can you meet me?*

At Cromheld's Wood. Aye, surely. Gwen was fully awake now, and all compassion. *In half an hour's time. I shall fly.*

Aye, Mother. I thank you. Cordelia broke the contact and, already feeling a little better, hurried to doff her evening gown and don her travelling dress. Cromheld's Wood was halfway between Sir Julian's manor house and Castle Gallowglass. Cordelia caught up her broomstick, leaped astride it. It sank half a foot, then lifted and shot out through the window.

In the forest clearing half a mile away, Gwen prepared to do the same.

"Don't let her see you, dear." Rod had awakened as soon as he heard Gwen rising from her bedroll beside him in the tent.

"I shall not, husband," she assured him. "Indeed, I shall go past Cromheld's Wood and come back. If she doth see me, she shall think that I have come from Castle Gallowglass."

"Horrible to lie to our children this way, isn't it?"

"I do not lie, strictly," she said primly. "I merely leave matters open for her to believe as she wishes. Good night, husband. Do sleep—there is no need for you to be watchful and wakeful." She bent down to kiss him, lightly and quickly, then turned away to leap sidesaddle onto her broom.

"Good night, love," Rod called softly. He watched her go, diminishing into the night. As to the need for watchfulness and wakefulness, he had his own opinions. He sat up straight, very straight, legs folded in half-lotus. Closing his eyes, he concentrated on the mind of his son Geoffrey. It came clear . . . he could feel . . .

Passion.

Instantly, Rod severed the connection. Well, he certainly

wasn't going to learn anything about what was going on in the manor house that way.

For that matter, neither was Geoffrey.

Instead, Rod focussed on Alain's mind.

This was more difficult for Rod than for his wife or children—he had not been born to it or learned it as he grew up. He'd had the gift inborn within him, but it was only contact with Gwen that had brought it to life. Even then, he had blocked it, until Father Al had helped him to unlock it fully.

So he eavesdropped with his eyes closed, listening, feeling, sensing what Alain sensed . . .

. . . sensed a dream, one that featured his daughter, and that he had no business overhearing.

He severed that connection, too, but sat, wakeful in the dark, waiting, listening.

From a distance, Cordelia saw her mother, a lighter shred of cloud almost, a spark in the moonlight, circling down into Cromheld's Wood. No one else would have thought to look, of course. Cordelia breathed a silent prayer of thanks, and sent her broomstick arrowing after Gwen's.

She darted down to the ground, pulling up short and leaping off, running to her mother, saying "Oh!" and burying her face in Gwen's bosom.

Gwen held her for a timeless moment, folding her arms around Cordelia and holding her, a faint smile on her face. She could feel her daughter's turmoil, could tell what her trouble was—and it was a trouble that Gwen was delighted to discover in Cordelia. She had wondered if the child would ever fall in love, truly in love. There had been a few infatuations, but not nearly enough, to Gwen's mind— and certainly, nothing serious. "Yes, child," she said softly. "Now—what troubles thee? Speak!"

" 'Tis . . . Alain, Mother."

"Ah. Alain."

Then, in halting phrases, with sobs always beneath her voice but never quite in it, Cordelia explained.

She had always been fond of Alain, as she might be of a lapdog. She had always thought of him as being hers, but he had made such a wretched botch of his proposal, being frankly insulting, that she had turned him away.

Gwen found a sawn stump of a tree and sat, listening. She had heard this part before; she waited.

"He has always been so—been so—boring!" Cordelia clenched her fists, jamming them down at her sides. "There is no other word for it, Mother. Oh, aye, I have always had the comfortable feeling that I was quite his superior—but still, he was boring."

"And this . . . Forrest? The bandit?" Gwen interjected softly.

"Aye, the bandit! But he is a gentleman born, Mother!" Cordelia's eyes lit with enthusiasm. "He has been knighted! Yet he has strayed from the straight and narrow, that is quite sure. But he is—exciting. When he holds me, when he kisses me, I melt inside!"

"Yes," Gwen breathed, "yes." But she felt a frisson of fear for her daughter, for she knew that plans to reform a man failed far more often than they succeeded. She knew better than to say so at the moment, though; instead, she said only, "Does not that decide thee, daughter? What else dost need to know?"

"But he is so corrupted, Mother! Can I truly plight my troth to a knight who has abandoned his vows, and has given no sign that he will redeem himself? Who has looks that fairly undress me, aye—but undress every other damsel around him, too! Can I, Mother?" The words were wrenched out of her. "Can I trust him?"

Gwen breathed a hidden sigh of relief, then chose her words carefully. "Looking doth not breed mistrust, daughter."

Cordelia stared, appalled. "You do not mean that Father has regarded other women in that way! Not since he met *you*!"

"Well, no," Gwen admitted, then chose her words carefully again. "Not that I know of. If he hath, he hath certainly been quite circumspect . . ."

"Oh, Mother, you bandy words!" Cordelia said impatiently. "Father has never so much as glanced at another woman since he met you!"

"Not since he met me, aye. But before that, he looked at one other in that way, surely."

"Oh." Cordelia felt obscurely shocked. "Is it . . . anyone I know?"

Gwen debated within herself for a moment, then nodded. "Aye. It was Queen Catharine."

"The Queen!" Cordelia stared.

Gwen laughed softly, catching her daughter's hand with her own. "Oh, she was beautiful once, daughter."

"But she must have been so unlike you!"

"She was," Gwen admitted, "but at the last, it seemed your father preferred my sort, rather than hers."

"And . . . has he looked at her . . . again?"

"Not at all." Gwen smiled, feeling very complacent. "Or at least, not in the way we speak of. He doth look upon her as he would upon any friend, nothing more—and considerably less, for he must be ever wary, never sure when she will turn upon him."

Cordelia giggled, nodding. "Indeed, all men feel that way with her—even King Tuan, does he not?"

"Well, mayhap," Gwen admitted. "It pleases me to think that it may add spice to their marriage. I hope that I am right."

Cordelia sobered again, dropping her gaze, dropping her voice. "That is what I seek, too—one who will ever be true to me, who will never look at another woman once he has become my husband." She looked up at her mother. "But perhaps I am not so alluring as you were."

"And as I still am, to thy father," Gwen told her, with some asperity, "though only to your father, I doubt not. As to yourself, though—you do not know the limits of your allure yet, my dear, nor did I, at your age. Have you learned nothing of them, on this quest of yours?"

"Well . . ." Cordelia blushed, lowering her gaze again. "Tonight . . . I did seem to be . . . something of a favorite . . . with the young men. . . ."

"Show me," Gwen said.

Cordelia closed her eyes, remembering the sight of all the young men crowding around her, clamoring for her attention, for a dance with her. She remembered quick snatches of each dance, the partners changing with dizzying rapidity—though Alain's masked visage, and Forrest's, kept recurring. The scene was very vivid; she could see it all again, almost smell the flowers decking the hall, hear the chatter, the gay laughter . . .

Gwen gave a sigh of satisfaction. "Oh, I rejoice to see it! I knew thou wert a beauty, daughter, but I have waited long for the men of this world to see it!"

"And Father has prayed that they will not, I am sure," Cordelia answered, with irony. "Yet what am I to do now, Mother?" She spread her hands. "Not only one man has seen some beauty in me, but two!"

"Two?" Gwen frowned. "You speak of Alain?"

"Aye." Cordelia stood up and began pacing again. "I had thought that he regarded me only as his property, even as I thought of him. I believed that he had come to claim that which he thought was his by right of birth—and mayhap he did . . . But now . . ."

"Now what?" Gwen said; and again, "Show me, daughter, if it is not too private."

Cordelia closed her eyes and let herself remember the dances with Alain, his arm about her, his body pressing against hers . . . She broke off the memory. "More than that I will not show, Mother."

"As thou shouldst not," Gwen agreed. "I think I can guess the rest of it." Inwardly, she was delighted. "So, then. *Two* men make thee melt inside; there are *two* who make thee guess at pleasures thou wottest not of, not yet."

"Two. Aye." Cordelia looked down at her twisting hands. "I would never have thought that one of them would have been Alain!"

" 'Tis surprising," Gwen admitted, "though pleasant. And the other? What is he like, this paragon?"

"He is scarcely a paragon! Indeed, he is not at all suitable!" Cordelia cried. "Oh, aye, he is well formed—but he behaves abominably. Nay, any knight who would stoop to outlawry should no longer be called a knight, and is certainly no fit husband for a gentle lady!"

Gwen gazed off into space. "Do not think that thou shalt change him, daughter. No woman can ever change a man to become what she doth wish him to be. *Marriage* will change him, aye—not all at once, not in the moment the priest pronounces thee wed, not in a month, not even in a year, but gradually, little by little, he will change—as wilt thou thyself. Thou canst but hope that he will change more closely to that which thou dost wish him to be."

She looked back at her daughter. "Though love and affection, and thine unceasing reassurance, building him up in his own eyes, will make him stronger inside, and will help most wondrously. Still, when all is said and done, thou canst not know for certain what he will become; thou mayest but be sure that he *will* change, and if he doth love thee as well as thou dost love him, then, with good fortune, thou wilt grow together, to become more like one another."

Cordelia gazed into her eyes. "I think that you speak from knowledge and life, not from faith."

Gwen nodded slowly. "By Gramarye's standards, thy father was not at all suitable as a husband—nay, not suitable for any but a peasant. He had no family here, seest thou, and though he claimed to be nobly born, none could prove nor disprove it, for his folk were far, far way indeed, even on another star. And he was an adventurer—none can deny that, though 'twas for the good of other people he adventured, not for estates and a fortune. Surely he had no inheritance, other than Fess and his ship, for he was a second son of a second son."

She smiled at her daughter. "Then again, I too was not the most eligible. I was, by all accounts, a foundling, raised by elves, with only the knowledge that my mother had been gently born, and had died at my birth. *Her* father had been a knight, but he was dead, too, as was all her family. Oh, the elves raised me with assurances that my father was noble, but never told me his name—even though he still lives." For a moment, her eyes crinkled with mirth, though she was quick to hide it.

Cordelia was rather irritated. Whatever the jest was, her mother was not sharing it—and it had very little to do with her problems of the moment. "But did you and Father grow together? Or did you grow apart?"

"By Heaven's blessing, we have grown together," Gwen answered, "though there is no assurance that all the changes have been for the better. At least I had no concern that he would spend more time with friends at the tavern than he would with me—for he had no friends here, and had become persona non grata with the Crown, by the style in which he ended the first rebellion against Catharine. Surely the two of us were ever together, and rejoiced in one another's company. After our sojourn in Tir Chlis, though, he changed, and changed very badly."

"Yes, I remember," said Cordelia. "His temper . . ."

Gwen nodded. "Yet still were we in love. That, and the madness that came upon him when he ate the witch-moss chestnut, which still comes upon him ever and anon— those have been sore trials. And this was a most goodly man among men when we met, mind you!"

"These have been heavy burdens in truth," Cordelia murmured.

"They have indeed. Yet the elves had warned me as I grew that such as this happened to the best of men, from time to time—and women too, daughter! We are human, do not forget!"

"Trials that ended, you could bear." Cordelia came and sat by her mother, taking her hand to hold. "What was it that you could not bear, then?"

"His ever-abiding conviction that he was not good enough for me. Nay, say naught, do not deny it! It is there, and if thou dost think on it, thou shalt see it. This is the trial that does not end—that ever and anon must I build up his inner picture of himself, to shore it up, lest he leave me, ashamed of his weakness, ashamed of his lack of Talent, of his ugliness."

"But none of those are true!" Cordelia protested. "He is

comely even now, and must have been far more so when he was young! Aye, in a rough-hewn way, but comely still! And his talents have kept this land of Gramarye balanced 'twixt tyranny and lawlessness—though you have been of great aid to him there . . ."

"I have," Gwen said, "though I would not have undertaken it of myself, but would have left governance to the Queen, and I do not think that she would have called upon me, for she did not know me well—and I was too old to feel easy among the Royal Coven . . . Nay, it is your father who has brought me to such cares about governance, and it is his plans and strategies that have kept Catharine and Tuan on their thrones. He is a most puissant man, my dear, but he believes it not."

Gwen shrugged. "He doth believe that his success hath been good fortune, or that at most, he hath been able to bring others together, and it is they who have managed the troubles that have arisen, not he. Left to his own devices, he doth not believe well of himself. This has been my sorest trial—to always, always give and give, unceasing. But what I have received from him, in affection and outpouring of his love, is at least as much as I have given."

For a moment, Cordelia wondered fleetingly what trials her father would tell of in his lifelong courtship of her mother—but the thought was fleeting indeed, for it had little to do with her own troubles. "But such giving must be to only one, Mother. How shall I choose? And if I choose wrongly, how much grief shall I bring to them both?"

Gwen sighed. "This is a family disease, my dear—being too serious, too concerned for others' welfare. Nay, we seem to have the need, your father and I, to take others' burdens on our shoulders—and not the burdens of one person, or a few, but of all those on this Isle of Gramarye. Still, 'tis what has made us noble, I think—the feeling of obligation for others."

Cordelia became very thoughtful. "If I had not known you were speaking of us Gallowglasses, Mother, I would have thought 'twas Alain." She lifted her head swiftly, sharply. "Am I as dull as he?"

Gwen laughed softly. "Most certainly you are not, my dear! Your moods change like the sun's light in a field of sailing clouds. As soon as a man might begin to think you are serious, you suddenly laugh, and are gay. Nay, you have always been frolicsome, and have a sense of playfulness that Alain doth lack. Your own mercurial temperament offsets his stolidity quite well—and that is one of the reasons why you are well matched."

"Well matched?" Cordelia gazed into Gwen's eyes. "We should marry, then?"

"Oh, nay, nay!" Gwen raised a hand. "Simply because thou dost well together, because thou canst function well in tasks shared, does not mean you should marry. Only love can mean that. If thou dost love him, and he doth love thee, then wed him. If he doth not, be his friend, be one of the pillars upon which he can rest his kingdom—but do not be his wife. What can tell you that you should marry? Only love, my dear—only love."

Cordelia reddened. "It may be that love is telling me to wed someone else, Mother."

"If it *may* be, then it *is* not," Gwen said firmly.

"But do I love *them*?" Cordelia cried. "And do I love one, or do I love both?"

"Why, rejoice!" Gwen said softly. "Two men desire thee, two men kindle a burning within thee—and one of them is a rogue, while the other is a prince in every sense of the word. What choice is there, daughter?"

"But how can I be sure of either of them?" Cordelia cried. "I have seen how they look at that . . . that cat, Delilah! How I have matched her in beauty, I do not know, but I seem to have, this last night—yet I can surely never be as seductive as she! How can I be sure that either of them would cleave unto me, and not unto such as her? Can true love be a true defense? And which is my *true* love?"

"Ah." Gwen nodded slowly, her eyes glowing. "If you do not know yet, daughter, you must not say yes to either of them."

"Yes to which question?" Cordelia asked, guarded.

"Any question! Thou must not say yes to any question

that either doth ask thee!" Gwen said severely. "Not until thy whole heart, and thy whole body, and thy whole soul do answer 'Yes!' before thy lips and tongue have dreamed it."

"But how shall I know when that comes?"

"Thou shalt know, daughter," Gwen assured her. "Believe me, thou shalt know. But if thou must have some guide, here it is: If thou dost find thyself even asking the question, 'Am I in love?' then thou art not. When thou art in love, thou wilt know it beyond the shadow of a doubt. If thou dost wonder if thou art in love, then thou art not. Aye, if thou art in love, thou wilt know it—and there is no more to be said."

"Truly, good mother?" Cordelia asked, in a very small voice—and for a moment, Gwen saw her as a little girl again, a five-year-old clinging to Gwen's skirts. She stood up, smiling, and embraced her child. "It was true for me, my daughter—oh, how it was true, and is! I cannot say what was true for others, only for myself. If it is love, thou wilt know it. It will not be, 'Am I in love?' No, the voice within thee shall say, 'So this is love!' "

"Yet how if I love two?" Cordelia asked, still quite small. "And how if both love me?"

"Wait," Gwen advised. "Wait until thine heart has spoken for one, and only one, for the other is a liar. Wait, daughter—only wait."

In the sitting room of her suite, Chief Agent Finister paced the floor, still disguised as Lady Delilah. The mask of innocence was dropped; the clinging vine had fallen away, to be replaced by the whiplash. Her eyes flashed fire, every movement tense with barely suppressed rage.

Her lieutenants stood in respectful silence against the walls of the room, three of them men, two women. The men were nearly salivating, feeling themselves galvanized by the mere sight of their leader, felt every cell of their bodies respond, even now, when the lady was not being at all seductive—even now, when she was enraged and might very well attack one of them with lethal intent. But she was completely beautiful; every line, every gesture, every curve kindled desire within them.

The two women watched in mixed awe and envy—awe that a woman had gained the foremost position of power among the anarchists of Gramarye; envy of that power, and of the beauty that she had used as a tool and a weapon, to rise to that position.

"How dare she outshine me!" Delilah fumed as she paced the room. "How dare she win the Prince's eye—and how dare he be merely courteous to me, yet burning with ardor for *her*!"

No one dared answer.

"We must do away with her!" Delilah spun on her heel, jabbing a finger at one of the women. "Did Gerta take her that cup of poisoned wine?"

"Five or ten minutes ago, Chief," the woman said quickly. "As soon as you ordered it, the wine was prepared and sent up."

Delilah nodded, eyes burning. "We still dare not attempt an open assault—these Gallowglasses have proved too powerful in the past. But a poisoned cup, here in our headquarters, where everyone around them is one of our agents—aye, here we may have at them." She burst into rage again. "Where *is* the silly goose?"

There was a knock at the door. One of the men reached to swing it open, and Gerta entered.

"Well?" Delilah pounced upon her. "Did she drink it?"

"N-n-no, Chief."

"Not drink it! Did you not press it upon her?"

"I . . . I couldn't, Chief. She wasn't there."

"Not there!" Delilah halted, staring. Then, finally, she probed with her own mind, her eyes glazing for a moment. It was true—wherever Cordelia was, she was beyond Delilah's range.

Chief Agent Finister was a very powerful esper, but her range was very limited. Within that range, she was formidable, especially in the area of projective telepathy. She excelled at the crafting of witch-moss, and at inserting her own commands and thoughts into another person's mind at so deep a level that it amounted to instant hypnosis. This also made her able to kindle passion in any man, to make herself seem infinitely desirable. It was this last trait that she had used to win her office—coupled with extortion and assassination.

"Her broomstick was gone, too, Chief," Gerta supplied. "After all, she *is* a witch."

"She could be anywhere!" Delilah threw up her hands in disgust, turning on her heel to pace again. "Did the sentries not see her go? Did no one see where she sped?"

"None, Chief."

"Of course not!" Then, suddenly, Delilah stopped, lifting her head, a strange, feral gleam coming into her eye. "She is gone, she is fled. Now might we slay the Prince and be one step closer to loosing anarchy upon Gramarye!"

"He has a younger brother," one of the men protested.

"And when he comes of age to be susceptible to me, I shall slay him likewise! Then, when the King and Queen die, the barons shall vie to see who shall have the Crown—and war shall be loosed upon this island! Let us not waste the opportunity! Creep into his chamber, stab your daggers into his heart, run him through with your swords!" Her voice sank low, with an intensity that raised the hairs of her lieutenants. "For *I will see his blood*!"

Her men stared at her, appalled. Not a single one of them doubted the true reason for this murder. Oh, surely, it was excellent policy for the anarchists. Baron against baron, duke against duke—a chaos of war out of which a few strong warlords would arise. They would tear the land apart in their own turn until the peasants, sickened by war, would rise up and cut them down.

Then, guided by the anarchist cells, they would establish their own local governments which, carefully guided, would wither away, and the land would be left without government, without law, without oppression, guided only by custom and the natural morality inherent in each human being, the innate nobility of the species. This was their dream.

Of course, they blinded themselves to a few unpleasant truths that disagreed with their vision. They ignored some of the more base impulses of human beings, and the savage aspects of the natural social rules that arise even in the animal kingdom, plus the fact that there are always unbalanced humans who are motivated more by greed than by concern for their fellows—but all dreamers overlook a few things they do not wish to gaze upon.

Still, those reasons of policy were scarcely what had motivated Delilah to order this assassination. All of them knew that she had intended to captivate Alain, then marry him. What would have happened then was open to speculation. Many of them suspected that her real goal was personal power, and that she would forget the anarchist cause in an instant when it had served her purpose—or even turn against them, seek to wipe them out, as threats to her own position.

That didn't affect their loyalty, of course. It was based on fear and lust, on the men's side, and on the women's, on admiration and fear.

So none of them really believed Alain's assassination was a matter of policy. They all knew that Hell hath no fury like a woman scorned, and that, somehow, incredibly, unbelievably, Prince Alain had scorned their leader, the Lady Delilah, Chief Agent Finister, whom any one of the men would have given his life for—if, before death, he could have shared the ecstasies of her bed.

"His comrade," one of them ventured, "Geoffrey Gallowglass. He is a warlock, and a powerful one."

"Moreover," said another, "he is highly skilled with weapons—perhaps the most expert in all the land."

Delilah smiled, with cruel anticipation. "I made an appointment with him, to play a game of chess; he expects me even now."

The men all stiffened in jealousy.

"But he shall not find me." Delilah turned to one of her female lieutenants. "His weakness is women. Send him your most voluptuous, most accomplished assistant—and when he is deep in his revels with her, ignoring the world around him and least expecting attack, drive a dagger under his ribs. Then bring me his head."

The men all shuddered, but their jealousy was the only guarantee she needed.

"And what of the bandit Forrest?" one of the men protested. "Might he not come to the Prince's aid?"

"I doubt it, since they both sue for the same woman." Delilah tossed back her head, eyelids drooping. "But we shall make sure of him. I shall see to the bandit myself. He is not worth killing, that one—but he is certainly worth a few moments' attention." She glided out of the room.

The men all stared after her.

The women knew why Delilah was willing to do it—it was her victory over Cordelia, if not as she had originally planned it.

At that moment, each of the men would have slain Forrest happily, if by doing so, they could have changed places with him.

But since they could not, they went to slay Alain.

CHAPTER
~15~

Alain dreamed that Delilah was bending over him, loosening the fastenings of her gown—but she changed even as she loosened, becoming Cordelia; and even as she was sliding the gown down over her hips, she was murmuring with excitement, "Alain! Alain, wake up!"

But why was her voice urgent instead of seductive? And why were her ears growing into points? In fact, why was she turning into an elf?

"Crown Prince! Awaken!"

Alain's eyelids snapped open. It must have been a dream. Cordelia would never address him by his title.

He lay very still, and heard the voice again. "Waken, Crown Prince!"

Alain lay unmoving, his gaze flicking about the room. Then he saw the brownie woman, hanging from the bed-post, calling down, "Crown Prince, awaken!" She glanced nervously up at the door. "Waken, Prince Alain!"

"I have waked." Alain sat up.

"Praise be!" the elf breathed. "They come to slay thee, Prince! Catch up thy sword and flee!"

More than his sword—Alain, like most medieval folk, slept naked. He leaped out of bed and seized his hose. Fortunately, he had left all the points tied, and had only unbuckled the belt. Now he had only to wrestle the hose on, not pausing to smooth them out, and buckle up.

"Quickly, quickly!" the brownie woman hissed. "Wilt thou lose thy life for a pair of drawers? Surely 'tis better to live naked than to die clothed!"

If they had sent a male elf, Alain probably would have agreed—but as it was, he was embarrassed to be seen naked by a woman. Standing up, he buckled his belt, then caught up his baldric, throwing it over his head and drawing both sword and dagger.

Just in time. The door swung open, slowly, without a squeak.

Alain held his breath and stepped back against the wall. His impulse was to leap out and start stabbing, but he needed to be sure that the men were truly hostile before he would let himself strike a blow that might kill. If they were, he intended to make sure he had them all in sight before he began work.

One . . . two . . . and they held swords and daggers drawn! Three . . . four . . . five . . . none more came in; they moved toward the bed.

Silent as a cat, Alain circled opposite their direction, slipping behind the tapestry that hung on the wall. Peering around its edge, he watched the five men gather around the bed in the darkness. What cowards were they! So many men, to slay one poor sleeping knight! Anger boiled within him at the treachery. He tried to let it ebb, but not too far, for it held at bay the fear that had begun to pool in his stomach. He remembered what Geoffrey had told him—that all the swordsmen Alain had ever fought would never have dared to beat the Crown Prince. Had the bandits known who he was? Had the witch's henchmen?

But these men did not, or if they did, they did not care. Alain realized that he was about to discover whether or not he really was a capable swordsman. Why they wished to kill him, he did not ask—there would be time enough to understand it later.

"Light," the first man hissed.

A beam speared out. Alain blinked with surprise—he had not heard the sliding of a metal shutter, nor did he smell the flame-heated tin of a lantern. What manner of men were these?

He stepped out from behind the tapestry, circling behind their backs toward the door.

"He is fled!" the leader hissed. "Where . . . ?"

"There!" another man shouted, his finger spearing at Alain.

The leader spun wide-eyed, as Alain threw himself forward in a lunge, howling, "Havoc!"

The nearest man fell back, barely getting his sword around in time to parry—which was perfect, because Alain whirled his thrust into a slash, coming in low and cutting upward. The man cried out and fell back, holding his hands to his side. Alain braced himself and yanked the sword free as the man fell—but even as he did, he was catching the second swordsman's blade on his dagger. Not quite well enough—the blade nicked his shoulder, but Alain ignored the pain. He didn't even take time to riposte, only pulled the sword straight out of one man and stabbed it into the next. The second's sword managed to parry at the very last second, but Alain slipped his blade around the parry and thrust, scoring the man's thigh. The man howled and collapsed.

Alain sprang aside as the third man lunged. The edge scored the Prince's ribs and the pain burned, but he ignored it and swung backhanded, striking the man on the back of the head with the heel of his hilt even as he raised his dagger to block an assault by the fourth man. He leaped back as the two remaining men crowded him, their blades flickering. He parried, blocked, then slammed a kick into the midriff of the nearest and spun away toward the door.

The leader shouted and charged at him. He leaped aside

at the last second, and the man slammed into the wall. Before he could recover, Alain was out the door.

The leader shouted a curse, and his thrown dagger struck Alain on the back of the head. Dizzy for a second, he reeled back against the wall. Then his head cleared, and he leaped to his right, plastered himself back against the wall—and sure enough, the leader came charging out, yelling, "Stop him! Guards! Stop that man!"

Alain caught him in the right shoulder with his dagger. The man spun around, saw Alain's blade chopping down, and sprang aside with a howl of fright. His sword fell from numbed fingers—and one of the other men dragged himself out the door, gasping for breath, but cutting at Alain with his sword.

Alain leaped aside, then cut low, slicing the man's calf. It would have been a foul blow in a foil match, but here, it spared his opponent's life. The man cried out and collapsed.

But the leader was running away down the hall, crying, "A rescue! A rescue! Seize him!"

Alarm, and the old instinct to chase when you're winning, almost sent Alain after him, but prudence dictated that he find an escape.

"Flee, King's Son!" cried the brownie from the lintel.

In answer came shouting from around the corner, and the sound of boots running. The rattle of steel punctuated the drumming.

Alain whirled about and ran down the hallway, not knowing where he was going, a wild exhilaration beating in his breast, for he was alive, and his enemies were disabled. He decided that perhaps he was as good a swordsman as he had thought.

A section of panelled wall swung out before him. He jarred to a halt, dagger up, sword on guard, panting, the feet and the shouting swelling closer behind him. Alain stood, ready for whatever danger would come at him out of this secret door . . .

An elf leaped through, crying, "Inside, King's Son! Quickly, ere they come in sight of thee!"

Alain didn't argue. He ducked down and shot into the hole behind the panelling. The door clapped shut behind him, and he knelt in the darkened space, holding his breath, though his lungs clamored for air. The pounding feet came closer, the shouting was louder and louder, and his heart was hammering within him . . .

Then the feet were fading away, and the shouting with them.

Alain let the stale air explode out of his lungs, and gasped in fresh.

Little lights suddenly sprang up all about him. He pushed himself back against the wall, his blades coming up to guard, then saw elfin faces by the candle-sized flames of miniature torches.

"We will lead you to safety, Crown Prince!" the largest of them said. He was quite tall by their standards, a foot and a half high, with a look of incipient mayhem in his eyes.

"You are the Puck!" Alain panted.

"I am, and come to save you from the peril into which your own foolish glands have brought you. Will you come?"

But Alain stayed where he was, pushing himself upright slowly, wary of a ceiling that might strike his head. "Nay," he gasped, "I cannot flee!"

"What nonsense is this?" Puck demanded. "Let us hear no foolishness of proving your valor, youngling! This is no time to play games of honor! Come, and come quickly!"

"I cannot," Alain said. "The Lady Cordelia . . . if they have sought to slay me, they may seek to slay her . . . I must find her!"

Puck calmed, staring at him. "Even so," he said.

For a moment, it occurred to Alain to worry about Geoffrey . . .

Then he realized that he was being ridiculous.

"Follow," the elf told him. "I will lead you to a place that is near to her chamber."

"I follow," Alain answered. He slipped down the passageway after the ring of fairy lights, barely able to see where his next step should be. "I thank you, Wee Folk."

Puck exchanged glances with one of the other elves. It was rare that they met a mortal with a proper sense of gratitude. "Thou dost credit to thy parents and thine up-bringing," Puck answered.

Then, suddenly, he came to a halt. Tiny feet pattered toward them, a little torch bobbing up and down, lighting a brownie's face.

"What moves?" Puck demanded.

"Not the Lady Cordelia," the elf answered. "Her room is empty; she is fled."

"Thank heavens!" Alain sighed, then suddenly stiffened. "Or has she been taken?"

"We shall seek," the elf promised.

"Aye, we shall find her, if any may," Puck said. "Come now, King's Son. Thou must needs leave this house with us."

"Not until I know that she is fled, not taken!" Alain protested. "Nay, do not stay by me, good folk, but go seek her indeed! Although, if you would be so good as to leave me a light, I shall be safe enough here. Do you seek her out . . ." Then, as an afterthought, "And you might spare a thought for her brother. Warn him, too—I doubt not he shall need it."

Puck regarded him for a moment, weighing his instructions against one another. The lad was safe enough—and he did need to prove himself to himself . . . "We shall attempt it. Are you sure you shall be well, though, King's Son?"

"I am certain," he said. "Go. I shall amuse myself by prowling these secret hallways, to discover where they lead. Who knows but it may be of benefit?"

"Even as thou sayest," Puck pronounced. "Take care, and do not seek to fight a whole army by thyself."

"I shall not," Alain promised.

Of course, he didn't say anything about a squadron.

Puck went away with his little troop, well aware that he could not depend on the Prince to play it safe—not at his age, or with his overdeveloped sense of responsibility (or his being in love).

Of course, Puck wasn't about to let him really be alone.

Alain thought he was, though, and felt the sense of abandonment creeping in. He threw it off and, lit only by the miniature torch (which, he noticed, was not burning down at all), prowled the secret passage. What he was really seeking, of course, was another door into the manor house's rooms—in fact, as many doors as he could locate. If Cordelia was in the slightest danger, he intended to leap to her defense by the quickest route he could find.

Cordelia, of course, was in no danger at all, except, perhaps, from her own emotions.

She flew in through her chamber window as the sky was lightening, feeling bone-weary, but with some measure of peace within her. She was emotionally wrung out and ready to sleep until noon, at the very least—but, as she was about to take off her travelling dress, she paused, a vagrant image of Alain drifting into her mind. It was not the Alain she had always known, pompous and self-important, but the Alain she had met the night before, the masked face with the gentle but ardent kisses . . .

Then she remembered his face, staring at her aghast when he had been unmasked. She smiled, feeling very tender. She decided to seek him out, for she felt a sudden need to talk with him, heart to heart, mind to mind . . . perhaps even breasts to chest . . .

And if he was asleep? Well, so much the better. It would not hurt to catch him at a bit of a disadvantage. She laughed softly to herself and slipped out of her room.

Alain's chamber was all the way at the other end of the hall. She wondered idly who was his neighbor, and glanced at the panel next to Alain's.

Somehow, she was sure it was Delilah's.

Suddenly suspicious, she stepped up to Alain's door, hoping that she would not find the chamber empty. She turned the knob very quietly, pushed the door open, and slipped in.

The empty bed was almost a slap in her face.

For a moment, she raged inside—until she saw the overturned chair, the slashes in the tapestry, and realized that those stains on the floor were blood.

Jealously was instantly replaced by horror. What had happened to Alain? She whirled out of the room. If anyone knew, it would be Delilah.

Without the slightest attempt at discretion, she slammed through the door and strode in, ready to beard her rival in her den—or in her bed, which, with Delilah, was probably much the same thing . . .

But she was not there.

Cordelia stared, completely taken aback. She stepped farther in, then halted, amazed at the splendor of the sitting room, at its spaciousness, its silken hangings, the depth and softness of the carpet on the floor, the grace and delicacy of the occasional tables and upholstered chairs.

Then she looked more closely, for signs of the night's events. There was only the one glass, with wine dregs, sitting on a table by a chair, and another that seemed to have scarcely been touched, by the door. Cordelia was tempted, for she was thirsty, then remembered that Delilah might have sipped from it, and turned her back on it.

She glanced at the hearth; there were still coals glowing there. Then she surveyed the walls, all hung with rose-colored silk; there might be a platoon of guards hidden behind them. She listened with her mind, but found no one nearby, and ignored anyone outside the room, her attention focussed only on its mistress. The furniture was white and gold, and the carpet was Oriental, with patterns of a dusky rose on a cream background.

But there was no one there.

Her heart began to hammer within her breast. She wasn't sure whether she was more afraid of not finding Alain at all, or of finding him in Delilah's bed. Silent as a morning zephyr, she slipped across the carpet to the door in the far wall, turned the handle as quietly as she could, pushed it open, slipped in . . .

And saw no one.

The bed had not even been slept in. Now, suddenly, the rage of jealousy boiled up within her, but with terror right behind it. What *had* the witch done with Alain! Cordelia suddenly became tremendously afraid that when she found Delilah, she would find Alain, too. Why else would they both be gone from their beds?

She fled out into the hallway, then halted, in a quandary—where could she go? Where could she search?

Forrest! He would know! The saturnine, hot-eyed, bearded face of the bandit chieftain rose up before her mind's eye. She could depend on him to help her, surely, as he had in the woods, when Delilah's "sister" had attacked, with her henchmen. Certainly, if he were really in love with Cordelia, he would leap at the chance to help her—even if it meant helping his rival, too.

Which door was his? She did not know, but she suspected. She went to the other side of Delilah's door and turned the knob, softly, ever so softly ...

She recognized Forrest's boots and the costume he had worn as Dionysus, the night before. His doublet lay upon a stool—but that was all there was. His bed was empty; like Delilah's it had not been slept in.

Like Delilah's ...

Suspicion reared up in her mind again, anger roiling behind it. Who else? What had been happening while she had been talking with her mother?

She turned away to the door, seething. If Geoffrey was gone, too ...

Then she told herself she was being silly. Surely the strumpet could not seduce more than one man in a night—or a half-night, for the ball had ended an hour after midnight. She strode out the door and down the hall to Geoffrey's room.

She was about to burst in, but halted at the last second, though she was not sure why. She reached out with her mind instead ...

And almost collapsed with relief. To find only a dream of him riding, riding with the wind in his hair, wild and free, was a vastly pleasant surprise. She sighed, then turned the handle and opened the door as quietly as she could. She would wake him gently, tell him that she needed his help . . .

But what of the woman who lay beside him?

And the two armed men who lay sleeping on the floor, just inside the door?

What sort of twisted pleasures had her brother been pursuing, anyway?

Cordelia stared, outraged. Then all the morning's anger boiled up within her, and she strode across the floor, stepping over the two sleeping men and hissing, "Hussy!" She reached down, grasping a smooth, bare shoulder and snarling, "Strumpet!"

The girl opened her eyes halfway, a lazy smile on her lips, stretching with a sinuous undulation, turning her head up to look . . .

Then she saw Cordelia, and her eyes flew wide in shock.

"Get out from here!" Cordelia snapped. "Now! Instantly! Ere I claw your eyes blind and pull your hair out by the roots!"

The woman sat bolt upright, but her eyes narrowed as she clutched the bedclothes to her. She was in her early twenties, Cordelia guessed, and was quite well put together—lushly, in fact. "I am not your servant . . ."

Cordelia's hand came around with a ringing slap. The girl cried out and fell back, and it was Geoffrey's hands who held her up. "Peace, sister. 'Tis not your affair, after all."

"Nor was Alain yours!" Cordelia spat. "Out, tearsheet, or I shall do you more mischief than a whole tribe of elves!"

The girl darted a glance at the two men. "Bardolph! Morley! Aid me!"

The men lay still, not even snoring.

The woman stared in horror—and, for a moment, so did Cordelia.

"They are men who prefer to watch, not do, I suspect," Geoffrey said, very nonchalantly. "They crept in whiles we did disport ourselves, and I had some wish for privacy, so I put them to sleep."

The girl's glance swung up to him in fright, and she squirmed away from him toward the edge of the bed. "But . . . your embrace was so ardent, your kisses so fevered . . ."

"That I might overlook an intruder?" Geoffrey smiled, showing his teeth. "I am never so besotted that I cannot hear someone who fairly shouts his gloating glee, as their minds did."

"And you cast them into sleep without even . . . even . . ."

"Batting an eye?" Geoffrey shrugged. " 'Twas only a moment's distraction."

"Now will you get hence!" Cordelia raged. "Nay, do not pause to dress—take your tawdry garments with you, and get *out*!"

The girl didn't stay to argue any further—she leaped out of bed, catching up her clothing, and darted out the door with only one backward look of fright.

Cordelia gazed after her with more than a little contempt, seasoned by jealousy. "Your taste surely runs to the baroque, brother."

"A good guest takes what is offered." Geoffrey sounded amused.

Seething, Cordelia spun about, to see him propped up on one elbow, the sheet still draped across his hips, watching with an expression of great interest.

"You curmudgeon!" Cordelia said, with every ounce of contempt she could muster. "You lewd man, you libertine, you rake! How many women must you debauch before you realize the harm you do?"

Geoffrey started to answer.

"Nay, tell me not!" Cordelia snapped. "Great affairs of state cannot wait while you slake your desires!"

Geoffrey stared up at her, thinking that his sister was really very impressive—and had probably saved him a deal of trouble in disentangling him from one more set of lingering clutches. But he said only, "You may be sure that I dally only when there is time."

"Oh, do you indeed!" Cordelia snapped. "Nay, you are

like a dog who forgets all else when he scents one trace of a bitch in heat, and forsakes all duties to go padding after her, drooling!"

Geoffrey frowned. "Would you have me be a celibate? Nay, a monk, perhaps, never to enjoy the company of any woman who was not a nun!"

" 'Twas scarcely a nun who left here but now, and 'twas far more than her company that you did enjoy! Nay, while you did 'dally,' your friend Alain was beset by armed men and, for all I know, nearly slain!"

Geoffrey was out of bed, somehow contriving to slip his breeches on without completely giving up the cover of the sheet. "Armed men? Why, could you not fend them off, sister? Nay, do not answer—'twas not your place! A curse upon me, that I was not there!" He froze, staring up at her, frowning. "Nay, surely any number of armed men who came against him while you were watchful would have died in the attempt!"

Cordelia felt a stab of guilt, but told herself sternly that she was not Alain's keeper—not yet.

Geoffrey pulled on his doublet and buttoned it. "Therefore, if he was taken, you were not there."

"No," Cordelia said, biting down on shame. "I was not."

Geoffrey stilled, watching her. "Do not blame yourself, sister. You are not Alain's watchdog; you were not set to that task. Nay, it is the man who is supposed to guard the woman, not the woman the man. Yet if you did not witness it, how do you know he was set upon?"

"Why," she said, "because his room is in disarray, with tapestries slashed and furniture overturned—and there was blood on the floor!"

Geoffrey was moving toward the door before she finished the sentence, buckling his sword belt. "Proof enough. Let us go."

"How shall we find him?" Cordelia wailed. "And we must find him right quickly, for he may be in mortal danger!"

"His soul, mayhap," Geoffrey agreed, "but I doubt that his body is in any peril at all, blood or no blood. The man is a most excellent swordsman, Cordelia—he held me off for a good five minutes! Nay, we have only to find the Lady Delilah . . ." He was about to add, *and we shall find Alain*, but caught himself and said instead, ". . . for she will know where the bodies are, dead and living."

"Her chamber is empty," Cordelia said.

Geoffrey shrugged impatiently, opening the door and ushering her through. "That means only that she is not in her chamber. We shall find her, and she will know where Alain lies." He didn't like the sound of that, so he added, "Or stands and fights—where we may join him."

Alain stood deep within the manor house's bowels and had finally found a door, larger than the others, that would let him into the Great Hall. He opened it only a fraction of an inch, and was assailed with the sounds of men's voices barking commands to one another, while they scurried to put away the tables and take down all the decorations. It seemed odd that they would be so prompt about tidying up after the ball, but Alain didn't really give the matter much thought, only edged the door closed again and stood on the other side, sword in hand, waiting, listening to Sir Julian's voice bawling orders to search and to guard. Alain's face hardened at the words; the old man was commanding his men to seek out the Lady Cordelia and hale her before him, and to bring her brother with her, dead or alive.

Well. There was an outside chance that, if enough of them leaped upon Geoffrey in his sleep, they might be able to take him prisoner—but Alain doubted it mightily, especially since he had no doubt the elves were guarding Geoffrey as well as they had guarded him.

Cordelia, however, was another matter. She was so small, so fragile! Even with all her witch-powers, she could not fly if they kept her from her broomstick. Geoffrey, if worse came to worse, could simply disappear—but Cordelia could not, just as warlocks could not make brooms fly.

Alain stood in the darkness and the dank chill, shivering, lighted only by one elf-light. He hefted his sword in his hand, waiting for the moment when he would hear Sir

Julian's voice address the Lady Cordelia, when he would have the chance to leap to her aid.

Until then . . . ?

Well, if the commotion died down enough, if the voices faded away, he would risk stepping out to see the lay of the land. Perhaps he could hide behind an arras—what else were they for? Till then, he could only stand and wait—and shiver.

He did.

An elf-wife slipped out from behind the arras. "Lady Cordelia!"

Cordelia spun about, staring down at the diminutive person. "Hail, Wee One!" She dropped to her knee. "Have you news of the Crown Prince?"

"One of our folk did wake him ere the murderers did fall upon him," the elf told her. "He fought his way free. We brought him to the tunnels within this house's walls, and he doth prowl through them, seeking for sign of thee. We have bade him flee to save his own life, but he will not, till he is sure thou art safe. Canst thou move him, lady?"

"It appears I do." Cordelia blinked away mistiness. "Brave man! Praise Heaven he is well!" Then the remark about "tunnels" penetrated. Secret passages, obviously. "Is there no passage from those tunnels, into the free air outside?"

"Oh, aye! We bade him come with us, to leave this strange place—but he will not, so long as he fears for thy safety. In truth, he is certain that they wish to slay thee, so even though thy chamber was empty, he still doth prowl the passages, seeking sign of thee. He will not go out from this place until he can take thee with him, alive and well."

Cordelia nearly melted, right then and there. Her limbs felt weak again, and the strange warmness moved up inside her—most strange, considering she was not even with Alain, much less touching him. Her heart had dissolved in that warmth, she was sure—but she felt her brother's hand on her shoulder and pulled herself together.

"We must seek him," Geoffrey said softly.

"Aye." Cordelia smiled through a mist of tears and had to blink it away. She turned to the elf. "Tell him I am well—alive and well, and that I wish him to flee to safety."

"Assuredly, I shall." The elf-woman whisked back behind the arras, and was gone.

Cordelia rose and spoke to Geoffrey without looking at him. "Come. We must find him, protect him."

"Aye, we must indeed," said Geoffrey, loosening his sword in its scabbard, "for if I know Alain, he will be pigheaded enough to stay until he sees you with his own eyes."

"Oh, do you truly think he would?" she cried.

"I do not doubt it for an instant," Geoffrey said drily. "Let us seek him out, then. Since we know where he is, let us call back the elf-wife, find these tunnels, and seek him out directly."

Cordelia froze at a thought. "Nay! Let us finish the course we first set! Find the Lady Delilah."

"I am ever ready for that," he said with a grin.

Cordelia flashed him a glance of annoyance. "You are disgusting, brother. I confess I am glad of your aid, but not of your animal nature. Be assured that I do not wish to find the lady for the same reason that you do."

"I would scarcely think it! But say, sweet sister, what purpose there is in seeking her at all?"

"For that she is a shrew and destroyer beneath her beauty, brother, and if you have not seen it, be assured that I have."

Geoffrey frowned. "But we have learned that Alain is alive and well, and could therefore be in no danger from her. Should we not rather be seeking to find who set these assassins upon the Prince?" He stared, facts suddenly connecting in his head. "Surely you do not suspect the lady of the deed!"

"I would suspect her of anything," Cordelia returned, her eyes glittering. "Who do you *think* sent those men to fall upon him?"

Geoffrey frowned. "Say."

"The Lady Delilah! Do you not remember the dream we

shared? It was she who gave the orders! If anyone commanded Alain's death, it was she!"

"That was but a dream . . ."

"A dream that came from a telepath who did not shield her thoughts, thinking we slept! She did not realize her words would sift through our slumbers to form pictures in our minds!"

Geoffrey pursed his lips, not wanting to believe such malice of so beautiful a lady—but by the logic of war, it was what an enemy would do.

Cordelia's eyes narrowed as she watched the emotions pass across Geoffrey's face. "Believe it, brother, till we have proof otherwise—the more so since 'tis likely she gave other commands also. Did she not whip up your lust this night, then send a woman to satisfy it, thus holding your attention so that you would not be aware that Alain needed your aid?"

Geoffrey's face darkened with the blow to his pride, but he had to admit it made sense. "Aye." Then the logical conclusion hit him. "If so, 'twas she who sent the blackguards to slay me while I sought ecstasy!"

"I doubt it not," Cordelia agreed. Her face turned stony at the idea of the woman actually trying to kill her little brother. "We shall pay her back in her own coin."

There was something in the way she said it that gave even Geoffrey chills.

"But what of Alain?"

"The elves shall bring him my word, and he shall heed it, I hope, going out from this house. But we must make sure of that safety in other ways."

"By choking it at its source." Geoffrey smiled like a wolf.

Cordelia gave him a curt nod. "Do you still wish to believe the woman innocent? Then prove me wrong, brother. Find her."

CHAPTER
~16~

They searched. Delilah had not come back to her room, nor Forrest to his.

Geoffrey stood immobile in the center of Delilah's sitting room, eyes losing focus as he probed throughout the manor house with his mind. Finally, he nodded. "The room that was shielded."

"Of course!" Cordelia cried. "What malice does she brew in there?"

"Let us go see." Geoffrey turned to the door.

They ran through the hallways with no sound but the rustle of their garments, staying to the shadows (and there were a lot of those). Down below the Great Hall, down in the basement of the manor house, there where there should have been storerooms, they found an oaken door with men in livery standing sentry.

Geoffrey slipped his dagger out of its sheath, but Cordelia stayed it with a hand. "They are weary already, brother. They have watched through the night." She stared at the two men for a few seconds.

One of them raised a hand to stifle a yawn. As he finished, the other began.

"Stay awake," the first growled.

"No, *you* stay awake."

"I need to . . ."

"I just got to . . ."

Then both slumped to the floor. After a minute, each snored.

Cordelia and Geoffrey stole silently around the corner and up to the door.

"Softly," Geoffrey whispered. "Let us take them unawares."

Cordelia glared at the lock until it turned itself. Then she gave the door a gentle push with her hand, and it swung open silently, on well-oiled hinges.

There was only the one candle, but its glow reflected off data screens, holo-cube readers, holo-cube files—and an improvised bed, cushions clustered together, and on them, snorting and heaving, shuddering and gasping . . .

Cordelia froze, wide-eyed. She would have turned on her heel if she could have, but the sight held her, horrified, fascinated. She was intruding on a very private moment, but . . .

"Take your enemy while you can," Geoffrey breathed in her ear. "In fact, as she would have done to me." He stepped past her, gliding toward the bed like a shadow left by a moonbeam.

Cordelia shook off the spell, remembered the sleeping assassins and the bloodstains on Alain's floor, and followed.

Geoffrey levelled his sword and spoke very loudly. "Hold!"

Cordelia stood by, reaching out with her mind, ready to throw every movable object at . . .

(The man lifted his head, shocked, and found himself staring at a sword's tip.)

. . . at Forrest.

Cordelia stared, appalled. Inside her, she felt something sicken and shrivel.

The bandit chieftain saw it in her eyes. He scrambled out of the bed, remembered himself just in time, and whipped a corner of the sheet over his midriff, then raised his hands to Cordelia. "My lady, forgive! A moment's impulse . . . I weakened . . . Never again . . ."

His voice ran down as he saw the look on her face.

Beyond him, Delilah lay back against the pillows, half-covered by the rest of the sheet, watching Cordelia with a vindictive, triumphant smile.

Cordelia stood, stunned.

Delilah's gaze flicked to Geoffrey, filled with malice, one finger drawing a circle on the sheet over her breast, spiralling in. "Come, seize the moment—and me. You knew me for what I was; use me now, for you'll never have another chance."

Geoffrey's sword point swivelled to her throat.

She stared at him, indignant, affronted—for the look on his face was only one of amusement.

Forrest bowed his head, shamefaced.

But Delilah's eyes glinted malice at Geoffrey, and she laughed, low in her throat.

Geoffrey shrugged.

Suddenly, Cordelia was aware that she might not have been the only one who had been hurt by the scene. Her gaze darted up to her brother's face in concern.

Then she saw how the smile on his face widened, showing teeth. "I knew you for what you were, aye, and was quite willing to take you on those terms—nay, and still would be, for a night or two—but for nothing more."

Storm clouds began to gather on Cordelia's brow.

Geoffrey's swordtip moved slowly down Delilah's body, as though seeking the best point.

"Thrust, then," she said with contempt, "at least with the symbol, since you are too much afeard to use the referent."

"Geoffrey!" Cordelia cried, appalled.

Geoffrey gave her a quick glance before he looked back at his target. "Sister, I hope that you did not think that Forrest was anything more than Delilah was."

Cordelia's head snapped back, as though she had been slapped.

Geoffrey went on, circling his sword tip carelessly, nearer and nearer to the smooth skin. "Nay, the two of them are well matched, indeed."

Forrest rose to his knees, hands upraised in pleading. "Lady Cordelia! Sweet lady, forgive!"

"Never could I forgive such a lapse as this!" Cordelia retorted, infuriated. "How could you seek to humiliate me so?"

"To put you in the same class as myself?" Delilah said sweetly. "That is no humiliation, sweet innocent, but a compliment of the highest order."

"Speak not to me, lightskirt!" Cordelia turned on her, enraged. "Were I ever like you, I should wish to die ere I was thrown on the trash heap as a worn-out plaything for any man who wished!"

"Say rather, any man whom *I* wish!" Delilah writhed out of the bed and up to her feet, her eyes sparking with anger. She slipped past the sword's point, and her open palm cracked across Cordelia's cheek.

"Oh!" Cordelia pressed a hand to the hurt, indignant, anger building to an unprecedented explosion.

" 'Oh,' indeed!" Delilah stepped back laughing, leaning back, hands on her hips, naked and glorious in the candlelight. "Yes, any man I want, even yours! *Any* man of yours! Stay awhile, while I go to claim your Prince!"

Cordelia sprang forward, spitting, "False and hollow shell!" hands reaching, fingers hooked to scratch.

Alarmed, Forrest caught her, holding her wrists. "No, lady! You shall be hurt!"

"Let me go! Oh, let me go!" Cordelia raged, twisting and thrashing about in his hold.

"Aye, let her go!" Delilah taunted. "Let her follow! I shall have her Prince grappling me ere she can come!" Catching up her garments, she sprang to the door and ran out, bare feet pattering on the floor.

"Will you let me go!" Cordelia cried, still raging. "I must catch her, stop her, ere it is too late!"

"Why, lady, why?" Forrest implored. "You shall only go to your own hurt—for surely, Alain is no better than I!"

"Yes, sister, let be," Geoffrey said gently. "I would not wish you hurted more, if she is right—and I would not wish to spit Alain on my sword, if . . ."

"But do you not see?" Cordelia cried. "She knows he is the Prince!"

Geoffrey stared.

Forrest frowned. "What matters that?"

"That her men tried to assassinate Alain this night!" Geoffrey snapped, the implications immediately clear to him. "And if she knows who he truly is, it is sure that we guessed aright—it is she who set the assassins upon him! It is not his virtue or his heart that is threatened, but his life! Let be!"

Astounded, Forrest loosed his hold, and Cordelia sprang free.

They leaped after her, out into the hallway . . .

It was empty save for the two snoring sentries.

They stood, absolutely still, and heard the muffled sound of bare feet padding away, somewhere out of sight . . .

"The stairs!" Geoffrey snapped. "She can only have gone upward!"

"That would be novel," Cordelia said acidly, but she ran after Geoffrey.

Up the stairs they flew, into the entry hall, where they halted, looking about. There was no loose clothing on the floor, no hint as to where Delilah had gone—only the doors to the solar on the one side, and the Great Hall on the other.

Geoffrey strode toward the Great Hall. "She will be here, if she is anywhere. 'Tis the seat of power for a country squire."

They threw open the doors and strode in . . .

And armed men stepped out from the walls. A thicket of swords surrounded them.

At the end of the hall, on the dais, stood Delilah, clothed again now, hands on her hips, head thrown back, laughing long and loud.

Cordelia looked about her, stunned. The trestles and tables had not only been folded and set aside—they had
been taken out of the hall completely. The fire was dead,
the hearth cleaned and swept. The torches were gone from
their sconces, and the decorations had disappeared. Only
bare walls and bare floor met her gaze, bleak in the light
of the false dawn filtering through the tall windows.

Delilah laughed and laughed, revelling in their surprise.
"There is nothing here to throw, witch! How shall you
fight now, when there is nothing for your mind to move?"

Cordelia stared, aghast, realizing that she had walked
into a trap, and Geoffrey swore. "By Blue, and by all the
obscene slitherings from the dawn of time! You have laid
your snare carefully and well, lady!"

"And you are caught within it!" she cried in glee.

"You have been planning it long and well."

"Aye, since first I learned that Their Majesties would
command their son to wed! And you are caught, ensnared
more thoroughly than you could have imagined! Know
that you shall die this night, Sir Geoffrey!" Delilah's voice
suddenly softened, cozening. "Yet the condemned man
may have his last wish." Her hands went to the laces of
her bodice. "Come, take what you have sought so hard!
You may at least die in ecstasy."

Cordelia stared at her, horrified—but Geoffrey only
shook his head a little, with a knowing smile.

"Oh, do not fear for your manhood!" Delilah mocked.
"I well and truly do lust after you, and shall have my fill
of you soon enough, I warrant—you shall know a glorious
death."

"I think I shall know no death at all," Geoffrey purred.

"No? Surely you do not think you can fight one against
fifty, and win! And you shall not disappear from our
midst, for your sister cannot, and you are too concerned
with your piddling honor to leave her! There is nothing
here for your mind to throw, no weapons but your single
sword and dagger. How shall you fight?"

"With me at his back!" Alain burst out of the wainscot-
ting, the hidden door slamming open. He leaped, sword

slashing, to wound the nearest guardsman. The man cried out, and Alain parried a cut by another guard with his dagger, then drove home with the sword. The man screamed and spun away, clutching at his side—but Alain had already whirled away, stabbing and slashing. Ten men near him shouted, and jumped on him.

Geoffrey roared, and his sword spun, dagger stabbing with inhuman speed and force. Three men fell back, fountains of blood; a dozen more leaped away from the berserker. That opened the path to Alain, and the Prince was beside him in an instant, taking station between Cordelia and the armed men, setting his back against Geoffrey's, who was still weaving his web of steel. "To the death, old friend!"

"If die we must, Geoffrey!"

"No, not our deaths—theirs!"

But while they had been doing that, Cordelia had been busy with the others. A guardsman shot up ten feet off the floor, crying out in alarm. He had good reason; Cordelia's eyes narrowed, and the man hurtled straight toward Delilah. She sprang aside with a cry of fear, and two more men rocketed into the air and spun toward her.

"Nothing to throw, you say?" Cordelia cried. "Then have at thee!" And both soldiers slammed down onto the floor; Lady Delilah barely stepped aside in time.

Five men shouted and leaped at Cordelia—but this time, it was she who shot up into the air astride a spear, and the soldiers' swords slashed at one another. Shocked, they cried out, then turned to parrying—and from parrying, to cutting and thrusting at one another.

Cordelia's eyes narrowed.

Suddenly, swords all over the room slashed at the men next to them, as though they had taken on lives of their own. Their owners shouted with fear—but so did their targets. In moments, the whole room was a vast melee of ringing steel and cries of anger.

"Out upon them!" Delilah cried.

That brought her men to their senses; with titanic heaves, they wrestled back control over their weapons and leaped to strike at the Gallowglasses and the Prince. Alain and Geoffrey met and blunted their rush, protecting Cordelia—and leaving her free to tend to Delilah. Her heart swelled with joy at their loyalty, even as she focussed her mind on her fingertips, thinking of thickening air, molecules crowding more and more closely together, moving faster and faster—so that by the time she swung her arm down, throwing, it was a ball of flame that leaped from her hand.

Delilah dodged it easily, laughing, even as her hands described a circle—and a ring of fire sprang up about Cordelia. She cried out in alarm, then bit it off, thinking of rain, a cloudburst.

Brief as it was, her cry was drowned in the howls of pain from the guards, servants, and knights who were battering at Alain and Geoffrey. They leaped back, and the two young men gasped for breath, grinning. "The Lady Delilah fights well . . . for us," Geoffrey panted.

Apparently she realized it, too. The ring of fire died down as suddenly as it had sprung up, but Delilah's men hung back, wary, for a moment. Geoffrey grinned and swished his blade through a sword drill, but Alain only glared and held his on guard.

Cordelia, though, was ready the second the flames died. A cloudburst broke right above Delilah, appearing from nowhere, drenching her. Delilah coughed and spluttered in sheer surprise, then wiped her hair out of her eyes—just in time to see a circle of rope whirling down to settle around her. She gasped and glared at it; it burst into fire before it could tighten, and was gone.

The response had been too quick; Cordelia hadn't been working up her next spell.

They were all illusions, of course. The trick was to make them seem so real that the other witch's mind would accept them subconsciously, and really feel the heat from the flames and see the burns blistering her skin, even though her conscious mind knew better. Delilah, for example, was really wet—her hair hung lank and dripping, her clothes plastered to her body; her own mind was cooperating in keeping her so. But she knew the moisture was harmless, and ignored it as she hurled a fireball at Cordelia.

It was an empty gesture, of course—Cordelia damped the flames before the sphere was halfway there. It faded into the thin air it had been made from—but it had given Delilah time to work up something more subtle.

Alain lurched back against Cordelia, snarling—and throwing her off balance for a moment. His sword flashed like a heat-haze, his opponents dropping back with wounds—but more jumped in, in their place. There were at least three for each of her guardians, and they were hard-pressed indeed. She realized they couldn't last much longer . . .

A high, shrill battle-scream sounded, and the great black iron horse reared up behind the men who were slashing at Geoffrey. Fess's steel hooves lashed out, felling Delilah's men. He had heard the row, and broken from the castle stables, Cordelia realized—just in time to even the odds.

The men around Alain looked up, saw what was happening, and some of those at the back ran to attack Geoffrey, then leaped aside as steel teeth snapped at them.

Welcome as Fess was, he had distracted Cordelia too long. Suddenly, a huge snake was coiling around her. Its coils tightened; she couldn't breathe! Then the wedge-shaped head hovered in front of hers, and she would have screamed, if she had had breath. Its jaws opened, fangs curving down to tear . . .

But constrictors don't have viper's fangs, and pit vipers aren't big enough to wrap and squeeze. The fangs themselves made her realize all over again that the snake was only an illusion, projected by a master directly into the back of her mind; the fangs broke her unconscious belief in its reality more effectively than anything she could have thought of. She held her breath, eyes narrowing, glaring into that putrid maw, thinking of another form, another shape . . .

The snake sprouted hairs, hairs that thickened even as its head melted and shrank, reforming into the dead, sculptured face of a fox—and it was only a fur wrap made of a dozen foxes, each biting the other's tail, that coiled around her. She looked up at Delilah in triumph . . .

And saw a small snake, only three feet long, but one with a spreading hood and curving fangs, rearing up to strike at her.

Cordelia realized, in a way she never could have otherwise, that Delilah was a Futurian agent, raised in a modern culture, no matter where she had been born—for no native of Gramarye knew about cobras. Even to Cordelia, they were things from books—and she didn't doubt that they were so to Delilah, too. The woman probably didn't have any of the details right. It was a pitiful attempt at persuading her hindbrain, and she ignored it, knowing that its venom couldn't really hurt her. She thought at it, and it struck—but curved away from her, sailing back toward Delilah, and as it went, its head shrank into a handle, its body lengthened, its tail slimmed into a lash—and a bullwhip cracked over Delilah's head, then lashed about her shoulders.

Unprepared for it, Delilah cried out in pain; then she narrowed her eyes, and the bullwhip disappeared. She, too, had remembered that it was an illusion, though Cordelia noticed that the rents in her dress did not heal themselves.

Delilah glared, and a giant spider scuttled across the floor—but there was no Cordelia for it to frighten away. Delilah stared, lost for a moment, looking wildly about the hall, trying to find her adversary.

She never thought to look at her own men, of course, and didn't notice the guardsman in her livery who was working his way down the line of fighters, staying behind and only trading an occasional blow with Alain or Geoffrey—until he turned on Delilah and struck at her with his sword.

She screamed in fear, falling back, bleeding from a cut in her arm.

The guardsman swung his blade up for another slash.

Delilah realized who he must be, and glared at the man. Sure enough, his tunic stretched down, changing back into the tan and russet of Cordelia's riding dress. His face fined down, his helmet disappearing, and it was Cordelia who glared at her, eye to eye. The sword shrank and dwindled; it was only her extended index finger.

But Delilah had spent her time and effort in undoing Cordelia's illusion. The screech of rage from overhead took her by surprise, and the eagle that plunged to seize her gown in its claws as it buffeted her head with its wings made her shrink back with a scream of terror. Its dagger of a beak thrust right at Delilah's eyes . . .

. . . but a huge tawny paw reached up and swatted the eagle aside, and a lioness pounced to tear the eagle apart with one quick rip of its huge jaws. Then it turned on Cordelia, leaping . . .

And caromed off the belly of a huge bear, waddling toward Delilah on its hind legs, roaring in anger, its claws raised to slash.

The lion roared right back and sprang, teeth reaching for the bear's throat, but the bear swatted it aside and plunged after it. There was a moment's flurry of fur and claws . . . then the bear rose, its jaws dripping blood, its eyes afire with rage, a snarl ripping loose from its throat . . .

A snarl that was answered by a deep, throaty laugh as a huge man, eight feet tall and three feet wide, hideously ugly and entirely naked, strode toward it, a huge club swinging high in his ham of a hand.

The bear roared and struck—but the ogre swung the club in a blur, both hands and all his weight behind it. There was a sickening crunch, and the bear lay dead, its head caved in.

Then, drooling, the ogre reached for Cordelia with a gloating laugh.

Cordelia shrank back with a scream.

Alain heard her and leaped between herself and the ogre, but she knew he believed it to be real, that he could not stand against it.

The guardsmen whooped victory and leaped in where Alain had been.

Fess screamed and struck them down with his hooves, curving between Cordelia and the murderous agents.

Cordelia's scream echoed inside her own mind, now as much for Alain as for herself. In her heart, she reached out for the protection that had always been there in her childhood—her parents and her big brother. But her parents were miles away, and Magnus was light-years away . . .

Not his image, though. It came striding forth from behind her to do battle, as much bigger than she as he had seemed when she was five and he eight—which made him nine feet tall now, smiling in wicked anticipation of a fight, shouting, "Thou wouldst, wouldst thou? Then have at thee!"

Delilah screamed—and screamed, and screamed. "No! It cannot be you! I have banished you, I have maimed you, I have sent you fleeing to the farthest . . ."

And, for the moment, her mind was open, she was that terrified—open and unguarded, and her memories of Magnus clear for Cordelia to read. She stared, horrified—this was the woman who had trapped Magnus's heart, toyed with him, played with him, dashed his hopes and his dreams of love to flinders, burned the belief in feminine goodness out of him . . .

Then Delilah saw the huge Magnus grappling with the ogre, swinging the howling monster high and dashing it to the floor, and she threw back her head and laughed, mocking again, vindictive. "Of course! It was not he! You would call for your big brother, would you?"

"Witch!" Cordelia screamed, in full rage. "Have at thee!" Her face twisted with fury and hatred, and a bolt of pure energy sparked in the air between them. Then it was gone, but a huge explosion rocked the room, and Delilah doubled over in agony, hands pressed to her abdomen.

Cordelia strode through the smoke of that bolt of pure emotion, eyes burning, and snatched the woman's hair, hauling her head up. " 'Tis you who have murdered my brother's heart! Why, then, be sure that I shall murder you!"

And there were snakes, toads, salamanders, scorpions,

and spiders, all crawling over Delilah. She screamed, swatting at them, tearing at them—then remembered them for what they were, and stilled, glaring at the vermin . . .

The bolt cracked from Cordelia's head to Delilah's, pure energy, overloading Delilah's system with Cordelia's rage—for when last came to last, it was Cordelia who could feel more intensely, far more intensely, even in hatred and anger.

Delilah staggered, and suddenly, her own hands were slapping her face and tearing her hair.

She went crazy.

She screamed and twisted in the grip of a primal fear, turning to tear at Cordelia with hands crooked into claws, lashing out with a bolt of panic that startled Cordelia; it was far more than she had expected. She leaped back, the first taste of horror touching her as she realized that Delilah was completely out of control.

The woman thrashed about, tearing at invisible enemies—and a jumble of images began to appear on the floor of the Great Hall, flickering into being, then transforming into something else, then flickering out as new ones appeared. Snakes and worms and maggots crawling from rotten meat; bulbous vases breaking open, spilling rancid oil; huge nails hammering down into boards made of flesh that screamed and writhed, and more, more, on and on and on.

Cordelia stared, aghast, revulsed as much by what she was seeing as by what she had done.

But Delilah recovered, slowing, stilling, the jumble of images fading, lifting her eyes to Cordelia again—eyes that now bore not only hatred and rage, but also madness, stark madness.

For the first time, the cold fingers of Death seemed to touch Cordelia, and she realized that she really could die in this fight.

Panic surged, and she threw one more bolt of mental force at Delilah, with all her own fear and anger in it. The explosion rocked the hall, and Delilah slammed back against the panelling with a scream.

The guards had stilled their fight to watch; even Geoffrey and Alain had been caught in the spell of the beautiful witch's madness. Now, though, one of Delilah's men came back to himself with a shout, slashing past Geoffrey's guard at Cordelia.

She screamed and fell back, seizing his sword with a mental grip that froze it and held it immobile, afraid that Delilah would recover and seize her chance. Alain came out of his reverie with a howl and turned to cut the man down, but all Delilah's men shouted and attacked again . . .

Swords lifted above them, and fell; for each man, a knight towered over him, striking.

"Have at them!" bellowed a huge voice from the doorway, and a stream of men thundered into the room, halberd blades flailing. Behind them rode the King himself, sword slashing down from horseback, with the High Warlock beside him, parrying and cutting. Lady Gwendylon stood fiery with anger, a basket of stones in her hands, stones that sped with unerring accuracy to enemy swordsmen, while on a ledge above them, a grizzled, barrel-bodied dwarf bellowed, "Hold! Surrender yourselves, or die! Seize the false lady, seize the poisoner of hearts!"

But it was too late. Delilah was already gone. Psionics or trickery, she had vanished from their midst.

Just in time, too—so heavily outnumbered, the guardsmen threw up their hands and weapons with cries for mercy. In a few minutes, the King's soldiers had all the walking enemies herded into a corner, and a doctor and his assistants were tending to the moaning wounded, thin-lipped with disgust.

But Alain had no eyes for any of it. He leaped up beside Cordelia, crying, "My lady! Are you hurt? Upon my honor, if any have touched you, I shall have their heads!"

But Cordelia could only stare in amazement at this huge, bare-chested, golden-haired Adonis whose muscles played beneath a sheen of sweat like a statue of a young Greek god, sword in hand, eyes wide in concern. Rooted to the spot, she could only nod as his arm went about her waist, hugging her protectively against the huge, hardened muscles of his chest. She gazed up at him in mute astonishment, eyes wide, lips parted—and for a moment, he stared down at her in equal wonder.

Then his head bowed, his lips touched hers, and she knew only the wonder of his kiss, and the wrenching anguish and soaring ecstasy of a heart finally given, completely, in love.

Some while later, some immeasurable time that surely must have been only a few minutes, though it had seemed eternal bliss, Alain lifted his head and stood staring down into her eyes. She knew he was going to kiss her again, and willed it with her whole being—but someone coughed, and she herd King Tuan's voice saying, "I rejoice that the lady is well."

Alain turned to his father in surprise, and Cordelia saw before them her brother, grinning from ear to ear, and her mother, arms half-raised, with her father behind her, eyes glowing. She gave a little mew of protest and sank back against Alain's chest; his arm came up about her automatically even as he said, "My liege and father! How came you here?"

"Why, in caution and apprehension, my son," Tuan said, smiling, "and with the guidance of elves, alarmed at thy peril. Have you proved yourself in the ways of battle, then? And have you kept the lady safe?"

Alain looked down, and there was reverence in his eyes. "You are safe, are you not, my love?"

My love! Cordelia nestled against him, eyes brimming, and nodded, with a misty smile. Reassured, Alain answered with a secret smile of his own that stopped time for a few minutes, almost kissed her again, then remembered the proprieties and turned back to his father. "She is well, my liege—and she has kept me safe far more than I her!"

"Or as much, at least," Rod Gallowglass murmured, and his wife added, "So should it ever be."

Alain turned to him, becoming grave and formal even as

he moved. He inclined his head and said, "My lord. My lady. Have I your leave to court your daughter?"

Lord and Lady Gallowglass exchanged a brief and tender smile, then turned back to nod. "You may."

"The courtship is done," Cordelia murmured. "The lady is won."

Alain looked down at her, glowing with pride, then turned back to her mother and father. "May I also have your leave to ask her hand in marriage?"

Again, the secret smile. "You may."

King Tuan only beamed down. After all, he had given his permission before all this began.

But Alain had ceased to see them all. Sinking down on one knee, he gazed up at Cordelia, she his whole world, nothing else existing for the moment. "My lady," he breathed, "will you honor me, ennoble me, do me the greatest honor I can know—by giving me your hand?"

"Oh, yes, my love!" she cried and, as he leaped up and took her in his arms, she breathed, so softly that no one else could hear, "And all the rest of me, too."

Then there was no chance to say anything more, for her lips were sealed with his, and time had stopped again.